SUBZERO

CAMBRIA HEBERT

BearPaw Resort #4
SUBZERO

Alex

I waited.

I waited so long I actually started to think maybe—*just maybe*—the phone wouldn't ring.

Hoping perhaps the whisper of my name went unechoed. Perhaps I'd really been forgotten.

I knew better.

Deep inside me, past the optimism I would be left in peace, I recognized. Once something freezes so deep it falls into negative temperatures not even hope can survive.

I knew the phone would ring. Deep in the drawer where I kept it locked away from prying eyes and curious ears, the sound erupted, shattering the silence.

My hand shot out before my eyes even opened, my mind awake before the rest of me. Halfway through the first ring, I answered, pressing it to my ear and peering through the onyx darkness shrouding the ceiling.

I didn't have to say anything. Whoever was on the other end knew I was there.

"There's a job."

I sat up in bed, the darkness of the room shrouding everything, including the sound of my voice. "You know I'm out."

"That's why it has to be you."

I digested that. My eyes shut. I battled back a thousand feelings, including shadows that could scare away even the darkest of night.

"You owe me." He reminded.

I did owe him.

I wasn't the kind of man who let a debt go unpaid. It wasn't how I was wired. "Where and when?" I asked.

"I'll be in touch."

The line went dead.

I pulled the phone down and snapped it in half, pulling the battery out for good measure. That was my only untraceable point of contact, but it was now compromised.

I lay back down, though all traces of sleep had vanished. I was alert, mind churning, reliving some of the past and wondering just how badly this shit was going to leak into my present.

The point of contact might be destroyed, but it didn't matter.

He'd find me.

I'd take the job, no matter how fucked up it might be.

Why?

It's what we did.

Sabrina

The unmistakable stink of dirty diaper wrinkled my nose. It didn't matter how many of these bombs I changed. I still wondered, every single time, how something so small and cute could produce such heinous crap.

Literally.

I worked quickly, locking down that shit (again, literally), and tossed it into a nearby bin that was supposed to suppress the stank.

It still lingered.

"Incoming," a familiar voice said over me as a new child with an equally horrid "present" was placed before me.

Oh. So maybe the bin did lock out odor. Maybe the lingering scent, which was now a full-blown gag-fest, was due to the fact that there was yet another diaper to be changed.

* * *

I groaned and jolted, rolling onto my back and blinking groggily at the ceiling. It was dark and the movement of the fan overhead was proof I'd been having a dream. Well, more like a nightmare.

Even knowing I was home in my bed, my nose crinkled and I took a tentative whiff as if testing out the air quality, making certain that there definitely was not diaper pollution up in here.

The only scent that greeted me was that of the fabric softener I used on my sheets.

Still groggy, I sat up, pushing the blankets around my thighs and glancing over at the clock on the bedside table. It was the middle of the night. I still had a few hours before I had to be up. Hopefully, that dream wasn't a premonition of how my upcoming day was going to go.

Before lying back down, I reached for the tall glass of water nearby and took a sip, letting the cool drink slide down my dry throat. Halfway to setting it back down, movement on the other side of the room made me pause.

The liquid in the glass swished around as I glanced over immediately, knowing something was wrong.

The long yellow curtain hanging around the window was moving. Billowing in a breeze that was not from the overhead fan.

Quietly, I slipped from the bed, clutching the glass so tight my knuckles ached. Creeping to the window, my heart jackhammered in my chest but then abruptly stuttered and faltered when I saw the window was partially open as though someone had forgotten to shut it all the way.

The screen on the outside was slit so drastically that it flapped around in the night breeze.

Instinct kicked in then. My brother's voice filled my head.

Assess then act.

My assessment was there was someone in my apartment. It didn't matter that I was on the fourth floor of the building and the guy would have to be Spider-man to even get in through the window.

I didn't cut the screen and open my window.

And since I lived alone, that meant someone else did it, someone who knew I wouldn't answer the door and invite them in if they knocked.

Get out of the house. Stay calm, my brother's voice instructed.

There was only one point of exit and entry in my place. The front door. Unless, of course, you were Spider-man, which I was not. That meant I had to walk through my place where someone was probably lurking.

I moved soundlessly over the carpet, pressing close to the wall. After listening for what felt like twenty-five long years and hearing nothing, I risked it and peeked out into the hall. It was empty, so I slipped out, moving with my back to the wall toward the front where the door was.

The end of the hall approached, and my throat was constricted from holding in the panic rising inside me.

Panic later. Get out now.

The white door leading out into the hallway came into sight. I halted at the end of the hall, still pressed to the side, and debated on my chances if I just made a run for it. It would take two seconds to get to the door, another two to deal with the locks. Once I was out in the hall, I could scream like a banshee and let the neighbors all call the cops.

Plan made, I blew out a breath and started forward.

The second I lunged, someone else darted out in front of me. A hard, heavy hand clamped around my wrist, and a screech built in the back of my throat and leaked out through my still-closed lips.

Instantly, I fell back, forcing all my weight away from the intruder. He wasn't thrown off balance as I was hoping (and as my brother said would happen), and he didn't loosen his grip on my arm.

Realizing the glass was still in my hand, I flicked my wrist and threw all the contents at the attacker, drenching him.

A low curse filled the room, but I barely heard it. He'd let go, and I stumbled back but used the momentum to slam the glass into the wall. It shattered, leaving me with a broken shard still clutched in my hand.

Like a hellcat, I lunged, brandishing the glass like a giant knife. This asshole was between me and the door, and the only way I was clearly getting out was to go through him.

I twisted away from my first attempt to slice him, but I rebounded and spun, lashing out to his other side. The glass sliced down his forearm. I felt the tear of skin.

Still gripping the weapon, I ran forward, smacking into the door, and threw the lock.

Just before I could fall out into the hallway, he grabbed me from behind. I began kicking and jabbed the glass into the arm around my waist. "Fuck!" he swore quietly.

I was just about to slam my palm into the glass still sticking out of him when he spoke. "Goddammit, Brina!" he grunted. "It's me!"

I went slack against him, then stiffened again and spun.

My brother stood there heaving, a hand pressed over his bleeding arm. He was dressed all kidnapper-ish, and even in the dark I could see his glare.

"Don't look at me like that," I snapped. "You deserved it."

"Next time, go for an artery," he quipped.

I rolled my eyes. That was Daniel—forever telling me what I did wrong. It didn't matter he was the one who broke into my house and scared the crap out of me. It didn't even matter that I stabbed him with glass… It only mattered that I didn't do it good enough.

"This better not be some kind of sick teaching drill in home invasion self-defense," I told him. "I have to work tomorrow."

"You aren't going to work tomorrow," he said, moving so soundlessly it made me feel as if every step I took was like a bull in a china shop. His arm swept around me, and he moved us away from the door, toward some shadows deeper in the room.

"You know how I feel about you bossing me around."

"Shh!" He insisted, giving me a little shake.

There was a noise toward the back of the apartment. The sound of a door opening and closing.

"Motherfucker," Daniel intoned, and cold chills swept down my back.

My heart rate, which hadn't yet recovered from before, was now throbbing against my chest, almost as though it were trying to escape.

I pressed a hand to it, hoping to keep it in.

"Move," Daniel mouthed, placing his body in front of mine and producing a large black gun with a suppressor on the end from nowhere.

He took aim as he walked toward the door, basically pushing me along with him.

The barest hint of movement across the room was all he needed. Daniel fired, and the sound of a body dropping made my stomach ache.

"Go," he ordered, his voice tactical and emotionless. I heard him, but my feet didn't move. I stood there staring at the dark lump on my carpet. It wasn't moving or making a sound.

My brother just killed someone in my apartment.

He hadn't even needed a light to do it.

He cursed, reached around us, opened the door, then, still keeping the gun trained on the hallway, wrapped his free arm around my waist and lifted. Out in the hall, he sat me down, giving me a shove. "Move, Brina."

I started up then, rushing toward the elevator.

"No," he said behind me.

I veered right and went into the stairwell. My feet hit the first step as Daniel wrapped his arm around me again and lifted, picking me up off the steps and hauling me back.

I didn't make a sound. I knew better, but when he started going up the stairs instead of down, I rotated and gave him a glare.

Using the long black nozzle on the gun, he pressed it against his lips, telling me to stay silent.

On the next landing, Daniel sat me down, motioning for me to stay, and planted in front of me. Still using his own body as a shield, he crouched and peered through the railings down at the flights below.

The muscles in my neck were so tight pain radiated up the back of my skull and behind my eye. I tugged on my ear as if that would somehow relieve some of the tension. When my brother's already tight body stiffened further, I held my breath.

He shot off another two rounds, the sound slightly louder in here because of the echoing stairwell.

Something rolled down the steps below… Not something. Someone.

I pressed against the wall and put my hand over my mouth to muffle any sound I might accidentally make. I stared at the back of my brother's head and remembered all the horsey rides he used to give me and the Barbie movies he endured when I was little and didn't have anyone else to watch them with.

How could that boy have turned into this?

I knew how. Hell, I didn't even judge him for it.

But I would be unbalanced if I didn't sit here astonished as my brother, my best friend, showed me exactly what he was capable of.

I don't know how much time passed, but after a while, my brother moved, rotating his head on his shoulders, then slowly standing. He kept the gun out but held it down at his side. His free hand reached out to me.

I stared at it, noting the rivulets of dark streaking his forearm and dripping into his palm. I wanted to apologize for it, but my voice wouldn't work and he'd probably scold me for talking anyway.

Instead, I slipped my hand into his, disregarding the blood that I knew would be smeared on my palm. He pulled me along with him as we slinked down the stairs, having to step over a dead body… and then a second one, which had indeed rolled down the stairs.

On the bottom floor, he pulled me out of the stairwell and into the maintenance hallway leading toward the back of the building. He pushed my back to the wall and stood in front of me as we moved down the corridor as one unit.

Only when we got to the door leading out onto the street did he relent enough to put his gun in the back of his pants.

Daniel moved out onto the street first, gesturing toward me.

There was an unmarked car that looked like a hunk of junk parked beside a giant dumpster. I knew without being told to get in. I climbed into the back and crouched behind the seats so no one would know there was a passenger.

I had no idea what was going on, but I knew my brother well enough to know this was what he would want me to do.

He didn't look back at me, he didn't say anything at all as he got in the car and started it up. We drove in silence for a long time, so long my ankles fell asleep and I became increasingly cranky from the crouched position I was in.

The sky was starting to lighten when, finally, my brother, spoke. "Clear."

Unfolding from the position, I groaned and then promptly fell over because my sleeping lower half was numb and tingly.

"Gumdrops!" I swore as I shoved up, using his seat as leverage.

He snorted at my choice of cussword.

"Yeah, yeah," I muttered and climbed between the seats to fall into the passenger side. I made sure to knock into him a few times just because he deserved it.

When I was finally settled, he gave me a look.

I sighed. "You saved my life back there."

"I'm the reason your life needed saving."

See? I couldn't even be mad when he never cut me any slack. That was Daniel. He didn't cut anyone any slack. Not even himself.

"What did you get involved in this time?" I asked, leaning my head back against the headrest. "Shit!" I burst out suddenly.

Daniel glanced over sharply. "What?"

"I'm not wearing any pants!"

He made a sound. "Gee, Brina. Next time I'll stop the bad guys and ask them if we can have a timeout so my little sis can put on some pants before they shoot her."

"Jackass."

"Being nice doesn't keep you alive."

I'd heard that so many times it was a wonder I didn't dream about that instead of poopy diapers.

I watched as we passed a sign. We were heading out of town. I looked at my brother, who was still young but so incredibly old. "How bad is it this time, Bear?" I whispered.

"You can't go home, honey."

And that's how I knew it was bad. Not because he said I couldn't go home, but because he didn't even blink when I called him by the nickname I knew he didn't like.

Alex

I had no clue where I was. Lost wasn't even an adjective I could use to describe it. Not even the most state-of-the-art GPS system could locate my team and me.

There was no way of knowing what country we'd crossed into because the amount of time we spent on a plane blurred together, as did the last place my feet actually touched the ground. Hell, we were so far off grid this place might not even belong to any country at all. Maybe it was the land version of the ocean, owned by no one, governed only by the ones with balls enough to be here.

I didn't think of where I was as a place anyway. It wasn't a destination anyone would ever want to travel. It was why we were here.

We came to places no one knew existed. The armpit of the armpits of the world, where drugs ruled and no one was safe.

Sand was everywhere, creating a gritty crust on everything it touched, including skin. During the day, I knew it was hot as Satan's ball sack, but we'd be long gone before the sun even came up. Night was colder here. The drastic change of climate between night and day was just one more thing to deter people from coming.

We 'chuted out of a plane about four miles back, using only pure skill and instinct to land in unfamiliar territory. I heard a few low curses when we started hitting the ground, but I stayed silent. Once regrouped, we moved out as a unit, so in sync with each other we could have been the same body.

I wasn't sure what we'd be walking into tonight. Even if we'd had a full report to go on (which we didn't), it wouldn't matter. I always employed the mindset that I was walking into a completely unknown scenario. Being complacent got you killed.

During the four-mile hike, we barely spoke. My muscles worked beneath my gear. My finger stayed tense on the trigger. Despite the chill, sweat beaded down my temple and slid over my chest beneath my uniform.

Four miles wasn't anything. It was sort of like a walk in the park. The last place we went into was ten miles, and the place before that, I stopped logging at fourteen.

We slowed as we approached the village. Calling it that was a mere courtesy. Nothing about this place was remotely inhabitable by most human standards. Yet people lived here. Squatting in huts that had barely enough room to lie in.

The sound of a child crying cut through the darkness, and I shared a look with Mercer. I hated missions when kids were fucking involved. Kids shouldn't be in places like this with people like this. In the very beginning, I would get mad at the women who had them, until I realized they didn't have a choice either. So many of the kids born into these kinds of places were results of rape, abuse, or just the fact that it was all these people knew.

"Let's just get this done," Mercer said to everyone.

We all moved, grim but confident. Our team was like a well-oiled machine at this point. We barely even had to talk about what we were going to do when we got somewhere. We read each other, and we had a system that never failed.

Lithely, I moved into position, backing up against a shack that I didn't dare put any weight on. I waited for the two men I could still see to do the same. Adrenaline coursed through me, but I forced my body calm and waited.

Two of my teammates would be moving in right now, doing the job we were sent here to do.

It would be in and out. Easy.

Until all hell broke loose.

The sound of rapid gunfire from weapons that most definitely were not the ones we came equipped with cut through the night. I tensed but stayed in position because acting rash would be stupid.

More fire and the sound of cries and screams erupted.

"Ambush!" a familiar voice yelled, and I lunged from around the structure, weapon ready.

I surveyed the scene in seconds. People were running around, screaming and yelling, some naked and some partly clothed. Gun fire continued to reign, bullets hitting the ground with such force and speed the sand and dust created a haze. The bonfire in the center of the village seemed to glow ominously, backlighting one of my teammates as he stumbled forward.

He was hit.

I rushed forward, knowing the other guys would cover me, and shoved my shoulder up into his armpit as he collapsed against me. I half carried his weight as he wheezed, eyes picking up some movement in the place I had just come from.

I fired off a few rounds, taking out the guy before he could shoot first.

Bullets hit the ground behind us, kicking up sand and making every muscle in my body tense. I turned, using my body as a blockade for my wounded brother, and opened fire as I pushed him back.

The sound of a nearby explosion muffled all sound, making everything go blissfully silent for long moments and making me feel as if everything was put into slow motion. When we were in the clear, my brother fell onto the ground, clutching his side, blood spilling out from between his fingers.

I knelt, grabbing his neck and forcing him to look up. "Where's Wells?" I demanded, though I knew he wouldn't be able to hear my voice over the gunfight and chaos.

His lips thinned, and he shook his head once.

They killed him? These animalistic motherfuckers killed my teammate? My brother?

Movement in my peripheral brought me back to the moment. I lifted my gun and shot, dropping whoever it was.

Mind spinning as the pandemonium continued, I went on autopilot and let my training take over. I dragged my wounded mate over to the side where he had some concealment and was out of the line of fire, then made sure he had a loaded weapon in his hand.

Before I rushed back into the fight, I met his eyes. Beneath the pain, I saw the bleakness, the guilt he already felt at the loss of his friend.

This wasn't supposed to happen tonight. Someone sold us out. Somehow, someone got intel we were coming, and we'd walked right into a fucking ambush.

Bodies were everywhere as I ran back into the melee. From what I could tell, the remaining three of us were holding them back.

Mercer was closest to me, and as he fought, he yelled, "In there!"

I started forward, then noticed the creeper coming up behind Merc, a dirty blade in his hand and a rag covering the lower half of his face. I dropped him.

Merc kept fighting, and I rushed around the fire, wondering why this was such a fucking blood bath.

Then I realized. I heard laughter. It twisted in my chest, making my stomach revolt.

They were taking out their own people. Yes, this had been an ambush to take us out, but they had turned on everyone else here, too.

Sweat dripped into my eyes and slipped between my lips. Ignoring it, I fought my way into the small building Merc had indicated, taking out the man watching the door and the one perched on the roof. He fell with a cry and then landed with a sickening thump nearby.

There was a man standing over my fallen comrade's body. He stood leisurely, as if the war waging around him and the dead American at his feet was relaxing. We locked eyes, and he smiled.

He pointed to my brother and said something in a language I didn't quite understand. I didn't have to understand his words exactly, though, because the second he was done, he began to laugh again.

Cold plummeted over me. I welcomed the numbness it offered.

Something inside me switched off at the same time something else switched on…

* * *

A heavy hand fell onto my shoulder, and I reacted instantly. In seconds, I had the body slammed down on my desk, my hand at their throat.

"It's me," the man under me choked out.

I blinked. The past faded away, giving way to the present even as the sound of gunfire and screams echoed through my head. *There was a lot of blood that night… so much blood.*

"Shit," I said, pulling back from my best friend. "Liam."

He stayed down for another minute, watching me, but not with fear in his eyes. Liam wasn't afraid of me, even when he probably should be.

"I wasn't thinking," I told him, reaching down to grab the front of his shirt and haul him off my desk.

He leapt up and cleared his throat. "Thought I might have pissed you off."

I smiled, though I didn't feel the humor in the situation. "I'm sorry."

"Minor."

It wasn't minor, though. Getting that call brought up a lot of shit for me. A lot of shit I wanted to leave buried.

Liam hitched his chin at me. "What's going on?"

"Nothing," I said, gazing out the window overlooking the ski slopes. An intense urge to strap into a pair of skis and stand at the top of a trail clutched my chest. "I was just deep in thought. I didn't hear you come in."

"If you think I believe that, you're an asshole."

The side of my mouth lifted. "I don't want to talk about it right now."

"I can respect that."

"So, ah, what'd you come in here for? What's up?" I tried to inject normalcy in my voice. I tried not to hear the still-echoing gunfire and distant flashes of my hands grabbing bodies.

"Nothing important," he answered. I felt him watching me, measuring me.

"You mind if I take off early today? The powder is calling my name."

A beat passed before he answered, "The call of the mountain is strong."

"You'd know better than anybody."

He flashed a smile. "Probably. But I think you might come in second."

On my way past, I slapped him on the back. "I'll see you tomorrow."

"Alex," he called out, and I turned back.

"Yeah?"

"You want some company on the slopes?"

"Naw," I answered. "I think I'll tear it up solo today."

He nodded, not offended at all. "You know you can talk to me, right? I got your back no matter what."

Some of the tension in me eased. "Yeah, bro. I know. Thanks."

Liam already knew about the shit that haunted me. It's not like I was afraid if I told him, it would change anything about our friendship. Didn't mean I wanted to bring it up, though.

It was already resurrected inside me.

Sabrina

It was dark again when I felt the car finally come to a stop. Nudging one eye open, I peered out, half expecting some offensive, too-bright streetlight all gas stations seemed equipped with to nearly blind me.

When that didn't happen, I opened both and stared out. From my hunched-over position in the passenger seat, I could see about a million stars.

More stars than I'd ever seen before in my entire life.

I blinked, thinking maybe I somehow had something in my eye, but no. When I refocused, the stars were still there, winking overhead like diamonds just waiting for someone to scoop them up. They glittered against a night sky that looked like royal velvet and stretched farther than any ocean I'd ever visited.

Still staring at the sky, I sat up. "Where are we?"

We were in a different car now. Not the beater from before. At some point during the day—when the sun was still high in the sky—my bother ditched that car, and we took off in a black SUV.

I didn't ask where he got it or why he had an SUV stashed along the interstate somewhere. This was Daniel I was talking about. He had contingency plans for his contingency plans. Hell, he probably had a car stashed in every single state.

I'm serious. My brother made doomsday preppers look like wieners. And honestly, he wouldn't tell me if I asked anyway.

Plausible deniability and all that.

"Is this truck stolen?" I asked abruptly.

He glanced at me with one raised eyebrow. "Would I drive my baby sister around in a stolen vehicle?"

I snorted. "Yes."

"I need you to do something for me."

I sighed. "I just asked you two questions, and instead of answering, you tell me you need a favor."

Daniel rubbed a hand over his face. He looked exhausted. "Colorado and no."

I perked up, surprised he actually told me something. Two somethings! "What are we doing in Colorado?" I asked, gazing around with renewed interest. There were a lot of trees, a road that might not even be a road (it wasn't paved), and what looked like a lot of mountains.

Daniel's hand slid over mine, drawing my attention to where he clasped it in my lap. "I have to leave for a while."

"Like a job?" I asked, feeling my stomach dip. Suddenly, I felt like a little girl again. That moment he'd come home and said the same thing.

I remembered that hollow, aching pit in the base of my stomach as I stood at the window and watched him leave for bootcamp. I was twelve. Daniel was eighteen. And I remembered knowing that day everything would change.

I was right.

And now here I sat, eight years later, no longer a little girl but still needing my brother as though I were. I had that feeling again. I instinctively knew everything was going to change again.

"I have to tie up some loose ends," he explained. "I can't come home until it's done. You know I won't take any kinds of risks with you."

Slowly, I nodded. "So those men in my apartment…"

"You're my weakness, Brin-brin." He cupped the side of my head, and something raw opened up inside me. "You always have been."

Those men wanted to kill me so they could hurt my brother. Hurt him for probably trying to stop them from being a waste of human space. My brother was a lot of things—a killer one of them. But he didn't kill frivolously. He killed deliberately. When he had to. When the world was better off without the scum he was wiping out.

"I'm sorry," I said. It seemed maybe his life would be less complicated if he didn't have me as his weak spot.

"I'm not," he said, rubbing his palm against my hair. I lifted my eyes, and he smiled gently. "You're pretty cool for a sister."

I shoved him back, and he laughed.

"I need you to stay here for a while. Until I'm sure no one else is going to come looking for you."

"Why here?"

"It's safe."

I glanced around again, not really sure why he thought Colorado was a safe place. He'd never mentioned this place before. As I rotated, I noticed a house out the back window of the SUV. I glanced at Daniel and then back out the window. "Whose house is that?"

"A friend."

"You don't have friends."

"A brother."

I felt my eyes narrow. "Daniel…"

He sighed. "Look. I know you think you can take care of yourself—"

"I can."

"I know." He allowed. "I made sure of it."

"Then—"

"It's different this time." His words were harsh, and I drew back. He glanced away, then back again. "There are some dangerous, bad people out to get me, and they think the best way to do that is through you."

I opened my mouth, but he spoke before I could.

"They're right."

All the air deflated from my lungs. "Daniel—"

"I went into the army for a better life. Not just for me, but for you. I just wanted to take care of you… make sure you always had what you needed." He laughed humorlessly, released my hand, and shoved his through his hair. "I could have done that with some stupid admin job."

I smirked. "You weren't built for a desk job, Bear."

"I'm sorry I dragged you into this. I'm sorry about a lot of shit… I do love you, though, Sabrina. More than anyone else on earth."

"Same," I said, my heart swelling just a little.

"Maybe bringing you here will make up for some of the shit I've pulled," he said, almost as if he were rationalizing to himself.

I perked up. "Why here?"

His eyes became shuttered and the corner of his lips turned down into a grimace.

"Daniel…" A tingle of warning brushed over me.

"Promise me you'll stay here. I can't go out there if I think you're not being protected."

"Who's in that house, Daniel?" I stabbed my finger toward the back window and the A-frame cabin nestled in the trees.

"Probably the only other man on this planet who would go as far as I would to keep you safe."

A funny feeling wormed around inside me, and I grew uncomfortable, beginning to fidget in my seat. I didn't like that answer.

I also didn't like that his answer brought up a name in the back of my mind. A name that instantly dissolved into feelings tightening my diaphragm and making my insides tremble.

"You didn't…" My voice was hoarse and deep. "You wouldn't…"

Daniel sighed. "Get out of the car, Sabrina."

I didn't listen. Not because I was being stubborn. I was stubborn, but not even that character trait could break through the feelings and dread swirling inside me. I was stuck to the seat as if I'd been glued. My throat worked, trying to swallow spit my mouth didn't even have. My tongue was dry; my lips were dry.

I was being irrational. Getting all wound up for nothing. I knew whoever was inside that small A-frame wasn't who I'd conjured in my mind with my brother's words.

He was gone. Vanished from my life almost as if he hadn't been there at all. Sometimes I found myself wondering if perhaps he was just a figment of my imagination.

The sound of the door opening beside me startled me, and I jolted, pressing a hand against my chest and collapsing against the seat.

"Drama is not a good look on you, sis."

I gave him a depreciating look. "Who's in there?"

"I want you to know…" His jaw worked and his eyes slid to the side. I could tell he was nearly choking on whatever it was he wanted to say, which naturally made me want to hear it.

"Yes?" I invited.

He gave me a dry look but then turned serious again. "I'm sorry for the shit I pulled a few years back. I—" His eyes softened. "You were so young. It was my job to protect you."

Holy knicker-knackers. He is talking about him.

When I found the words to speak, they scraped out of my throat. "If you're protecting me, then why bring me here? This isn't protection, Daniel." *It's pain.*

"I told you. I was wrong."

He didn't tell me.

"I just did," he replied exasperated. Apparently, that thought had come out of my mouth without me realizing.

I was spiraling. Spiraling back a few years. Spiraling back into heartache and anger. My palms were clammy, and the trembling inside me had only grown.

I couldn't be here. I think I'd rather take my chances with whoever it was that wanted to kill me.

At least then I'd be dead and not walking around with my heart ripped out. *Again.*

"No," I said. My final answer. My absolute decree.

I might have been "too young" back then, but I wasn't now. I wasn't going to allow this. The amount of control my brother had over my life was scary. Enough was enough.

Wind swirled around my body, reaching out and slipping over my bare arms like cool silk. I drew in a deep breath, feeling just the slightest relief from the emotions assaulting me. The crispness to the air strengthened me. The cold seemed to harden my resolve. Overhead, the trees rustled, creating their own sort of song, a compliment to the temperature in the breeze.

Fall.

A season I wasn't that familiar with.

A season I had mostly seen on TV and in stores when late August rolled around.

Was this what it felt like? A kiss to your skin, the swirl of new beginnings in the air? Stars blinking like precious diamonds and cute wooden cottages tucked into mountains?

I'd been so preoccupied with the place around us I didn't even notice the reaction to my decree.

It wasn't a good one.

I shrieked as Daniel bulldozed into the seat of the SUV, locked his arms around my waist, and towed me out. "Daniel Mason Mercer, what the hell are you doing?" I demanded, though it came out more breathless than I intended because the jerk tossed me over his shoulder like I was a freaking sack of potatoes that weighed no more than a feather.

"I'm sorry, but this is for your own good," he remarked, not even winded.

I pounded on his back, hard enough that my hands stung, but he didn't even flinch. He didn't break his long strides across the yard, which was dotted with leaves… *How charming.*

His shoulder jammed into my stomach, and I lurched. "*Ugh*," I groaned. "Put me down!"

"No."

"I'm going to puke down your back."

"Wouldn't be the first time."

"That was one time, and I was drunk!" I hollered.

His shoulders shook with silent laughter. It made my stomach hurt worse.

"You're going to pay for this." I vowed.

"I'll take all the revenge you care to dish out, Brin-brin. As long as you're here to dish it out, I don't care."

The fight drained out of me instantaneously. I stopped struggling. He said the words lightly, but I heard what he didn't inflect. My brother was not an overreactor. He was not dramatic. He was actually the opposite. So cool that sometimes he came off as emotionless.

I knew better.

And I also knew he was worried.

He stopped walking. The arm holding me tightened just a little. "Brina?"

"I'm here," I whispered.

He grunted and started walking again. "Should have pretended to pass out. That might have worked."

"Jerk."

His chuckle floated behind him as he took the first wooden step leading up onto a deck.

"Wait!" I gasped, lifting my torso just a little.

His foot paused on the second step.

"Just tell me it's not him."

"You know I can't do that."

I collapsed against him again, feeling all the blood rushing to my head. I was dizzy and off balance, and it wasn't because I was upside down. "Why would you do this to me?"

He started walking again, and I thought maybe he didn't hear the whispered words.

The sound of a door being pulled open made my entire body tense so tight I hummed.

Daniel hadn't even knocked yet. He was still at the top of the stairs.

No one said anything, but the air changed completely.

Gone was the crisp autumn night.

Now the atmosphere was polluted with thick, sticky tension and unnatural foreboding.

I felt Daniel glance over his shoulder toward me, but I didn't lift my head. I couldn't. Everything inside me was focused on the person I couldn't see. The person I knew filled an entire doorway. A person I thought I would never in a million years see again.

"I'm not doing this to you," my brother said softly. "I'm doing this *for* you."

Alex

I felt the disturbance before the SUV even came into view. I was up and at the window when the black ride rolled to a slow stop not far from my place.

No headlights. License plate conveniently obscured by mud.

My fingers tightened on the gun at my side as I stood still, watching. Waiting.

No interior lights came on over whoever was inside. No movement came for a short while. Awareness prickled along my scalp and down my arms insistently, almost as if my own calm were fooling my mind into thinking I wasn't paying attention.

I was.

Oh, I was.

The best attack always started with stillness.

I knew it could be Mercer. Just days ago, he vowed to find me. It could be whoever Mercer pissed off, too. I wasn't complacent enough to believe whoever it was wasn't a threat. Complacency led in one direction: the grave.

In a thrust of movement, someone got out of the driver's side and stalked around the front of the truck, disappearing momentarily. I crouched low beneath the window, levelling my gun on the windowsill in the direction of the man.

He came into view again, his movements frustrated and a little jerky. All his attention was focused on the inside of the car, but his body language was something else entirely.

He was primed, cognizant of his surroundings, and clearly prepared to pull out the gun I knew was stashed in the back of his jeans.

Familiarity assailed me. I hadn't seen Mercer in a while, but I knew him instantly. The training in me recognized the training in him, and the unbreakable bond that we would have the rest of our lives settled between my shoulders.

Still, I didn't lower the gun. I didn't relent my stance at all.

Mercer wasn't here for a family reunion. He hadn't just come by for a beer and a memory.

The passenger door was pulled open, and he all but glared inside.

Oh no…

I shook my head, the first flash of distraction coming over me. I shoved it away violently and refocused.

Mercer's lips moved. His shoulders tensed. Whoever was in that car was pushing all his buttons.

Oh, hells no…

With a blast of movement, Mercer lunged into the car. When he drew back, he tossed a woman over his shoulder. He slammed the door of the SUV and spun. Long, dark hair whipped around before being shielded by his bulk.

"*Fuck.*" The curse slipped out of my lips. It was the only reaction I would allow myself to have. At least in that second.

All the others? You know, the immediate gut tightening, quickening of breath, and bunching of every single muscle in my body. I shoved them back.

I shoved them so hard it made my insides ache.

I didn't focus on Mercer or the woman he was hauling. Instead, I focused around him. To the yard, the familiar shapes and sounds of my home, and the way everything here should be feeling.

It wasn't until his boots hit the bottom step that I pulled back.

All was clear.

At least for the next, oh, twelve seconds. The second I opened that door and confirmed who that long, silky hair belonged to, shit was going to hit the fan.

Not that I needed confirmation. My body knew exactly what my eyes had yet to verify. I didn't have to see her face. I felt her. The air nearly crackled with her presence and my reaction to it.

What the fuck was Mercer trying to pull?

Tucking the gun in the waistband of my sweats, I stalked to the door and pulled it open.

Mercer paused at the top, and our eyes met.

We didn't say anything. Silence rang out like a crack of lightning in the center of a thunderstorm.

This is the job? My eyes belayed the pair.

He gave a curt nod.

He must have been fucking desperate to bring her here.

"No," I said, the coldness in my tone surprising even me. It had been a while since I'd let out this side of me.

"Ice," Mercer said, calling me by the name no one had used in years. "Hear me out."

I started to shake my head, my chest so tight it hurt to breathe. It hurt to stand.

"Alex?"

The whisper cut through me unlike anything else. Slicing me nearly in two and filleting me. I schooled my face into a mask of nothing, something I clearly hadn't forgotten how to do. I didn't let him see just how fucking wrecked just a whisper left me.

The softest of sounds. The most tentative of inflection.

My name.

My name on the lips of a woman who was completely off-limits. A woman who goddamn owned me regardless.

"She needs you," Mercer said, going right for the jugular.

"I do not!" Sabrina rebuked, fury in her tone. I heard the slap of her hand against the back of his legs.

My lips twitched. More of my insides spilled out.

I stepped sideways, motioning with my chin for him to come inside.

Relief flooded his features, and it was as if all the anxiety he'd just let go of was heaped on top of the dose I was already buried under.

"This isn't an agreement," I said quietly when he stepped past.

My body was taut, and I pushed back against the door so I didn't accidently get brushed by her swishing hair. It was hard, so goddamn hard not to look down, not to seek out her hazel gaze.

Instead, I focused on her ass. It was right there on display. Round. Tight.

Not mine.

"You alone?" Mercer asked, going farther into my place.

"You already know I am."

Mercer probably knew what color underwear I had on. There was no way he brought her here without knowing all about my life first.

The second I spoke, it seemed to break whatever invisible barrier had been between us. She lifted, staring through curtains of deep-brown hair right where I stood.

Our eyes crashed.

The room tilted.

I knew I was a goner.

6

Sabrina

He wasn't wearing a shirt.

His body was just as ripped as I remembered, but it didn't even matter. As mouthwatering and stare-inducing as his abs and chest were, his eyes held me.

Lordy, lordy his eyes.

They were so piercing I was convinced he could see right through me. I couldn't look away, entranced by the icy-blue shade, which was pale yet somehow still saturated. Sometimes that stare glinted silver and sometimes it looked like a cloudless sky on a bright-blue day. And sometimes it was a mix of both. The color was even more startling against his deep-toned skin, giving him an edge of dark and light.

I was assaulted almost violently with the first collision of our stares. He still affected me so deeply that a rush of anger burned the tops of my ears.

So much for growing out of a "schoolgirl crush."

"I had no idea he was bringing me here," I said abruptly, finally able to break the hold he had on me and drop my gaze.

"Well, that makes two of us." Alex's voice was gruff. God, just the sound made my knees weak.

Of course, Daniel chose that moment to swing me back onto my feet. My legs dipped beneath me, betraying the strong, sturdy image I wanted to portray.

"Whoa," my brother said, reaching to steady me.

I smacked his hand away and glared at him. "I'm fine."

I felt Alex's eyes watching me. Studying me in the intense way he had. I refused to look at him. Being in his presence was hard enough.

"We're leaving," I announced and started past Daniel.

"No, *we* aren't. You're staying."

"Staying?" Alex queried. I could practically feel the way his brows climbed up his forehead.

"You owe me," Daniel intoned, stepping toward Alex. "This is the job."

"I'm not a job. I'm a person."

"Right now, you're a pain in the ass," Daniel snapped. I could tell he was nearing the end of his patience.

Well, so was I! "Allow me to relieve you of said pain," I mouthed and started for the door.

Alex side-stepped, moving in front of me and using his body as a blockade. I stopped abruptly, teetering on my feet, terrified I might accidentally touch him.

"Where are my shoes?" I asked suddenly, after all this time realizing I wasn't wearing any.

"Probably with the rest of your clothes," Alex muttered.

My eyes flashed up. Renewed awareness flowed through me, and my throat tightened. I glanced down my body, fully grasping the state of my dress… or rather *un*dress.

Dear Lord, I was in my pajamas! A tank top, shorts that weren't exactly intended for the public eye, and… nothing else.

No socks.

No bra.

With a silent yelp, I glanced down at the girls and nearly died where I stood. My nipples were hard. Might has well be flashing neon lights as I stood there in front of Alex.

I started to cross my arms over my chest, totally embarrassed. Then I stopped. Screw that. Screw both of these guys!

"Well, I didn't have time to put on clothes because people were trying to murder me!"

Alex's eyes narrowed, and a chill climbed over the room. It spread slowly, methodically, making gooseflesh rise along my arms. Cold like this was ominous. The farther it spread, the scarier it seemed.

"Someone tried to kill you?" he asked, whisper-soft.

I couldn't speak, so I nodded instead.

Alex's eyes flashed and then flicked to Daniel.

"I killed them. All four of them."

"Four!" I gasped. "I only saw three."

"I know," Daniel replied, grim.

Alex nodded as if he approved of the murders and then dragged his eyes up my body again. I fidgeted, feeling the caress.

And yes, it was a caress.

I might hate him. He might hate me. But damn. When Alex looked at me, I *felt* it. I knew my legs were long, but he made me feel like they really were a mile high because it seemed to take forever for him to get to the top.

Something flashed across his face before he looked away. Jaw locked, he stalked out of the room.

Maybe stalked was a bad word to describe how he moved. He didn't stalk like he was angry, heavy-footed, or took up a lot of space around him.

No. Alex was lithe. He was sort of like a panther in a jungle he'd explored a million times over. Even if he was in a place he'd never been and not his own home, he moved so assuredly, so light-footed no one would ever be the wiser.

When he was gone, a hiss seeped out of me, and I spun to Daniel, giving him an evil, evil glare.

"Yeah, yeah," he said.

Realizing the path to the door was no longer blocked, I took off, my bare feet slapping over the wood as I rushed.

"Stop."

The command was low, firm, and it rooted me in place. Pissed off at my body for obeying, I turned to glare over my shoulder.

Alex was back, prowling toward me with something in his hands. It was red, gray, and white. I divided my stare between him and what he was holding. His mouth was drawn in a taut line. His body seemed tight and coiled, as though he expected me to fight.

I wanted to.

I couldn't. As much as he brought out that hellcat in me, he also tamed it.

When he got close, I tensed and sucked in a breath. Wariness washed over me, and the urge to bolt was back full force.

"Calm down," he said low, almost as if he were trying to soothe a spooked horse.

The thing in his hands lifted when he pulled apart the two sides. It was a plaid flannel shirt, and it looked worn and soft. That was the best kind of shirt, wasn't it?

"Here." He motioned for my arms. He wanted me to put on his shirt?

My thighs clenched together. I shook my head.

"You're freezing. I can see your goose bumps from across the room."

I wondered if my goose bumps also included my puckered nipples. That thought made my eyes narrow, and I looked up. He smirked as if he could read my thoughts.

I had a choice here:

1.) Tell him to go to hell and let my nips in all their glory command the room.

Or…

2.) I could put on the shirt, because being half naked in front of my brother and *him* was majorly embarrassing.

Sighing, I lifted my arms, and he helped me into the flannel like it was a coat. Thank goodness my back was to him because my eyes closed for the briefest of moments when the material fell around me and a scent I thought I'd forgotten wafted up to my nose.

He smelled good. So frickin' good. I didn't even know how to describe it except it was Alex. No one else smelled like him, and yes, I knew because I might have been a little stalkery back in the day and went to the men's cologne department and smelled every single thing they had to try and find something that reminded me of him.

There was nothing. Because he was unique.

I felt his palms hover over my shoulders as if he wanted to smooth the shirt over my arms, but he drew back instead.

I grabbed the front of the shirt and turned, tugging it a little farther around me, allowing the fabric to swallow me up. I was cold, and I knew after a few minutes, I wouldn't be anymore.

Alex hadn't stepped away, so when I was fully around, his chest blocked my view of everything. He gazed down, intensity dripping from every single pore. His eyes sought mine, but I refused to look up. Instead, I focused really hard on one of the buttons across my chest, trying with trembling fingers to get the little button through the hole.

On the third try, I bit my lip to keep from groaning in frustration. I couldn't do this while he was standing this close! My hands didn't work. My brain didn't work…

Long-fingered, sure hands appeared where I was focused. He went to brush mine out of the way, but I jolted back before he could touch them. He didn't react to that. Instead, he pulled the shirt around and deftly did up a few buttons, covering my exposed chest.

I swallowed, the action so thick I knew he heard.

The second the shirt was secured, he dropped his hands and pivoted away, giving me a few moments of blessed privacy. I drew in a shuddering breath and glanced up, studying the lines and sinew of his broad, bare back.

God, he looked incredible.

"If I worried I made the wrong call earlier, I sure as hell don't now." My brother spoke.

I stiffened and moved forward, giving Alex a wide berth. I could feel the fabric of his shirt brush against my legs and tickle the backs of my thighs.

"I need to talk to Ice," my brother said.

I batted my lashes and spoke sweetly. "Who?"

He raised a dark brow in reply.

I sighed and glanced in the direction where Ice, aka Alex, was standing but didn't look at him. "May I use your bathroom, please?"

"Through the bedroom," he replied.

The skin on my scalp tingled when I stepped into the dark bedroom. The scent I knew as Alex intensified. Intimacy flowed over me, and my stomach flipped upside down. I was in his bedroom, in his personal space.

Heart thundering, I went into the adjoining bathroom, flipped on the light, and shut the door. I sagged against it instantly, knees shaking.

My brother had to know I couldn't stay here. I wouldn't.

Alex

"I need you to protect my sister." Mercer cut right to the chase, something I would have done if he hadn't.

"And you can't because…?" I baited.

"I'm the reason she needs protecting."

"How bad is it?" I asked, even though I knew if he was on my doorstep, it was pretty fucking bad.

"They sent four men for her," he spat, stepping closer and lowering his voice. "You know four men aren't necessary for a one-woman job, unless they planned on having some fun before they finished her off."

My back teeth came together with enough force that my jaw radiated with a crack of pain. Sabrina was a lot of things—a pain in the ass at the top of that list—but the thought of shit being done to her that I knew was possible had the actual ability to bring me to my knees.

I kept my tone neutral, my voice clipped. "Who are we talking about here?"

"Foreign nationals."

"On our fucking soil." I snarled.

"Yeah, well… my last job got messy. And the mess followed me home."

I cursed.

"I have to take care of this, but I can't do that if I know she's sitting at home with a bull's-eye on her back."

I crossed my arms over my chest. "You could have taken her to anyone."

"Anyone isn't you."

"I've been out for a few years now. I'm rusty."

He laughed. "That was a fucking waste of breath, and you know it. Guys like us don't get rusty. Out or not, this shit is ingrained, and that's not something that will ever change."

I started to say something else, but he held up his hand. He looked fucking tired. Dark circles under his eyes, lines around his mouth, and an odor that made me wonder about the last time he was able to take a shower.

I'd known Mercer for years. We'd been in situations together that most people only ever came close to in a movie theater. He was always my top choice to have at my back when we dropped (literally by plane) into some fucked-up hole on the map for a mission. He'd saved my life more than once. I'd done the same for him.

He wasn't a friend, not really. But we were bonded by loyalty and trust. My relationship with Mercer wasn't at all like the one I had with Liam. But I considered both of them my brothers.

I'd go to hell and back for Liam. I'd been to hell and back with Merc.

"I know you still got it. You ordered a hit on fucking Perry Crone, for Christ's sake."

"I didn't order a hit."

"What would you call it?" He challenged.

I shrugged. "He was terrorizing my pregnant sister. Putting my nephew in danger. I wasn't about to let my bro do something with consequences he would have to live with forever."

He grunted knowingly. Killing left a mark on you, whether you did it once or a hundred times, for good or for bad. I was already marked the fuck up. I wouldn't let Liam be, too.

"Your sister hooked up with Liam?" he asked, puzzled.

"I shook my head. Not my blood sister. My chosen one."

He nodded, understanding. "And now my sister needs you."

"She's not my sister."

"I think we both know she's a hell of a lot more than that."

I dropped my arms and tensed. "You got amnesia? A few years ago, you didn't want me to even look in her direction. You forbade it."

I sensed movement in the doorway of my bedroom, but I didn't glance in her direction. Sabrina was listening, but it wouldn't influence any of the words I spoke.

"And you walked. You walked all the way out of the army."

Shrugging, I replied, "I missed home."

"That all it was?" He challenged, but without heat.

I just stared at him, not looking away, not fidgeting. No reaction. After a few, Mercer chuckled. "You haven't changed a bit."

I had, but the parts he was referring to were still there.

"She was young, man. So goddamn young. I didn't want her in this life."

"Yet here you are," I said, sweeping out an arm.

His eyes flashed. "Here we are. And I'm man enough to admit I was wrong. I shouldn't have forced you two apart. It's probably the only thing in my life I regret. Well, that and bringing the heat down on her in the first place."

"I would have done the same," I said, giving him that. It was the truth.

Sabrina had been barely eighteen. I was twenty-four, and I did some gritty shit for a living. Six years might not be so bad if I'd had a desk job and not something that added even more years to my age.

"I honestly didn't think she'd ever forgive me. In fact, I'm not sure she ever did."

I was staring at Mercer, but all my attention, all my awareness was directed toward my bedroom where I knew she was hovering in the shadows. I wanted to look over. I wanted to reach in and pull her out into the light and stare in her hazel eyes. I wanted to know if she'd forgiven her brother… if she'd forgiven me.

"I'm trying to make it right." Mercer went on.

I scoffed. "This isn't some matchmaking trip or even some way to try and make amends. You wouldn't be here right now if you didn't need me."

"You're right. But from the second I stepped into this house I felt it. I saw it. It's still there."

The sound of a throat clearing burst into the room, and Mercer looked around as Sabrina walked in. "Your man time is up."

Mercer glanced back at me, dropping some of the guard in his eyes. "You are the only one who will protect her like I would. You're the only one I trust with my sister."

How ironic. A few years ago, it was just the opposite.

Almost as if he heard my thoughts, he answered, "You earned it when you respected me enough to walk. If there is anyone out there who might even come close to being good enough for my sister, it's you."

Sabrina stiffened, her eyes spearing him. "What the hell, Daniel? You're acting like you're trying to barter my arranged marriage. Stop it. You don't get a say in my love life." She flushed, glancing at me, then quickly away. "Not anymore."

We ignored her.

Which pissed her off.

"I'm making coffee," she announced and stormed toward the kitchen. When she drew level with me, she stopped. "You have some, right?"

My lips twitched. God. She was exactly the same. Still as fucking feisty and gorgeous as ever. "In the tin on the counter."

She went into the kitchen, and I heard her moving around. A second later, she exclaimed, "A Keurig! I thought I'd have to use that instant crap and then go find a cow to milk just for some cream."

"It's Colorado," I called out. "Not a third world country."

"You'll do it?" Daniel asked, watching me.

"I'm still six years older than her. She's still only twenty."

"She'll be twenty-one next month."

"And I'll be twenty-seven in a few."

"Just… don't hurt her, okay?"

I raised an eyebrow. "You giving me your blessing with your sister?"

He swallowed. "I guess I am."

I digested that, rocking back on my heels. Stuffing my hands into the sweats I'd thrown on, I watched him. This definitely wasn't fun for him. It gave me a sick kind of satisfaction because of all the shit he'd pulled before.

Cocking my head to the side, I said, "You think just because you bring her here, tell me to have at it, that I'm going to do it? What makes you think I even still want her?"

"I didn't tell you to have at it," Mercer said, harsh. Then he glanced up. "You do."

I shook my head.

"That's not what this is about anyway. This is about her life. Her not being taken hostage, used up, and tortured before dying alone."

Actual pain lanced through me at his harsh words. Mental flashes of women I'd seen during my time in the army—women I'd rescued, some I'd been forced to leave behind—assaulted me.

Not Sabrina. Never Sabrina.

"You don't want her anymore? Fine. But at least protect her."

"I'm impressed," Sabrina said, coming back into the room, carrying two mugs. "Your fridge is actually stocked. And you had creamer. The good kind."

"I like to eat," I commented as she handed over one of the mugs to her brother.

"You need this." When he took it, her nose wrinkled. "You also need a shower."

"I've been busy," he said, taking a swig of the brew.

Sabrina glanced over her shoulder at me. Long, deep-brown hair fell down her back. It was knotted and tangled, making it look like she'd been rolling around in bed. Her golden-green eyes were tired, anxiety tightened her face, and her lips were chapped. My shirt—my favorite flannel—draped over her body, the collar sticking up to caress her jaw when she glanced around.

My guts tightened, and in my pockets, my hands balled into fists.

"You're a terrible cook." She remembered.

I shrugged and glanced away. "My sister is a chef."

Her face clouded with confusion.

Mercer's voice drew her around. Relief poured over me when she looked away. "The boarder's wife."

"Right," she said. "I read he got married."

I stiffened. "You read up on Liam?"

"He's an Olympic medalist. He was in the news a lot last year."

My shoulders unbunched just a little. Of course. You'd have to live under a rock not to know Liam Mattison.

"I'll do it," I announced, making a decision I knew I shouldn't.

Daniel seemed to visibly sag, then stepped around Sabrina to thrust his hand out toward me. "Thank you."

I took his hand, solidifying the promise I just made.

"What?" Sabrina exclaimed, coming over and knocking her brother's arm so his hand came out of mine. "I gave you time to talk. I took a minute and made some coffee. That in NO way was me agreeing to any of this." She swung around to Daniel. "I am *not* staying here."

"Yes. You are."

Sabrina stepped up to her brother. She was little taller than average, about five feet six, with long sinful legs and a round ass that made this brother want to cry. But she was no match for Mercer, who outweighed her by at least seventy pounds and was over six feet tall. Not to mention she lacked the savagery that I knew damn well lived within him.

She didn't back down. Either she knew damn well he wouldn't hurt her, or she just didn't care. My guess was both. Her bare toes hit against his booted feet, and she poked a finger into his chest, shoving her face close.

"Daniel Mason Mercer, you are *not* the boss of me. You might be the only family I have left… You might even be more father than brother, but I'm drawing the line! I love you, but enough is enough. I know you're worried about me, but I can take care of myself. We're leaving." She sniffed when she finished laying down the law.

Mercer was looking at her patiently, as if he was used to this.

When he didn't say anything, she nodded once. "I'll be in the car."

On her way out, she paused and thrust the nearly empty coffee cup at me. "Thanks for the joe. See you never."

I took the cup, and she continued. At the door, she paused and declared, "I'm keeping the shirt!"

Then she left.

I glanced down at the mug, then over at Mercer. "What else do I need to know in order to protect her?"

Now that she was out of earshot, we could finish our conversation before we both made her come back inside.

Sabrina

I waited.

Then I waited some more.

A sound of acute frustration filled the interior of the SUV, and I dropped my bare feet off the dashboard. My hair whipped around when I moved to glare out the back window at the A-frame.

Why did his house have to be so charming? Why did he have to still look like eye candy? Why couldn't he smell bad like my brother?

It didn't matter. We were leaving. I wasn't going to see him again.

I sank back into the seat, pressing a hand to the center of my chest and rubbing. It hurt to see him again. It hurt more than I realized it would. I thought I'd gotten over him.

Liar.

Fine. I at least thought that if I ever had to be in the same room with him again, it wouldn't nearly rip me in half.

Damn Daniel for bringing me here. For making me relive something that took a chunk out of my heart, leaving it incomplete for all eternity.

I'd made peace with it, with that chunk out of my heart. At least I thought I had.

Daniel still failed to come out of the house. Impatience and anger crowded beneath my skin. Clearly, he hadn't gotten the memo. You know, the one where I stated clearly that I wasn't staying.

Fine. If he wanted to stay so bad, he could.

I was leaving.

Shoving open the car door, I stalked through the yard. Stopped. Stared up at the starry sky and blew out a breath. I needed a plan. Glancing around, my eyes fell on something rather obnoxious on the side of the house.

I laughed. "This is just too easy."

In my haste to close the distance between me and my new transportation, I stepped on a branch, which could have probably doubled as a knife.

"Ow!" I swore, bending at the waist and stumbling. Grabbing my ankle, I hopped around on one foot before balancing to pull it up and glance down. The stupid bark-covered offender was sticking out of the bottom of my foot.

I yanked it out and tossed it down, glancing back to my foot. There was a smear of blood there, but it wasn't like I had a Band-aid… or a sock, so I kept moving.

A few steps later, I doubled back and picked up the stabby branch. I might need it later.

There was no movement or loud yelling inside the house as I passed, and I couldn't help but wonder what they were talking about. I heard the things Daniel said to Alex when I was in the bathroom. My goodness, he practically asked Alex to marry me!

That ship had sailed, buddy.

Of all the nerve—*really*! He threw such a momentous fit when he realized something was happening between his "baby sister" and his seasoned teammate, to the point that Alex actually left town and left me absolutely crushed. I didn't speak to him for months.

Clearly, he hadn't learned his lesson. 'Cause here we were.

I was out.

Luckily for me, the giant Hummer was unlocked, which frankly made me snort out loud. What kind of ex-special forces secret op leaves his car unlocked?

Oh well, it was my good fortune.

The door creaked a little when I opened it, which made me wince and glance up at the house. When Alex didn't burst out hollering, I figured I was in the clear. Climbing inside, I scooted down into the driver's seat to look under the dash.

It had been a while since I hotwired a car… but it was like riding a bike, right? I smirked, feeling a little gleeful imaging Alex's face when he heard his car start up and drive away.

That would almost be worth hanging around for.

It was dark, and the wiring was hard to get to. Cursing, I slid down onto the floor, having plenty of space because Alex's long legs required the seat to be pushed back. My toe stubbed on the piece of the dash I'd pulled off, and I leaned my forehead against the leather seat and sucked in a breath.

I seriously needed to get some shoes.

Getting back to work, I grew more frustrated because hotwiring a car was hard in the dark. I perked up and looked toward the glove box, realizing that a guy like Alex probably had a flashlight inside.

I scooted up and reached for it just as a large, unfamiliar hand clamped down on my outstretched arm.

I screamed.

Alex

I agreed to protect her. That didn't mean I was going to try and pick up where we left off nearly three years ago.

That ship had sailed.

I wasn't interested anymore. Sabrina made it *very* clear she wasn't either.

I didn't care about her like that. Not anymore.

A shrill scream cut through the night somewhere outside.

The purest form of panic coldcocked me right across the face. Even though my heart was literally leaping in my chest and the stickiest form of dread clung to me, I went cold.

My ability to go utterly calm and methodical during even the hairiest of situations was what earned me the nickname Ice. That and the fact that I killed without blinking an eye.

I moved fast, knocking back Mercer who was shitting his pants trying to rush across the floor. The house shook when I wrenched open the door and rushed outside, gun drawn, eyes scanning the yard.

"Sabrina!" I yelled, not even so much a quiver of fear in my voice.

But, oh, there was fear. So. Much. Fear.

I was going to gut whoever was out here, whoever even thought they would hurt her.

"Put me down!" she yelled.

I leapt off the deck, not bothering with the steps, and rotated to where her voice came from.

"Now! Or I'll bite your ass!"

What the…?

"Sabrina!" Daniel roared, rushing past me, clearly not hearing the odd threat.

"Ow!" A much deeper voice swore.

A much deeper, familiar voice.

I bolted forward, throwing myself at Daniel, ramming into him as he shot the gun he'd been brandishing.

"Down!" I roared.

A scuffle of movement met the corner of my eye as Daniel and I hit the ground.

Sabrina screeched.

I landed on top of Daniel, instantly disarming him of the gun and leaping up.

"Liam!" I called, rushing over to where they'd been.

He was on the ground, his body draped over Sabrina like a shield.

"Jesus Christ! Are you hit?" I demanded, dropping onto a knee to assess.

He glanced up, hair in his face. "Nah, I'm straight."

I blew out a relieved breath. Then Sabrina groaned.

The gun I held with both hands hit the dirt, and I hit my knees. "Kitten," I rasped out, shoving Liam away and reaching for her. "Kitten, honey, where are you hit?"

I gripped her shoulders and pulled her into me, scanning her face, her neck, her shoulders, panicking, searching for a bullet wound, looking for blood.

Her eyes popped open. "Alex," she whispered.

My stare sprang to hers. "Tell me, baby. Tell me where you're hit."

She sighed a little and snuggled close, then suddenly stiffened and wrenched away. I went to grab her back, still freaking the fuck out, but she yelled, "I'm not shot!"

I reached for her anyway. She grasped my hand and glared at me. "Alex! I'm not shot!"

I fell back onto my haunches, still gripping her hand so she had to move a little with me. "You aren't?"

"No." She held her arms out. "See?"

Anger filled my throat. "Then what the fuck were you groaning on the ground for?"

Good God! She took nearly twenty years off my life!

"Because this creep threw me on the ground and jumped on me!"

Daniel came out of nowhere, grabbing up Liam by the back of his neck and putting him a choke hold.

I lurched up and shook my head. "It's Liam."

Daniel dropped him immediately. "My bad."

"You're fucking lucky you didn't put a bullet in him," I swore.

"Sorry," Daniel said, sheepish.

Liam straightened his shirt and glanced at me, lifting a brow. "Kitten? Honey? Baby?"

"Fuck you, Mattison."

He turned to Sabrina. "You have a real name?"

She crossed her arms over her chest and sniffed. "You're bigger on TV."

Liam grinned. "Still took you to the ground."

"You better watch yourself." I warned him.

Liam took my threat mildly, squinting at me. "I take it you know this little criminal?"

Sabrina gasped.

I laughed.

Daniel stared between us all as though he wasn't sure how to react. Right now, he was taking my word that Liam was good people, but if Liam pushed him, then I'd be breaking up a fight.

"What'd she do?" I asked, smirking.

"I caught her trying to hotwire the Hummer."

The smirk dropped. "What?" I growled, glaring at Sabrina.

Daniel started muttering and cursing under his breath.

"He attacked me!" Sabrina declared.

Liam rolled his eyes. "I pulled her out of the front seat, and *she* attacked *me*."

"I taught her well." Daniel grunted.

"I probably already have bruises," Liam muttered, rubbing his ass.

"I've had just about enough of overbearing men thinking they can toss me over their shoulder and—"

"He tossed you over his shoulder?"

Liam heard the cool, flat tone I used and held up his hands. "She was trying to run. I was just looking out for you."

I frowned.

I didn't want him touching her. I didn't want anyone touching her.

"You better not have messed up my ride." I warned Sabrina.

She made a rude sound.

"Why couldn't you have just hotwired *your* SUV?" I wondered.

She looked offended. "I wasn't about to leave Daniel without any kind of transportation."

I made a face. "But I didn't need any?"

"Not my problem."

Liam was watching us, dividing apprising looks between me and Sabrina during the exchange. He took a step toward me. "Who is this?"

I sighed. "This is Sabrina."

His eyes widened. "*Sabrina*, Sabrina?"

I nodded.

He whistled beneath his breath. "That explains it, then."

"Explains what?" she asked, curious.

"What got him to hand over his favorite shirt."

I tossed my hands in the air. "She was half naked!"

"How did that happen?" Liam ribbed, wagging his eyebrows.

"That's my sister," Daniel intoned, stepping up to Liam.

Liam stuck his hand between them and introduced himself. After a moment, Daniel did the same.

I felt Sabrina's eyes. "You told him about me?"

I needed a drink. A stiff one. "I told him about my time in the army." I rebuked.

She glanced away and fell silent.

"Everyone, in the house," I snapped, picking up the guns and gesturing for them to all go ahead.

As Liam and Sabrina went up the stairs, I grabbed the back of Daniel's neck. "You shoot at my best friend again and I will put a bullet in you."

"Noted."

He wasn't offended. Why would he be? I was giving him a heads-up. Frankly, it was a downright courtesy.

I barely had the door shut when a phone started ringing. We all looked at Liam because no one else had one on them.

He answered instantly. "Hey, sweetheart." He paused. "Yeah, everything's fine." He glanced at me and listened. "He has some company is all. I'm telling you—" His words cut off and he sighed, stretching the phone out to me. "Bells wants to talk to you."

I grabbed the phone. "Yo! Girl who got away!"

"Why do you have visitors in the middle of the night?"

"How do you know I have visitors in the middle of the night?" I countered.

She made a frustrated sound. "Because when I got up with the baby, I looked out the window and saw a light on in the distance."

My brows knit. "Shaw okay?" I glanced up at Liam. He nodded.

"Yes." Her voice softened. "He's a baby. Sometimes he wakes up."

"I still think you must have a telescope angled at my place from that fancy mansion y'all be shacking up in."

"We aren't shacking up!" Liam growled. He hated when I said that. And when I called their newly built home a mansion. Naturally, I said it often.

Bellamy laughed in my ear. "Maybe we do."

"No other way you could see over here."

"I was just worried. I had a feeling. Liam said he'd check."

"Ah," I said, glancing at Liam. He met my eyes and nodded.

Bellamy was prone to "feelings," ones she refused to ignore. I couldn't blame her after everything she'd been through. Hell, if she didn't listen to her gut when it screamed at her then, she'd probably be dead.

I was touched. "You were worried about me, Bells?"

Liam made a noise. He didn't like when I called her that either. I grinned.

"Well, yeah."

"Don't be, okay? I'm fine. I'll send your boy home so he can tell you in person."

"I'm coming over tomorrow." She warned as if she were planning to catch me doing something I shouldn't.

My eyes strayed to Sabrina. *Hell.*

"Anytime," I replied, my eyes still on the brunette in my kitchen.

Liam took the phone, said a few more words, and then ended the call.

Sabrina was watching me, veiled interest in her eyes as she clearly listened to my conversation with Liam's wife, Bellamy.

"My other sister," I explained, not really sure why I felt I needed to.

"Like I care," she quipped and looked away.

Liam chuckled beneath his breath. I glared at him.

"So, ah…" He spoke up. "What's up with the late-night visit and the hotwiring?"

"Long story," I muttered. "I'll fill you in tomorrow."

"Need to know." Daniel reminded me.

I nodded. Liam needed to know, and I was going to tell him, whether or not Daniel wanted me to. My house. My rules.

Liam knew I'd tell him, so he didn't even react to Daniel's statement.

I turned toward my best friend. "Thanks for coming by. I appreciate it."

"Minor," he said, holding out a fist. I slammed mine into it. "Need me to hang around?"

"Nah, I got this."

He nodded and glanced at Daniel. "Thanks for having shitty aim."

Daniel's eyes flashed. "Ice pushed me out of the way."

Liam glanced at me at the use of my old army nickname. I shrugged.

He turned around, facing Sabrina. She lifted her chin, stubbornness reflected in her eyes.

"Nice to finally meet you, *Kitten*," he said, a total shit-eating grin on his face.

I grabbed the back of his shirt and leaned in. "Never again." I threatened.

He'd better never call her that again.

He threw his head back and laughed. Asshole.

When the laughter settled, he glanced back at Sabrina. "If you ever need anything, just let me know. Everyone around here knows how to find me."

She seemed surprised. Liam's acceptance was immediate and honest.

"Uh, thanks," she said, swallowing. He started away, and she called after him. "But I won't be around to need anything."

"If you say so." He chuckled, then let himself out the door.

I closed the door behind us when we stepped out onto the deck. "Bellamy had a feeling, huh?"

He nodded. "I knew she wouldn't go back to sleep until I made sure you were okay."

I smiled. I liked that girl.

"Maybe I was a little worried, too. The last time we talked, you weren't yourself."

I tossed my head toward the house. "Mercer had called. Brought some shit up."

Liam nodded, understanding. "And now he's here."

"Sabrina is going to be staying for a while."

"Just a while?" He goaded.

"Someone's after Mercer. Thinks the best way to hurt him is to hurt her."

"I really fucking hate men who hurt women," Liam growled, his face going dark. I knew he was thinking about Bellamy and everything she'd been through.

"Word." I agreed.

"All right. We'll talk later. I'll cover you at work tomorrow. Think you might need the time." He glanced back toward the house, lips twitching.

I nodded.

Partway down the steps, he turned back. "Bro?"

I answered. "Bro."

"You never told me how hot she is."

My tongue ran over my teeth and my eyes narrowed. "Don't look at her."

Liam smiled slowly. "Oh yeah. This is going to fun."

I gave him the finger, but he was too busy laughing as he sauntered away.

Sabrina

Alex offered my brother the use of his shower, who was about to say no when I pointed down the hall and glared. He'd been going well over twenty-four hours without any sleep, and before that, I had no idea. I honestly didn't have a clue how he was still on his feet.

Daniel relented and followed Alex down the hall to get a towel and a fresh change of clothes.

When they were gone, I blew out a breath. My stomach was in knots and my nerves were shot. I was a tough woman. I'd been through a lot in my life, and I honestly knew I could get through anything, but I was rattled.

Watching my brother kill men in front of me. Knowing the men he killed really wanted to kill me. Changing cars on back roads I didn't even know existed and stopping only at gas stations that were so insidious Daniel didn't even let me out of the car was enough to unnerve anyone.

And all that ended here.

With a man who broke my heart so badly I knew deep down I wouldn't love again. Yes, I blamed Daniel for it… but not all of it.

Alex could have stayed. He could have fought for me. For us.

He didn't. He left and he never looked back, disappearing and making it so I couldn't even reach out if I'd wanted to.

Rubbing the back of my neck and tugging once more on my ear, I glanced at the large triangular window looking out over the yard. The walls were wood, a deep honey color, and beams framed the window, the bottom of the glass met a large window seat that was screaming for some cushions and a blanket.

The window would be adorable if it were framed in string lights. Not on the outside, but in here where they could be enjoyed year round, lending a cozy glow to the definite cabin feel.

The room changed before he even entered. I felt his presence first. The cabin felt suddenly crowded, though I was standing there alone.

Even after all this time, my body still anticipated him, even after all the pain.

I kept my back turned, not wanting to look at him. I wasn't going down this path again. Holding my breath, I listened for the sounds of his movement, though there weren't any. Alex was a large man, but he moved like he was small.

I knew it was training, the same kind my brother had, and even though I practically lived with it, I was still always amazed.

I felt him stop partway into the room. I felt his eyes raking over me the same way I would rake over him if I had the chance to look at him without him looking back. My body tensed even though I tried to force it to remain relaxed. I couldn't not react to him. To his eyes. To his presence, to the way I knew his piercing stare fixed on me.

He chuckled quietly, obviously noting the way I stiffened. I amused him. I didn't think any of this was entertaining. My brother dragged me here, and they both stood around discussing what I was going to do like I was a child, like I wasn't capable of making choices for myself.

"I don't know why you laugh," I said, keeping my body turned away as if the view outside was worthy of so much staring. In truth, all I could see was the dark night. "You left to get away from me, yet here I am."

His silence was anything but. The crowded room seemed to overflow with unspoken words, tension, and… Was that surprise? I took a moment, pressing my lips together and inhaling slowly through my nose. I was tired, but I was not weak.

"As soon as Daniel gets a few more minutes to breathe, we'll be out of here." *You can go back to the life you so desperately wanted without me.*

"I didn't say I wanted you to go."

All that nervous energy? The flock of stupid and annoying butterflies filling up my stomach and chest? They died.

Everything in me dropped like the heaviest of stones to the bottom of a deep, murky lake. I felt when it hit, and I imagined a million dead butterflies lying motionless and weighing so much more than they ever could when they were in flight.

You never said you wanted me to stay.

He made a soft noise. Then I heard him moving away toward the kitchen. "I'll be outside. I'm going to check the perimeter."

I wondered if anything could ever shake his control.

The door closed quietly with a low click. I avoided watching him descend off the deck, glancing away until I knew if I looked, he'd already have melted into the shadows.

Only then did I let out a shaky breath and drop my guard enough that my body ached from the released tension I'd been so coiled with.

Pushing my hair behind both ears, I stared down my body, gazing over his shirt and then down to my bare feet.

It amazed me I'd gone this entire trip and didn't realize I'd left my house with nothing but a small pair of pajamas. I wondered how long it would have taken for me to notice had it not been for Alex's comment.

Not much later, Daniel entered the room, and I turned from the window, watching him rub a towel over his head, drying the hair he didn't have. His hair was dark brown like mine, but he kept it buzzed off. The only time I'd ever seen it long since he'd joined the army was when he'd just come home from a lengthy mission and it was almost to his chin. He'd had a beard, too. Something else I'd never seen.

I asked about it, and he said it'd been a way of blending in. Whatever that meant. The day after he got back, though, all the hair disappeared and he was back to looking like the brother I knew.

"You look better," I remarked and then smiled. "Smell better, too."

"Har-har." He tossed the wet towel at me. I caught it with one hand and threw it back. Daniel snagged it out of the air and draped it over his shoulder.

He wasn't wearing a shirt. He had that draped over his shoulder, too. His chest and shoulders were covered in tattoos, most of them just elaborate designs. Some of them I was pretty sure were symbols or things from other cultures, but I never questioned him about them because I knew he would only tell me half a truth.

I pondered sometimes what it would be like walking around with permanent ink on your body, knowing that some of it probably had only been a way of survival or of "blending in" and probably didn't even align with any of his personal beliefs. Like his body didn't just belong to him, but to the army and the missions he took.

Only a select few would ever know just how much he sacrificed, the countless people he saved. He'd belonged to a very secret special forces team—the same one as Alex. They'd both since left that team, but my brother still contracted jobs, unlike Alex who had walked away.

He cleared his throat, and I drew my eyes from the tattoos and up to his brown eyes framed with incredibly dark lashes.

"You want some more coffee?"

He grunted. "If I drink any more coffee, I'll be pissing brown the rest of my life."

"That was graphic," I said, making a face. "How about some water instead?"

He nodded.

I went into the kitchen, struck once more that I was in Alex's house and I was just walking around like I lived here. Of all the awkwardness and tension between me and Alex, this was the least of it. Even now, even after everything, I was still comfortable moving around his house. Probably because coffee and water, the bathroom, and clean clothes were a necessity. They were material objects that didn't really matter.

I reached into the fridge and grabbed a basic bottle of water and handed it behind me to my brother. Then, seeing all the ingredients, I reached back in and pulled out all the makings for a sandwich.

The bread was thick and looked homemade. I sliced off two wide pieces and set them on a paper towel. My stomach grumbled at the delicious scent of the sourdough, something I really loved. Daniel and I had lived off power bars and basic packaged crap the entire way here. He hadn't wanted to stop anywhere beyond those seedy gas stations, so food options were limited.

Daniel drained the water as I slathered the bread with mayo and added cheese, turkey, and some tomato slices. Once done, I slid the sandwich across the counter toward my brother and pointed at it. "Eat that."

"What about you?"

"I'm not hungry." I lied. Well, it wasn't exactly a lie. My body might be hungry, but the rest of me couldn't even think about food.

He picked it up and took a massive bite.

I piled the stuff back in the fridge and wondered about Alex's self-proclaimed sister. The one who was close enough to him to keep his fridge stocked with more than bachelor food and how much time she spent with him. What was their relationship like? What side of Alex did she get to see? There were so many of them.

I felt the bitter tinge of jealousy when I wondered if perhaps this woman got to see all of them.

I busied myself getting another bottle of water for Daniel and handing it over, along with a banana that seemed perfectly ripe.

"I see you've made yourself at home," he said, polishing off the sandwich.

"Hardly. You look like you're about to fall down. I'm just making sure you don't."

He grunted. "Takes a lot more than this to bring me down."

I slumped, sort of sad this kind of thing was so normal to him it didn't even faze him. Daniel noted my momentary pity party and set the water down, came around the counter, and pulled me into a bear hug.

I reached around him, digging the pads of my fingers into his solid back.

"How you doing, Brin-brin?"

I lifted my head. "You brought me here, and you still need to ask?"

His eyes darkened a bit, but his resolve never wavered. "This is the best place for you right now."

I laughed and pulled away. "You can't actually mean that. I mean this"—I spread my arms out, indicating the house—"is exactly what you *never* wanted."

His face shuttered, and his arms crossed over his chest. "I was wrong."

"Yeah, yeah. You said that ten minutes ago."

He smiled briefly. "It's still true."

"Well, it's too late. I won't stay here. Take me anywhere else, and I won't complain once."

He rolled his eyes. "Yeah right. The world would cave in on itself."

My eyes narrowed. "I will kick you. And it will hurt. You taught me how."

His teeth flashed. Pulling the black T-shirt Alex gave him off his shoulder, he shrugged it on. The material skimmed over his fit body nicely, and I knew it must have been a tighter fit on Alex because he was a little bigger than my brother.

"I don't have time to cajole you. I don't have time to beg. The hard, cold truth is that the men after me are mean motherfuckers who would take a woman like you and break her in ways you can't even imagine." He glanced away, then back, letting me see the naked truth right in his eyes.

I drew in a breath, caught not by his words, but by the haunted and tortured look he wore.

"I've seen it firsthand. I've heard keens and cries… pleas for death that will rattle around inside me until I die. And that was from their own women, Sabrina. That is nothing compared to what they would do to a woman of one of their enemies."

Unable to stop myself, I shivered. My toes curled into the floor, and I tugged the too-long sleeves of the flannel over my hands, tucking them inside.

I wanted to ask him why we couldn't just call the police, but I held back. I knew why. What my brother did went well beyond the scope of the police. Involving them would only get more people killed. Good people who didn't deserve to die.

"What about Rush?" I asked, thinking of another one of the men who'd been on their team. "He can protect me."

He shook his head once. "The only man who will protect you the same way I would is Alex. I think you know that."

I did know that. I felt it. I felt so many things I wish I didn't. Still, I resisted. "It's not right to ask him to do this. You and me, we're family. But Alex... he walked away."

"Because I asked him to."

I sucked in a breath. "Excuse me?"

"It's not like I made it a secret that I did not want my brother hooking up with my little sister. Especially since you were barely legal."

"We all know. You threw a large man fit."

"A man fit?" he asked, blinking.

"Like a temper tantrum the little boys at my daycare throw. Except you didn't throw toys and snacks. You threw punches and insults."

I thought back to the last night I'd seen Alex. The night my brother walked in on us kissing. His head damn near exploded. If he'd had his gun on him in that moment, Alex would have had a bullet in him somewhere. The two went at it hard. Punching, kicking, breaking furniture. It hadn't mattered how much I yelled for them to stop. It was like I hadn't yelled at all.

I left partway through. They'd been so busy hitting each other that they didn't even know I'd left.

That was the last time I saw Alex. He never even said good-bye.

"Whatever," he muttered. "I told him to keep his hands off. He didn't listen."

"But apparently he listened when you told him to leave." I fumed.

"He did the right thing. Something I respect him for."

"Well, as long as *you* think so."

Daniel grabbed my arm, pulling me back around. "I've apologized more than I'd care to. I won't keep doing it." Gentling his tone and his eyes, he let go and stepped forward. "The point is he's the best option— the *only* option—to protect you while I'm out there trying to clean this mess up."

I lifted my chin and refused to meet his eyes.

"Please," he said softly. "You can hate me and blame me every day for the rest of your life. You can even give me the silent treatment and make me go to chick movies every time we hang out. I'll take any anger you want to dish out at me for this… but please just say you'll stay here. If they get ahold of you…" The horror in his voice drew my eyes. His fear was so real, the anxiety so palpable, I reached for his hand. "It will break me."

All the anger and fight drained out of me. Not even the intense anger and discomfort I felt around Alex was a match for my brother in pain. "I could never hate you, Bear."

"I'm so sorry I brought this on you," he whispered.

I made a sound and moved forward. He wrapped his arms around my shoulders and hugged me close.

"I'll kill every last one of them. I'll make sure you're safe again."

I didn't want him to kill for me. I knew he had to.

I pulled away, but he put a palm to the back of my head and stared down.

"I'll stay. I'll stay here with Alex until you say it's safe to come home."

His eyes closed briefly, and his nostrils flared. "Thank you." He pressed his forehead against mine and smiled. "Thank you."

"You owe me." I warned.

He chuckled and pulled back. I did a doubletake at his sudden transformation. He looked about five years younger instantly. The lines around his mouth were softened, and the tension I hadn't even realized was clinging to him whisked away.

"Please stop worrying about me," I implored.

"Not possible."

I swallowed. "I know you miss Dad."

He stilled, his body going ramrod straight. "What?" he whispered, shocked by what I said.

"You were old enough to remember him when he left… I never was. I only know what he looks like because I've seen pictures. But not you. You have actual memories, and I know that sometimes, underneath the anger that he abandoned us, you miss him."

"Sabrina…" He shifted uncomfortably.

"Not remembering him isn't why I don't miss him." I forged on, wanting to get this out before my throat tightened so much with emotion I wouldn't be able to speak. "I don't miss him—having a father—because I never needed one. I had you."

He sucked in a breath.

"You never treated me like the annoying little sister I know I was." I flashed a grin. "Still am."

He chuckled.

"You let me climb into your bed when it stormed outside, and you're the one I yelled for in the middle of the night when I was sick or couldn't sleep. You always came. Always."

"Brina—"

I held up my hand and shook my head. I had to say this. I don't know why, but I had to.

"You taught me how to ride a bike. You beat up Tommy Graham in the third grade because he said I had buck teeth and bug eyes. You're the one who took me school supply shopping and to the store for girl stuff when I started my period and freaked out. Then later, when I was sixteen, you took leave for two weeks so you could come home and teach me how to drive. You bought me a car, Daniel. You might be my brother by birth, but in my heart, you're my father, mother, *and* brother. I can't even miss the family we never really had because I've always had you."

He put his hands on his hips and looked at the floor.

He sniffed.

Without looking up, he reached out and hugged me again, pressing his cheek to the top of my head. "I love you, Brina."

"I love you, too."

If staying here with Alex could repay even a fraction of everything Daniel had done for me in my life, then I would do it.

Before he pulled back, he kissed the top of my head, then swiped at his face with his hand. "Fuck," he muttered, pulling away finally to snag the bottle of water and drain it.

The door opened, and Alex poked his head in. "Is it safe to come in?"

The plastic bottle made a loud crunching sound when Daniel smashed it in his fist. "Yeah, man. Come on in."

He did, and I avoided looking at him. Instead, I began wiping off the counter where I'd made the sandwich.

"All clear," he told my brother, setting his gun in front of him like it wasn't a deadly weapon and instead something as mundane as a mug of coffee.

"Good to know."

"You think you were followed at all?"

Daniel shook his head. "No. I took the long way."

When there was nothing left to clean up, I was forced to turn around.

"You make sandwiches?" Alex asked me.

I nodded.

"Where's mine?"

That got me to look up. "Let's get one thing straight. I might be staying here, but I am not going to cook and clean for you."

He smiled. It was the kind of smile that could resurrect the dead butterflies in my gut. In fact, it did.

Damn him.

"As much as I would love to stay and watch the show, I've got to split," Daniel commented, clearly amused.

"Already?" I said. "You should get some sleep."

"I don't have time for sleep. I've gotta get some distance between me and this place before first light. I've already been here longer than I wanted to be."

I made a sound and looked at Alex for help convincing him to stay.

Alex shrugged. "He's right."

"I'll be in touch when I can," Daniel told Alex, who nodded. He stepped up to him and stuck out his hand, offering it to Alex. "If something happens to her, I'll come back here and make you wish you'd never been born."

I made a sound.

"I'd expect nothing less," Alex said, shaking my brother's hand.

Daniel moved away from him and held his hand out to me. I stuffed mine in his, and we walked toward the door. My chest was tightening again, and tears threatened the backs of my eyes. I shoved them down and ignored the squeezing feeling of my heart. I knew he had to go. I'd seen him off a hundred times before. I'd worried about him and scoured the news, making sure there weren't any disasters on the other side of the world he could have been killed in.

I'd done it all more than once.

It never made the next time any easier.

In fact, stepping outside with him now, it felt like the first time all over again, and I couldn't shake the feeling that I might never see him again.

I stayed on the top step, but he moved down them enough so when he turned back, we were eye level with each other.

"Try not to bust his balls too much, huh?"

"No promises."

He smiled. "Yeah, didn't think so."

"Hurry back," I whispered.

He nodded. "I will."

"Be careful, okay? My life isn't worth yours."

His eyes roamed my face, and a tender smile lifted his lips. He didn't say anything to what I said because I knew he didn't want to argue anymore. Instead, he glanced behind me at Alex's house. "You should see where that leads. You've got my blessing."

It was too late for me and Alex, but like him, I didn't really want to argue anymore.

"Catch you on the flipside," I quipped, using the same line we always did when he had to leave.

Leaning forward, he kissed my forehead, then stepped off the deck and headed toward the SUV.

I stood and watched, my fingernails biting into my palms. Just as he was about to be swallowed by the darkness, I called out, "Bear!"

He stopped and turned and smiled.

I smiled back.

Even after the SUV drove away with no headlights and the sound of the engine couldn't even be heard, I stood there. My gaze strayed from where he'd been up to the sky and the millions of stars floating overhead.

A little while later, Alex came out the back door, shutting it softly behind him. He came and stood beside me, stuffing his hands into the pockets of his sweats, and took up the same stance as me, and we both stared up at the sky.

We didn't say anything, and neither of us acknowledged the tears that eventually forced their way down my cheeks.

Alex

The instant I heard the approach of a car in the distance, I was up and out of the chair I'd been sleeping in.

I moved lithely toward the window overlooking the kitchen sink and out to the side of the house. The second Bellamy's SUV nudged into sight, I tucked the gun back in my sweats and turned to drop a pod into the Keurig.

While it was brewing, I went to the doorway and glanced into the living room where Sabrina was curled up on the couch. I didn't even try to stop the surge of tenderness I felt seeing her there. I was powerless against it. She made me feel like this almost from the first moment I saw her in Mercer's old place.

The guys had gone for beers and poker to blow off some steam between some intense missions, and there she was, perched at the table, looking like a flower blossoming in the dead of winter. She was settled at the card table, chips all lined up neatly, with a look in her eye that promised she would wipe the floor with all us "big bad soldiers."

She damn near did, too.

I'd felt such intense jealousy when I'd thought she was Mercer's girl. Then he announced she was his sister, and an unstoppable attraction roared to life.

I liked Merc, but in those following days, I liked him a little more. I hung out with him more than I might have, on the off chance she might be around, too.

I let it go too far, though. I was grabbed by the heart and led around until I looked up one day and realized how deep I'd fucked up.

Sabrina shifted, just barely. The small movement was like a loud bang to me because my attention jolted back to her, appraising to make sure nothing was wrong.

It wasn't. She was just shifting in sleep. I was gut punched seeing her last night. I was still gut punched seeing her in the morning light. Fuck. The feeling honestly never fully went away when she was around. Here we were almost three years later, and I still felt it.

She refused to sleep in my bed last night.

I stuffed down an audible laugh when I pictured her face when she asked where her room was, and I told her this place was a one-bedroom. Like I was the big bad wolf who was going to drag her back to that bed and eat her alive.

God. I fucking wanted to.

Instead, I grabbed some blankets and a pillow and handed them over. Once she was asleep, I slumped in the chair near the couch and dozed off and on the rest of the night, periodically waking up to stare at her.

Outside, Bellamy hollered to Charlie, and I snickered. She brought that damn dog everywhere she went. Liam still had a sore ass that he lost his loyal friend to his woman.

I pulled open the back door as she was coming up the steps, trying to wrangle Shaw, a bag of groceries, and a St. Bernard that weighed more than she did.

"Charlie!" she called out, seeing me. "Where's Alex? Come see!"

The dog was nosing around the leaves in the yard as a nippy wind cut through the morning. "Charlie!" I called out, and he gave a woof and shot toward us.

I realized my mistake almost the second I yelled, and Bellamy gave a little shriek as the dog bounded up the stairs, pushing by her. She teetered on the step and cursed, rushing forward.

She righted herself, thank fuck, but I reached out and steadied her anyway. "Girl, will there ever come a time in life when you don't put me into cardiac arrest?"

She laughed.

At the top of the steps, the baby in her arms started making noises and held his arms out to me.

"There's my man!" I said, reaching in to snatch him up immediately. I held him up over my head, and he kicked his little legs. "Dude! What you been eating? You're almost as big as me!"

He laughed, and I pulled him in. I never thought I was a kid person. Until Liam had a son and I became an uncle. From the second I first held him, I had a soft spot for the kid.

"Say hi to Uncle Alex," Bellamy said, gazing at the baby, who had a mini-size BearPaw Resort beanie on his head. Shaw lifted his hand and waved at me. I waved back 'cause I couldn't leave my little bro hanging.

Charlie gave a deep woof by the door, and we all turned to go in.

Shaw pointed at the dog and made a woofing type of sound.

"Tell him who's boss." I encouraged and pushed the door in. Charlie burst into the kitchen and went immediately toward the tin sitting on the counter that had his dog treats in it.

They'd been there since Bellamy stayed with me for a while last year, and I never bothered to take them to Liam's place. They already had a container, and since

Charlie was here so much, it just made sense to keep them.

He glanced at me and then back at the jar. I shook my head, so he turned his gaze to Bellamy.

"I brought groceries," she said, ignoring the dog and setting a large bag on the counter. An apple rolled out, and I caught it before it landed on the floor. Shaw reached for it, curious, and I held it out to him so he could clutch it in his hands.

"He's going to drool all over that." She warned.

I shrugged. "You know you don't have to bring me groceries every time you come over," I told her for like the twenty thousandth time.

She waved away my words and began pulling stuff out to set on the counter. "So?" she asked, gazing at me.

Charlie gave a huff because we weren't paying attention to him.

I raised my eyes. "So?"

"Is she here?" she asked, her voice a little hushed, but not low enough.

"Who?" I played dumb.

She stopped unpacking groceries and put her hands on her hips. She was dressed in a pair of leggings, jeans, and a loose sweater. Her blond hair was in a knot on her head, and it bobbed around when she swung to give me a look.

"You tell your Uncle Alex to stop joking with Mommy!" she said to Shaw, reaching out to tickle him on his round belly.

The baby opened his mouth and gave a dramatic laugh. Then fell against my shoulder and left his head there for a snuggle.

See? Damn. Babies were like the most innocent things ever.

I rubbed his back, movement from the doorway making me glance up. Charlie noted quicker than me and barked, lunging to put himself between the stranger and Bellamy.

"I think you mean me," Sabrina said.

Bellamy's blue eyes widened, and she whirled with a small gasp. "Hi!" she said. Then almost instantly, she added, "I'm sorry! We were being loud, and I just assumed you were asleep in the bedroom."

Charlie barked more, seeing Bellamy's start. Bells reached out and put a hand on his head. "It's okay. She's a friend."

Charlie stopped barking and wagged his tail.

Sabrina glanced up from the dog and tilted her head, gazing at Bellamy. "Why would I be in Alex's bed?"

Bellamy seemed startled, then recovered instantly. "Because when I stayed here, Alex wouldn't let me sleep on the couch."

"You stayed here?" Sabrina asked curiously. Her long, dark hair was still tangled, and her cheeks were pink from sleep.

"For a little while." Bellamy nodded and cleared her throat. "I tried to get away with sleeping out here, but he waited 'til I fell asleep and carried me back to the bedroom."

"Stubborn," I muttered.

"Me or you?" she asked sweetly, turning to glance at me over her shoulder.

I could feel Sabrina watching us, measuring our relationship and trying to decide how close I was with Liam's wife. I could have told Bellamy not to stop by until I thought Sabrina was ready to meet people, but I dismissed it instantly. Liam, Bells, and Shaw were my family. I wasn't going to keep them away.

Shaw began wiggling all over the place, trying to get down so he could check out the new lady.

"Hold your horses," I told him, putting him on his feet. Bellamy reached over and took the apple he was clutching so I could hold each of his hands.

He started out wobbling all over the place but putting one foot in front of the other.

"Don't let go." Bellamy reminded me.

I scoffed. "I got this."

"This is your son?" Sabrina asked, her voice much friendlier and softer as she looked down at the baby.

That got me to look at her. Whatever it was I heard in her voice. She was smiling at him, coming forward with a gentleness to her features.

Bellamy nodded. "Mine and Liam's son. I think you met Liam last night? His name is Shaw. He'll be one next month."

A year already. Damn.

"Yeah, I met Liam last night."

Bellamy smiled. "I'm Bellamy, Liam's wife."

"Sabrina," she replied, smiling. She never smiled at me like that. "I, ah…" She glanced at me, then away. "Alex and my brother used to work together."

Bellamy nodded. I knew Liam probably filled her in. "You'll be staying for a while?"

Sabrina nodded and turned back to Shaw. "I didn't know you had a nephew," she said as Shaw wobble-walked over to her. He stopped and looked up, his blue eyes studying the new person.

Sabrina dropped down to his level and smiled. "Hi there, handsome. How are you?"

He twisted his hand out of mine and reached toward her. Sabrina looked over at Bellamy. "Is it okay?"

Bellamy smiled. "Of course."

Sabrina reached out and picked him up, straightening to her full height. I swallowed thickly, completely ensnared by the sight of Sabrina with my nephew in her arms. She turned partially away, bouncing him in the most natural way. I'd seen Bellamy do it with him a thousand times, but seeing her was something else entirely.

A stirring somewhere in the deepest part of me tugged to the point I almost recoiled.

Sabrina patted his back and smiled down. "Aren't you a handsome little guy?"

"He looks like his daddy," Bellamy said proudly.

"Poor kid," I muttered. Bells elbowed me.

Shaw pointed toward the living room. "You want to go out there?" Sabrina asked, turning and walking with him. Her hair swayed a little, and his little fist reached around and grabbed a strand. I couldn't look away. A primal instinct roared to life watching her with him… a bone-deep urge rising up within.

I want that. With her.

"What's out here?" she asked as Charlie bounced over, watching her with the baby. I knew the dog would stick close as long as "his" baby was in the arms of a stranger.

"Oh, he has a basket of toys over by the fireplace. He probably wants to show you," Bellamy called, watching them.

"Over here?" Sabrina asked Shaw, bouncing him a little more as she walked. He pointed again, showing her exactly where his toys were.

"Wow!" she exclaimed, kneeling while still supporting him. "These are all your toys?" She looked between him and the basket in front of them. "What a lucky little boy!"

Shaw wiggled out of her hold, and she kept hold of him as she pulled the basket into the room and then carefully sat him on the floor in front of it.

He pointed to one sticking out of the top. His favorite. It was the loudest damn thing in the house. I was pretty sure that was why Liam sent it over here, 'cause his ass was tired of hearing it.

Sabrina pulled it out and hit a couple buttons. Shaw clapped and pointed to another one, and she pushed it, too.

I felt Bellamy staring, but couldn't look away from them. They made a sight sitting in front of the fireplace, her wearing my shirt and baby toys strewn about...

A hand hit me in the middle. I jolted and looked down.

"What?"

Bells gave me a knowing look, and I knew I'd been caught. I shook my head slightly, telling her she better not make a big deal out of it. I saw the sparkle in her eye and the smile on her lips. I wanted to groan. All the times I gave her and Liam a hard time were about to come back and haunt me, weren't they?

"You really like kids," Bellamy called out to Sabrina and went closer to them. "Do you have any of your own?"

My back went straight, and a low growl built in my throat. "Hell no, she don't have kids!"

"I could," Sabrina replied, still smiling at Shaw. "You haven't seen me in three years. That's plenty of time to have a baby."

"*Oh, hell no!*" I intoned. The thought of some guy between her legs made me want to rage.

Sabrina turned from the baby, her golden gaze pinning me. "You don't think I'd make a good mother?"

"No. I mean, yes, of course. I… *Hell.*" I turned away. "I need coffee."

"I work at a daycare center," Sabrina told Bellamy. "I love kids."

"Well, they clearly love you, too," Bellamy replied. After a second of more loud kid music, Bellamy spoke over it. "I hope I didn't upset you before, when I said I thought you'd be in Alex's bed. I really didn't mean to imply anything other than he's a gentleman and usually gives up his bed to guests."

Some of my hackles lowered when I realized Bellamy wasn't going to say anything crazy.

"Alex?" Sabrina scoffed. "A gentleman?"

"I heard that!" I grouched, adding cream to my coffee.

"He carried you to his bed?" Sabrina asked, her voice kind of low, but not so low that my eagle ears didn't hear.

Was that jealousy? My lips curved up, and I moved closer to hear what Bells would say.

"It was nothing. Liam and Alex think they can haul me around because I'm smaller than them," she said lightly.

"So's Brina, but I was scared if I picked her up, she'd kick me in my nuts!" I cackled, coming into the room.

Bellamy gasped and looked at Shaw. "That better not be one of his first words!"

I grimaced. "Sorry."

Shaw was making a hobby out of pulling everything out of the basket to pile on the floor. He even took Charlie one of the dog toys in the basket and laid it at his feet.

"That was very nice of you," Bellamy told Shaw. "Charlie likes that toy."

Shaw smiled and went back to his task.

She was a good mom. One of the best I'd seen. She lit up every time she was around Shaw, and I knew Liam was ready to try for another.

"I can't believe you have baby toys," Sabrina said, glancing at me.

"That's my nephew! Of course I got toys," I said, offended. "Like I'd be having my namesake over here and not have no toys."

"Your namesake?"

Bellamy nodded. "Renshaw William Alexander Mattison." She paused to grin. "It's a mouthful. I know. But I had to name him after all three of the men in his life."

"Who is Renshaw?" Sabrina asked, curious.

Bellamy's face fell just slightly, then brightened again. I wondered if there would ever come a time when her light didn't dim just a little from the past.

"He's Liam's dad. Shaw's grandpa," I answered for her. Clearing my throat, I said, "He passed."

"Oh, I'm sorry."

"It's okay." Bellamy smiled and then got up from the floor. "I need to put away the groceries."

"I can do that," I insisted.

She waved me off. "Drink your coffee. Play with your nephew. It will give me a few seconds of peace."

Charlie darted after her, and her laughter filled the house. "Good boy," she crooned, and I rolled my eyes.

He came back into the room with a treat and lay down by Shaw to eat it.

"I'm making breakfast!" Bellamy called out.

"She spends a lot of time here?" Sabrina asked, keeping her voice conversational.

"Liam, too," I replied.

Her face shuttered, and she turned back to the baby to play with him. I couldn't understand why, but it felt like that answer somehow made her angry.

I watched them for a few, being distracted by the mile-long, olive-toned leg stretching from beneath my shirt and across the floor.

Shaw rolled a yellow ball toward her, and she caught it, making him clap. She laughed and rolled it back, then clapped when he stopped it.

My heart turned over.

What the fuck had I gotten myself into?

Sabrina

I was jealous. I didn't want to be. I tried not to be. That's the thing with feelings, though. You can't stop them, and though I tried so freaking hard, I couldn't change mine either.

Alex had a family here, a big one. I knew his parents were around and his sister. He also had a family he chose in Liam, Bellamy, and his nephew. I wanted to dislike them, especially Bellamy because she was so comfortable in his house. It was clear she had taken on the role of taking care of him.

Alex would never admit it, but it was true. Men needed someone to take care of them. In that way, they were like the little kids I took care of at the daycare. Yes, grown men were capable of being on their own, handling the basics of caring for themselves, but I always thought they needed someone.

Hell, without me, Daniel would have a cardboard box as a coffee table and would probably wear dirty clothes out of the hamper and sleep on his mattress with a sleeping bag instead of sheets.

While Alex did seem a little more civilized in that sense (but, hey, he'd had parents to teach him better), I could tell he relied on Bellamy. She was the reason his fridge was stocked, the reason he had dog treats on his kitchen counter and a basket of baby toys in the living room. It was obvious to me he loved her. Not in a romantic way, but in a way that still made me jealous.

Any kind of love that Alex bestowed on someone would be worth having.

I wondered what she had that I didn't.

What was it about her that he allowed in? Why he didn't push her out of his life like he did me?

Was I unlovable to him? Had I just been a challenge, his teammate's kid sister who was off-limits, making her desirable?

If I'd been more, he wouldn't have left like he did. He wouldn't have let my bonehead brother chase him away.

"I left some things in the car. Will you keep an eye on the baby while I get them?" Bellamy asked Alex after we'd all had breakfast, consisting of French toast, bacon, scrambled eggs, and fruit.

I was used to grabbing a coffee and a granola bar to eat on my way to work in the mornings. This kind of spread was practically more than I ate in an entire workday. When you were chasing after toddlers, finding time to eat was pretty much impossible. By the time I got home in the evenings, I was too tired to even bother making anything.

I was kind of jealous of that, too. Of her ability to make something Alex plowed through like a bulldozer.

"You got it, girl who got away," Alex replied, glancing at Shaw who was sitting in a booster seat that strapped onto a dining chair and had a yellow tray. Alex kept that at his house, too.

When she was gone, the giant dog rushing after her, I glanced up from my plate. "Why do you call her that?"

"'Cause it annoys her." Alex cackled.

"Everything about you is annoying." I countered.

"Maaaamaaaaamaaaaa," Shaw called out, making a mess of the scrambled eggs on the tray in front of him.

"Mommy is coming right back," Alex told him.

"Maaa," Shaw yelled again. I could tell he wasn't at all bothered to be left here with his uncle, but he just wanted to yell.

"Slow your roll, little man," Alex said, sitting forward to point to some egg. "You gonna eat that?"

Shaw threw it on the floor, then laughed.

"You're just like your daddy," Alex muttered.

Seeing him with his nephew made my chest ache. Sitting here at the kitchen table with the scent of coffee, maple syrup, and bacon mixing in the air, dirty dishes on the table, and the morning sun filtering through the windows was almost surreal.

I'd daydreamed of something like this for so long. Imagined what could have been if he'd never left. I hadn't known if he liked kids or even if he wanted them. But seeing him now in these surroundings caused a rush of pain from the past to throb inside me.

Pain I thought I let go of.

"You want some juice?" I asked Shaw, pushing it all aside and trying to ignore Alex. His sippy cup was nearby, and I grabbed it, not surprised at all how sticky the entire outside of the cup was. There was even a small piece of French toast stuck to the side. "Here you go." I offered the cup. He glanced at me and smiled before reaching his chubby hands out for the handles.

I couldn't resist brushing a hand over the light hair on his head as he drank.

When he was done, he made an "ahhh" sound, then threw the cup on the floor, too.

"Some people's kids," Alex quipped, leaning down to get the cup and place it on the table just out of reach. Shaw reached for it, and Alex clucked his tongue. "I know your games. I'm not falling for it."

I felt his eyes settle on me. I didn't have to look to know when he gazed at me. I felt it. I felt him. "Bellamy and Liam knew each other way back in the day. Some shit happened to push them apart. Liam never really moved on in the relationship sense."

"The girl who got away," I mused.

"But then she came back and they got another chance." The tone of his voice beckoned me, and so did his words.

I looked up. His wintry eyes pierced my heart.

Clearing my throat, I glanced away. "I guess they were meant to be."

Bellamy bustled back inside, and I nearly fell out of my chair with relief. I jolted up, getting away from the table and turning toward her. "Need some help?" I asked, even though she was only carrying a large shopping bag.

"Actually, this is for you." She handed the bag over.

"For me?"

"Liam thought you might need some clothes."

My eyes widened. "You brought me some clothes?" I don't know why, but that made me feel so guilty for not wanting to like her.

The truth was Bellamy was impossible not to like.

She waved a hand before going to the sink to get a cloth that I assumed she would use to clean up her son. "It's nothing exciting, just some stuff I had in my closet. I figured it would at least get you through until you manage to get some things of your own."

I glanced into the sack, noting the different fabrics and colors. "I, uh, didn't really have a lot of time to pack."

"Been there," she said, and just from her tone, I could tell she actually had.

Bellamy turned her attention to cleaning off Shaw and peppering his face with kisses. "You're so sticky!" she exclaimed, making him laugh.

"Daaaaadaaaa," he told her.

"Daddy is at work. We'll see him later."

"Thank you," I said, still touched she'd brought me some clothes. It would be nice to get out of the pajamas and Alex's shirt.

Shaw began fussing, his lower lip wobbly in a sad pout. "Daaa." He whimpered, then began to cry.

Bellamy sighed. "He's a daddy's boy."

Alex rose from the table, towering over both Bellamy and the baby. "Step aside."

Bellamy did, and Alex scooped him out of the chair, tucking him into his arms. The baby looked even smaller against him. "No need for all that." He snagged a piece of bacon off the table and held it out to Shaw.

"Charlie!" he beckoned.

The dog rushed over and sat down, gazing up at both of them with drool hanging from his giant mouth.

"Here, give this to Charlie," Alex told Shaw.

His face lit up, and he took the bacon, holding it out. Because Alex was holding him and he didn't know to hold it low, Alex had to squat a bit so the bacon was level with the dog. Charlie glanced at Alex before going for the snack.

"Easy." Alex warned him, and his tail beat against the floor before the dog gently took the bacon from the baby.

Shaw laughed and beamed. Alex swiped a stray tear off his pudgy cheek while Bellamy smiled.

The ache in my chest turned painful, feeling like someone was squeezing my heart and making it impossible to breathe.

"I think I'll just go get out of this shirt. Put on some pants," I said, taking the bag and hot-footing it from the room.

I closed myself in Alex's bedroom, sagging once I was blissfully alone. In the past couple days, I'd been battered with emotions. Seeing Alex out there in such an intimate setting, doing things with people I'd always wanted him to do with me was just too much.

I needed some space. Some time to process and think. Daniel was out there right now, probably doing something beyond dangerous, and I was here because I was his weak spot. It was all I should focus on right now. About my actual family... not the one I didn't have.

The bag of clothes contained a basic pair of black leggings, which felt like heaven to pull on. There was also a pair of socks (good-bye bare feet!), a sports bra that was actually a little loose in the boobage area (because I was seriously lacking in that department), and an oversize long-sleeve hooded T-shirt in an army green color.

I could have cried when I saw a few simple toiletries, including a brush and a ponytail holder. Clearly, she had been in a similar situation because she knew just how important these little things were.

I went into his bathroom, avoiding thinking about the butterflies that fluttered around when I set my items on the counter alongside his.

I thought those stupid butterflies died.

It took a long time to brush the tangles out of my fine hair, and when I was done, I pulled it up into a bun on the top of my head to hopefully keep it from getting that way again. Once I finished up in the bathroom, I gathered all the items and made sure his space looked exactly as it had before I entered.

Being dressed made me feel more together. Readier to deal with the day ahead. I stuffed my lone pair of pajamas into the bag with the few other outfits she'd so kindly packed and then glanced at the flannel I'd tossed on his bed.

Liam commented it was Alex's favorite shirt. Why had he given me that one to wear?

Probably because it was the first one his hand closed over in the dark. Don't be making more out of it than there is, Sabrina. Don't be stupid.

Straightening my spine, I grabbed up the soft, worn fabric and tossed it farther up on his bed. I wouldn't be needing it anymore.

The bedroom door swung open, and Alex strode in.

I spun around and glared. "Don't you knock?"

"This is my room."

"I could have been naked."

"All the more reason not to knock." He wagged his eyebrows.

"In your dreams, pal."

He smiled, a slow kind of knowing smile, and my stomach dipped.

"Whatever. I'm done in here." I started to charge past, the bag hitting against my leg as I went.

Alex clotheslined his arm out, hooking me around the waist and lifting. My feet left the ground for a fraction of a second as he towed me back.

I glared up at him. "Excuse you."

"What's wrong?" he asked, catching me off guard.

I forgot he was annoying me. "What?"

"Something is wrong, and I want to know what it is."

I forgot how in tune he always seemed to be with me. I sniffed, looking away. "Nothing is wrong."

The soft, playful way he whispered, "Liar," made the muscles in my lower abdomen clench.

"Look," I snapped, angry. "I might be forced to stay here for a *short* while, but let's get something straight."

His lips jerked like he was trying not to smile, and my frustration increased tenfold.

"You are not privy to my thoughts and feelings. You do not get to ask personal questions, and if you do, I won't answer them. I'm only here because my brother insisted, so let's not get caught up in pretending we care about each other."

The smile disappeared as I laid down the law.

His eyes narrowed and regarded me coolly, penetrating the air with a distinct chill. "So it's like that, huh?"

I nodded briskly.

He shifted, stepping close. So close his scent wafted around me. "You do care, kitten. You care more than you want to."

A tingle of awareness brushed down my spine. I shoved him back with both my hands. He stumbled, his eyes widening with surprise.

"Get over yourself," I spat and marched toward the door.

"Sabrina."

I stopped, commanded by his voice. I didn't turn around, though. I stared straight ahead at the door, planning my escape.

"I do, too," he whispered.

Desire sparked within me, threatening to become a raging fire. I swallowed, then fled, running from the room and his words.

Alex

I walked into Liam's office, and his eyebrows shot halfway up his head when he saw me.

"I'm going to have to call you back," he abruptly said into the phone pressed against his ear and then hung up.

Dropping into the seat across from his massive desk, I said, "I hope that wasn't someone we needed cash from, because we ain't getting it now."

He didn't seem very concerned. "What are you doing here?"

"I work here."

"I thought you were taking some time."

I sighed loudly. "It's been two days."

Liam laughed.

I glared at him.

Then he laughed some more. "Things not going well on the home front?"

I rubbed a hand over my face. "She's driving me fucking crazy."

Leaning back in his desk chair, Liam kicked up his feet and propped them on his desk. His hands planted over his middle, and he grinned like a cat with a full belly. "Tell me more."

"Frankly, I'm offended at the amount of joy you're getting outta this, Mattison."

A low, deep chuckle filled the room, and I rolled my eyes. He kicked out of the chair and strode across the room to a bar cart, where he pulled out two longneck beers from underneath.

"You gotta beer fridge in here?" I demanded, offended. "All I got is some shitty coffee maker."

He handed over the frosty bottle and sat down beside me. "Where is she right now?"

"Downstairs checking out some of the shops and shit. She was curious about the resort."

"You're cool with it?"

"I never would have left her down there if I didn't think she was safe," I snapped.

"Testy," Liam drawled.

I snarled and lifted the beer to my mouth. After I swallowed, I said, "There's so much tension in my house. I'm surprised the roof hasn't blown off. We skirt around each other and barely talk. When we do, it's to argue."

"Might as well get it over with and just have sex already."

I made a sound. "I want her so fucking bad."

Liam scoffed. "Then what's the problem?"

"She's the problem!" I burst out, leaping from the seat to pace the room. "She's off-limits. The only reason she's here is because she has to be. This is a job. I owed Mercer."

"Because of me."

I glanced around at Liam, a question in my gaze.

He cleared his throat. "You owed him for something you set up last year, right?"

We never talked about what went down with Perry Crone and the details of how his demise came to be. It didn't really matter because getting rid of him—for good—was all that mattered.

"It's not a big deal," I commented.

"The fuck it isn't. You're dragged back into this shit because of what you did for me and Bells."

"I did what I did with open eyes. I'm a big boy. I made my choices."

"You should have let me take care of him," Liam rumbled, going to the window to look out.

"What? No."

"I'm glad that fucker is gone, but sometimes I still wish I'd been the one to send him into hell."

"It doesn't matter how he got there, just that Satan is twisting his balls right now."

Liam turned, his stare flat. "And when someone comes for Sabrina, will it matter then?"

My tongue ran over my teeth as I seethed. God help the man who came for Brina. Just thinking about it made my scalp prickle and my hands clench with the desire to kill.

It was like a bucket of cold water.

That right there. That was exactly what I'd been wanting to keep Liam from having to live with. *The desire to kill.* Once you take one life, it somehow becomes easier to take another. It's a heavy burden on a man's soul, a constant battle. It wasn't as if I walked around wanting to off everyone I saw, but when you were faced with a threat or a severe injustice, it was easier to reach the conclusion that taking it out permanently was the best solution.

Urgency thumped under my skin and made me paranoid. I grabbed the cell out of my pocket and hit a button. On the second ring, I started for the door.

"What?" She picked up before the third, stopping me.

"What took so long to answer the GD phone?"

"It rang twice, you moron."

I stared up at the ceiling and tried to hold on to my temper. Didn't she understand that she made me crazy? "And I'm asking why you didn't answer on the first ring," I asked through gritted teeth.

"I was making out in the bathroom with some random ski dude I met."

A mean sound rumbled out of me, anger coming fast. See? This is what I mean… I had the sudden desire to kill whoever she was lying about. A guy who didn't even exist was now on my hit list. "Tell him to have a seat at the bar and enjoy a drink on the house. It's the last one he'll ever have."

There was a brief, poignant pause on the other end of the line.

"Brina!" I yelled.

"I was in line for a coffee."

I said a little prayer to Baby Jesus and all his lambs.

Behind me, Liam started to laugh.

I held my hand up in the air, displaying what I thought of that. He laughed louder.

"Is there something you needed?" she asked, her voice cautious. Clearly, she sensed my mood, because she dialed way back on the sarcasm.

"I just wanted to make sure everything was okay down there. Nothing out of the ordinary?"

"You just saw me ten minutes ago."

"And I want to know if you're okay," I said, holding on to what little patience I had left.

"I'm fine, Alex."

The way she said my name made my fingers tighten around my cell and my cock twitch in my jeans. The thought of her kissing anyone else but me set my blood to boiling. "I changed my mind about you being alone down there. Come up to the executive level and down the hall to Liam's office. Just ask one of the receptionists where to go."

"You can't be serious."

My reply was cool and calm. "You can come up, or I will come down and get you."

"Did something happen?" she asked. I could hear the worry in her voice. "Is it Daniel?"

I scared her. *Stupid.*

I blew out a breath and forced myself to relax. Strange, I didn't even have to work to gentle my voice, though. It was like my body responded to her anxiety and automatically worked to soothe it. "No, kitten, nothing happened. I would just prefer if you were up here."

"I'll be right up."

My eyes shut briefly. "Thank you."

I turned back to Liam as I was jamming the phone into my jeans. He was smirking.

"Don't even fuck—"

"You have it so bad." He cut me off, a cheese-eating expression on his face.

"Yeah, yeah," I muttered. "It doesn't matter. Like I said, she's off-limits."

"Why?"

The simple question drew me up short. I blinked. For the span of a heartbeat, I couldn't think of one logical reason I couldn't just take her.

Then I remembered. "I hurt her, bro. Bad."

Liam cocked his head to the side. "She wasn't the only one who got hurt."

My eyes lifted.

He nodded. "I might have been prisoner to a hospital bed, jacked up on pills, and generally screwed up when you came home from the army, but even I could see how much you left behind when you walked."

"I'm no good for her, Liam."

"Why don't you let her be the judge of that?"

I barked a laugh. "Oh, she would tell you the same thing, probably adding in some colorful hand gestures."

"Maybe she could teach you a thing or two," Liam quipped. "'Cause you giving me the finger on the daily is getting boring."

I laughed. It felt good.

The bottle of beer Liam was holding made a thunking sound when he set it on top of his desk. I was pretty sure he hadn't even had a sip of it, but I'd already downed half of mine.

"I saw the way she looked at you the other night. She might have been hotwiring the Hummer to get out of there, but I can guarantee she doesn't really want away from you."

"Look, I'm gonna need a few more days off. I'm having some shit delivered tomorrow, amping up my security at the house. And I'm still not comfortable leaving her alone for very long."

"Ten minutes seems to be your limit." Liam observed, his eyes laughing.

"That little brat told me she was making out in the bathroom with some ski fucker!"

Liam laughed out loud. "I like her."

I made a colorful gesture, suggesting he should suck my cock.

"Good one," he commended around some chortling. "She just wanted to get a rise out of you. Clearly, it worked."

Yeah. Yeah, I guess it did.

A tentative knock on the office door sounded, and I stalked forward and wrenched it open.

Liam's assistant squeaked in surprise and jolted backward.

"Sorry about that," I offered, smiling apologetically. "I was expecting someone else."

She recovered quickly and smiled back. "No problem, Mr. Carter." I gave her a look, and she giggled. "Alex."

"Liam's in here." I gestured into the room, but she didn't come closer.

"You said you *are* expecting someone?" she questioned.

I nodded and glanced beyond the doorway to see Sabrina standing there clutching a coffee and looking annoyed.

"Sure am," I drawled. "That would be her."

"See," Sabrina told the assistant. "I told you."

She flushed and looked at me apologetically. "I'm sorry. She tried to just walk right in. I stopped her. Sometimes guests wander up here…"

"It's okay. You didn't know." I allowed. "This is Sabrina. She's, ah…" I faltered for a second before saying, "A friend of the family. You'll probably see her around a bit."

"Of course. I'll make sure no one else stops her again."

"Thanks, doll."

Off to the side, Sabrina stiffened. I got immense satisfaction that my little pet name annoyed her.

The assistant giggled and went back to her desk, stopping briefly to apologize to Sabrina.

Once she was gone, I got a death glare. I was beginning to look forward to those glares. I just didn't think my day would be complete without them.

"I leave you alone for ten minutes…" I scoffed.

Sabrina rolled her eyes and brushed past me into the office. The second her shoulder brushed the fabric of my T-shirt, a current of electricity shocked me all the way to my toes.

Damn. I wanted her. I wanted her so much there was no denying it.

"Sabrina," Liam greeted. "How's BearPaw treating you?"

"It's a beautiful resort, well, the little bit I've seen of it so far."

"I see you found the little café downstairs. That's Bells's favorite one."

"I didn't have much time to look over the menu. I was being rushed," she replied, a dig at me.

Liam chuckled. "I, ah, have a meeting to get to, but how about we all have dinner tonight?"

"Who's we all?" Sabrina asked cautiously.

"Me, Bells, and you two," Liam said. "The Tavern, around seven?"

It sure beat the hell out of sitting around in the cabin, wanting to crawl out of my skin. "Sounds good. We'll be there."

Liam looked at Sabrina for her agreement as well. She nodded. "See you then."

"I'll call Bells. She'll be thrilled." On his way out the door, he stopped beside me. "Don't worry about work. You held the fort down for months when I was training for the Olympics last year. It's my turn to do the same."

"Thanks, man."

"See you guys later," he said, stepping out and flashing me a knowing look as he smoothly shut the door behind him.

"Seriously, Alex!" Sabrina burst out, pinning me with a heated glare. "Ten minutes! You only gave me ten minutes of peace!"

A low rumble moved through my chest, making me sound like warning thunder before a storm. I stalked forward, moving with purpose and intent. Her cheeks were flushed with anger and her eyes bright with annoyance. As I moved, so did she. For every step I took toward her, she took one away.

I grinned, feeling wolfish and predatory. Her hesitation only made my perusal sweeter. When her back came up against the large window, her eyes rounded because there was nowhere else to go. I saw the idea form before she moved, reaching out a hand to stop her from stepping off to the side.

"Alex," she said, breathless.

I took the paper cup out of her hand and set it behind us on Liam's desk, feeling her nervous stare the entire time. My eyes bounced between hers for one brief moment before I surged forward and took her lips.

14

Sabrina

I melted against the glass like it was a flame and not at all the cold, unforgiving surface it really was. Suddenly, the only sensation that existed was the feel off his full, seductive mouth grinding against mine. Like a floodgate being forced open, desire I thought I'd felt the last of barreled out, saturating every single cell within my body.

His hands smoothed over my hips, then glided around to hold the small of my back, pulling so I would arch into him as he hunched in to surround me even farther.

God. I missed this. Him.

The thought penetrated the thick haze swallowing me, enough to make me pull back just slightly. Alex's mouth followed, but I turned my cheek and whispered his name.

We can't do this. We—

The tip of his nose brushed up the side of my jaw, his lips connecting with my skin.

"Shut up and kiss me, kitten," he rasped.

And then we were kissing again. The way he owned my mouth took over all reason, and my knees buckled when his thick, capable tongue swept into my mouth.

I purred, living up to my nickname, and Alex gripped my waist, lifting me up his body. Instinctively, my legs wound around his waist, and he settled more firmly against me.

This man didn't just kiss. He licked and stroked; he sucked and nibbled. He took everything inside me and bent it to his will until I was simply putty in his hands, living and dying for the next brush of his mouth.

My fingertips dug into his dense shoulders, clinging to him as if he might let me go. We kissed until my lungs absolutely burned for a breath of air. Finally, when my body forced me to, I unlatched our mouths and gasped, my head falling back against the glass.

Alex didn't seem to need to breathe, instead latching onto my neck, licking and sucking deeply. I moaned and arched back farther, exposing my skin for his taking.

One of his hands slid up the side of my body, brushed back my hair, and then gripped the back of my head, holding me motionless while he continued to assault the delicate flesh beneath my ear.

My center throbbed and ached, making my thighs clench tighter around his body. A deep sound vibrated his chest, and I answered the call, lowering my head so our lips could lock together once more.

The phone on Liam's desk went rang a few times, but neither of us lifted our heads. When it went off again a moment later, Alex pulled back just slightly, but not enough to break the hold he had on any part of me.

My chest heaved, and the rest of my body felt feverish. My fingers had long since stopped gripping his shoulders and rested on either side of his neck.

I enjoyed the way his muscles bunched and moved when he eased back even more. Before pulling completely away, Alex came back, pressing a final lingering kiss directly on my lips as if he wanted to seal in the savage way he'd just gone at me.

I collapsed against the window, my body completely boneless, my legs still around him but trembling with effort. The pad of his thumb dragged along the underside of my lower lip, and I watched through hazy eyes as he stuck it into his mouth and sucked.

The look in his startling blue eyes was still predatory, hungry, and held a scary yet delicious promise that he wasn't done with me yet. "I like the way you taste, kitten."

I swallowed thickly, unable to formulate any kind of response.

His dark brow arched, and amusement sparked deep in his unusual eyes. "Is that all I got to do to get you to shut up? Kiss you?"

Oh no. That was no kiss. That was a total attack on my senses, a complete reprogramming of my body. A simple kiss wouldn't have stopped me from flinging back a blistering retort.

I pushed at his shoulder, telling him it was time to put me down. It was embarrassing just how easily I'd succumbed to him.

"One more thing." He spoke softly. "Don't even think about finding some ski loser around here to make out with." He caressed the top of my cheekbone with the backs of his fingers. "Because there isn't anyone on this earth who will ever kiss you like I do."

He slid me down his body, setting me back on my own two feet. My legs were shaking. Hell, my entire body trembled. He seemed completely in control (the big jerk) but kept a steadying hand on my hip while reaching behind him for the coffee I'd completely forgotten about.

His eyes met and held mine as he lifted the paper cup and took a sip. How anyone could make taking a sip of coffee erotic I would never understand. "Not bad," he mused after he swallowed.

Alex was completely amused at the way he'd wrecked me, completely arrogant about it, too. It was that arrogance that managed to blow away most of the fog I was lost in.

"If you want a coffee, go get your own," I snipped.

He chuckled, the sound coating me like sticky, sweet honey. "Oh, kitten. I don't want a coffee. I just want you to have to put your lips exactly where mine just were every time you take a sip."

I stared at his broad back, completely dumbfounded again as he strolled away, looking mighty proud of himself.

At the door, he glanced over his shoulder. "C'mon. I'll show you around before dinner."

I snapped out of the trance he'd put me in. I went forward, angry about the moment we just shared, angry that it was so easy for him to brush off. It was a good reminder for me not to get caught up in him.

"Don't touch me again," I told him, skirting around his body on my way out the door.

His velvet laugh echoed behind me. "Drink your coffee, Sabrina."

Damn him.

Alex

I was a damn fool.

Kissing her had not satiated any kind of craving I had for the woman sleeping on my couch. Instead, that damnable kiss has done the complete opposite.

I hungered for Sabrina in a way I never had before. I'd wanted her three years ago, but since that kiss in Liam's office, I could barely think straight.

I showed her around the resort like I said I would, but damn if I remembered most of it. Her scent lingered beneath my nose, her taste on my tongue.

Even my hands echoed with the memory of what it felt like to finally touch her.

I'd even traipsed around behind her like a puppy while she shopped for shit she said she needed.

What I needed was her under me and her bare thighs wrapped around my—

"I'm ready." Her voice cut into the fantasy I'd had probably a thousand times since earlier in the day.

I didn't turn from the window right away. Instead, I willed my hardening dick to chill the fuck out.

"Hel-loo?" she sang when I didn't turn around immediately.

I spun, ready to say something I knew would piss her off, but the second my eyes landed on her, any words died on my lips.

She was dressed in a pair of jeans that hugged her body like a glove. One of the knees was ripped, exposing a small patch of skin that made my mouth run dry. Her wine-colored sweater was loose and fell off one shoulder, exposing yet even more golden-toned skin. Dark hair fell over her shoulders and down her back like a glistening waterfall begging for my touch.

When she moved, a strand of it fell forward, stroking over her exposed collarbone with the movement.

I was staring, and she noticed, glancing down at her clothes and the tall brown boots on her feet. "Is something wrong?" she asked self-consciously. "I guess I went a little ham in the shops today. It's nice to actually be somewhere I can dress for fall…"

My God, she was fucking sexy.

"Are you still a virgin?" I demanded, pissed off.

Her hands fell to her sides and her cheeks flushed. "What?!"

"Are you?" I pressed.

"That is none of your business." She moved across the room toward the kitchen.

"That would be a no," I said, sour.

She stopped, her shoulders stiffening. When she turned back, her hair floated around her. "What does it even matter, Alex?"

"How many have there been?" I asked, not bothering to acknowledge her question.

She laughed and started to turn away.

I lunged forward and grabbed her wrist, pulling her around. "How many?"

She yanked her arm free. "How many women have you been with?"

I blanched. "That doesn't matter."

"Why not?"

"Because I don't care about any of them."

She made a sound. "But you slept with them anyway? That's just great, Alex. So upstanding."

"I'm not an upstanding guy."

She snorted. "You got that right."

I gave her a shake. "Sabrina. Answer me."

She lifted her chin. "Tell me why you want to know."

"Because I'm going out of my mind thinking about how many men have touched you because I walked away." I could have been her first. Her only.

Her eyes lifted, old pain shining through. "You just left."

"Sabrina…" I made a sound and reached for her, but she pulled back, denying us both.

"Two," she answered.

"Two?"

"Happy now?" she snapped and quickly put distance between us.

No. I wasn't happy now. But I was relieved there hadn't been more.

"Are we going to dinner or what?" she asked, her tone distant and hard.

I was a complete ass for forcing the answer out of her. I couldn't help it. Kissing her before and seeing her dressed like this now… Jealousy and desire warred beneath my skin, making me irrational and explosive.

"Yeah," I replied, grabbing my keys. "Let's go."

She was quiet the whole way to The Tavern. Yeah, it was a short trip, but the silence between us felt as if it lasted forever. The interior of the Hummer was dark, but it didn't stop me from glancing at her every few seconds as I searched for the right words.

I parked right beside Liam's orange Chevy Xtreme and shut off the engine.

"That's a really nice truck. I've never seen one like that before," she said, gazing out the window.

"It's Liam's. Thailand gave it to him."

"Like the country?" she asked, dubious.

I laughed. "Yep, the country."

"Wow," she mused, still staring at it.

"Perks of being an Olympic god."

"I never understood that."

I shut off the engine and turned in my seat toward her. "What?"

In the darkness, her body rotated toward mine. My stomach fluttered a little with her movement. I didn't know if it was the dark and the fact that it created a sense of intimacy or if I was just relieved that she was talking to me again.

Regardless, she was the only woman who ever had the power to make my stomach flutter.

"You know, that these big athletes get so much money and prestige and outrageous gifts just handed to them. It's like you said. Their ability to throw a ball or ride a snowboard somehow makes them a god."

I cocked my head to the side. "You don't think it does?"

She shook her head. I could see the way her eyes shined even in the dark. I felt the passion beneath the words even before she spoke. "I think there are people in this world who do things a lot more important, a lot more life-altering, and never get any recognition at all. They put their life on the line every single day and go places even these godlike athletes wouldn't dare, but no one will ever know."

"People like your brother?"

She tucked a strand of hair behind her ear and nodded. "People like you, too," she added quietly.

The center of my chest ached a little. "The stuff I've done is too gritty for most to ever consider it a good deed or to ever be cheered for like sports."

"Maybe. But it should still be acknowledged."

The way she was looking at me just then… like I was a hero or that I deserved a medal or something, it would have made me hard—hell, I would be eating it up—if it was true.

"I'm no hero," I deadpanned and left the Hummer. When she didn't get out, I went around and opened the passenger door.

Sabrina turned, facing me, hair falling around her face and a soft look in her eyes. "You're too hard on yourself."

I felt the bite of ice inside me. "If you knew the shit I've done, you wouldn't say that."

"You're right. I don't know, but I do know you're a good guy, Alex, and whatever you've done, you did it all because you had no choice."

And just like that, I was reminded why I wasn't Sabrina's first and why letting anything more happen between us would be wrong.

I reached into the cab and lifted, depositing her on the pavement, then slammed the door. I glanced back, trying not to notice how small she looked next to my monster ride and how the confusion she was feeling scrunched up her nose.

"C'mon," I said, gruff. "Liam and Bellamy are waiting." I started ahead, but when I didn't feel her follow, I stopped and glanced back.

"What did I say?" she asked, still in the same spot, watching me.

"Nothing."

She scoffed and folded her arms across her chest, glaring. That damn sweater dipped a little lower, exposing more of her shoulder, and a cool autumn breeze kicked up, blowing the hair back from her face.

I stomped forward, knowing my eyes flashed with the anger I felt. She didn't move. She didn't even flinch.

I leaned down so I could stare coldly into her eyes. "I'm not a good guy. I've killed people. Lots of people. Remember that."

Our stares warred for long moments before she drew in a breath. I expected her to say something sassy, to let me have it for being a dick.

The second she expelled her breath, her eyes softened. When she reached up, I was the one who flinched. I recovered quickly, realizing she was going to touch me. An unsolicited touch that I suddenly wanted so fucking bad, despite the ugly words I'd just hurled to push her away.

Most girls probably would have let it go, but not Sabrina. Her hand hovered, waiting until I calmed, and then she laid her palm against my cheek. "Maybe you could do with a little forgetting."

My eyes closed for a fraction of a second. "That's not really an option."

"Hey, Alex?"

"Yeah?"

Her lips curled upward, the smile putting a little twinkle in her eyes. "I like your Hummer better. Yellow is so much better than orange."

A weight I didn't even know I had over me lifted, and I laughed. Casually, I draped an arm across her shoulders and led her toward the building. "Better not tell Liam that. His truck is almost as famous as he is around here."

"It will be our secret." She promised.

Just before I opened the door to usher her inside, I dropped my arm and faced her. "I'm sorry about earlier."

"You're going to have to be more specific because you have a lot of things to be sorry for."

I scowled. "I do not."

She gave me a *yeah right* look.

I sighed. "I mean about asking about your personal life. Technically, it's not my business."

"Technically?" She scoffed. "Try not at all."

I stepped closer and dropped my voice. "I think we both know it's my business, whether we want it to be or not."

The soft openness of her gaze shuttered a bit. I hated that look. And right now, I had no clue why I was getting it. "That's *exactly* why it is not your business. Because *you* don't want it to be."

Sabrina planted her hand on my chest and shoved, then stepped ahead into The Tavern without a single glance back.

Sabrina

I needed a drink. A stiff one.

Thank goodness we were at a bar. I left Alex in the dust and beelined inside, barely taking in the relaxed cabin feel of the interior. The air was scented with pizza, and my stomach grumbled appreciatively. The place was pretty busy, and I recalled that Alex said it was a popular spot, not just for the guests here, but for the locals.

The giant old-fashioned stained-glass light fixture centered over the bar drew my eye, and I nearly collided with a barstool right in front of me.

"Whoa there," a deep voice said as a hand reached out to stop me.

"Crap," I muttered, jerking to a stop. A sexy chuckle off to my side made me look up and flush instantly. "I think you might have prevented a collision."

The man smiled, his white teeth flashing from beneath his dark beard. A lot of the guys up here had beards. *Must be the cold.*

Except Alex. Alex didn't have a beard… Hell, when I knew him three years ago, he didn't have any hair either. He did now, though. A whole dark head full of it. Sometimes I caught myself wondering what it would feel like to bury my hands in the thick mass of curls he kept super short on the sides but full on top.

The other morning, he'd come into the room, fresh from whatever workout he'd been punishing himself with, a red bandana tied around his head. Just thinking about the way he looked made my mouth run dry.

"I felt bad for the chair you were about to mow down."

I snapped back into the present. Right. I was talking to someone. Or rather, he thought I was paying attention to him, according to the way his mahogany eyes filled with humor.

I remembered the chair and how he stopped me from making a fool of myself and lightly laughed. "Well, I'm sure it's very grateful."

I realized he was still holding on to my arm and glanced down. He noticed too and released me. There was a glass of beer in his hand, and he reached out with his free one. "Beau."

I slipped my hand into his. "Sabrina."

"Haven't seen you around here before, Sabrina," he said. "You here on holiday?"

"Something like that," I replied vaguely, glancing at the bar.

The bartender caught me looking and started toward us.

"Hey," Beau said, lightly touching my elbow and making glance back. "Why don't you let me get you a drink and you come sit with us?"

"Us?" I asked.

He gestured with his chin to a large table toward the back that was filled with a bunch of other guys and a few women between them.

One of them looked a little familiar, but I wasn't exactly sure why. The second that thought filtered through my mind, my heart began pounding tenfold. Why did I recognize him if he was a stranger? All these people were strangers... Any one of them could be after me.

Maybe that semi-familiar face was one I'd seen in my apartment that night. Maybe he hadn't died.

Beau shifted, reminding me that he was waiting for a reply. I swallowed down the panic trying to take over and forced a smile. "Oh, that's sweet, but I actually have plans."

Beau smiled. "Just one drink? You know, as a thank-you for saving you from the barstool," he goaded.

The bartender behind the counter stepped close. "What can I get for you?"

Just over his shoulder was a large sign that read "Have ID Ready." Shit. So much for me having a drink or two. Not that it mattered this second anyway. All I wanted this moment was to get away.

"Just put what the lady wants on my tab," Beau told the bartender, a note of familiarity in his voice. "She's going to join me in the back."

"The hell she is!" Alex declared from behind.

I jumped and spun, startled. The second I saw him glowering close by with both feet planted on the floor as if he were preparing for a throwdown, the crippling anxiety abated. My heart rate actually slowed, making it easier to breathe. Alex might have pissed me off more than anyone on the face of this earth, but I knew I was safe with him.

Not that I'd ever tell him that.

"Oh, for heaven's sake." I started.

"What the fuck do you think you're doing, Beau?" Alex confronted him, ignoring me.

From across the room, I saw some movement and glanced over to see Liam weaving through the tables with a grim expression on his face.

Beau's eyes widened. I noticed none of his friends were rushing over the way Liam was. "I didn't realize she was here with someone… with you."

"You know each other?" I asked, bouncing my gaze between the men.

Beau nodded. "I'm a ski instructor here. I work with Alex."

Ohh. I glanced over my shoulder at the group of men he'd invited me to join. That's where I'd seen the other guy. He'd said hi to Alex as he was showing me around earlier.

Well, thank God he wasn't someone sent here to bring me to my doom! I let out a long, relieved sigh. It was so audible Alex glanced at me and frowned.

I waved away the look, glancing back to Beau's table where all of them were watching the unfolding scene nervously. I guess that made it clear who the top dogs were around here.

Liam arrived, shouldering himself into the conversation. "Guys."

The silence in the room grew thicker. Everyone in the place stopped to stare at Alex and Liam. It seemed everyone was holding their breath to see what would happen.

"I almost tripped over a chair. Beau stopped me," I said stupidly, feeling as though I were about to start babbling.

"Sounded to me like he was trying to get you drunk," Alex intoned, not taking his eyes off Beau.

"No." His eyes widened. "No way. I would never… I just… I didn't know she was with you."

"Now you know." Three small, seemingly ineffective words that suddenly had the power to frost over the entire restaurant.

"Alex," I said, embarrassment heating my cheeks. "Stop it."

Beau cleared his throat and glanced at me, then quickly away. "It was nice meeting you."

"Thanks for the save," I said.

Alex practically growled.

Liam's lips twitched. Was he laughing?

I glanced around toward our table where Bellamy was sitting. She caught my look and rolled her eyes. Well, if she didn't think this was a big deal, then neither should I. Right?

Beau retreated to his table, and the entire place started up again. Only a few people were left watching us with curious eyes.

"You boys causing trouble?" said an older woman with a no-nonsense attitude and clearly no fear at all, coming right up to the three of us.

Liam and Alex both relaxed. "No, ma'am," they replied in tandem.

My mouth fell open.

"That's good. I wouldn't want to have to kick yous out."

"Aww, you'd never do that to us, Sharon." Liam charmed.

She chuckled and patted him on the shoulder. "Oh, yes, I would. I don't care if you own this place or not. This is my kitchen."

"Yes, ma'am," Liam replied like he was good and scolded.

Sharon turned to me, giving me a once-over, then smiling. "Who's this?"

Alex cleared his throat. "Sabrina. She's staying with me for a while."

A look of surprise filtered through her eyes. She leaned forward and whispered, "I got to warn you, honey. This one sleeps with a gun." She gestured at Alex with a thumb.

I felt my eyes widen. Not because he slept with a gun. I already knew that. My brother slept with one, too. What surprised me was that this woman knew.

Alex groaned. "You answer the door one time with a gun…"

"You do it all the time," Liam and Sharon both said, amused.

Sharon didn't wait for Alex to introduce her. Instead, she stuck her hand out to me and did it herself. "I'm Sharon. I've been working around here since these two were in diapers. I know firsthand their shit stinks just like everyone else's."

I laughed while we shook hands. "Sabrina, and I'm glad someone else knows their real odor."

Sharon winked at me. "Pizzas for the table?"

Liam nodded.

Alex glanced at me. "You cool with pizza?"

"Definitely." I nodded.

"Coming right up," Sharon declared. "Now you boys go sit down and stop scaring all my customers."

"Then tell your customers to stop hitting on my girl," Alex muttered.

I gasped and looked up quickly. *My girl.* Must have been a slip of the tongue. Him taking his responsibility to my brother too far.

Sharon patted me on the shoulder. "Go sit with Bellamy, honey. She'll show you how to handle them."

I watched Sharon walk away, stunned by the entire exchange.

"You cool?" Liam asked Alex.

"Yeah. I'm straight."

"Hey, Brina, how you doing?" Liam asked, once again catching me unprepared. I turned to answer as he swept in and kissed my cheek, giving me a one-armed hug.

"I'm good." I confirmed, surprised.

He chuckled and headed for the table. I stared after him. "Did he just call me Brina and kiss me on the cheek?"

"You're family." Alex was flippant, as if it should be obvious.

"No, I'm not," I refuted.

"You are. And now everyone in this place knows you're connected to me and Liam."

I sighed, feeling the stare of too many eyes. "You're just as bad as my brother."

"You'd do well to remember that." Alex warned, his eyes flashing as he glanced back to where Beau was sitting.

I don't know what I was thinking, how I actually allowed what I said next out of my mouth. Alex put his palm on my lower back and began leading me to our table, and the words just freaking tumbled right out. "I love my brother anyway."

Alex's entire hand spasmed against my back. I felt his fingertips curl into the fabric of my sweater, then let go. I felt his eyes. They almost burned a hole in the side of my face, but I refused to look up. I refused to even acknowledge what I'd just said.

Instead, I hot-footed it toward the table and slid into a seat right beside Bellamy, sending a plea into the universe that Alex wouldn't read too much into what I blurted but knowing damn well he would.

17

Alex

I spent the next week turning my A-frame cabin into a fortress as security parts and pieces arrived nearly every day. The more secure this place became, the tenser I grew.

When I came home from the army, I'd been a different guy than the one who left. My goofy, lackadaisical attitude was buried under death, bloodshed, and the reality of what this world was really like.

It took a long fucking time to re-shift everything inside me, to pull the more relaxed version of myself to the surface and stuff the shuttered, world-weary me below it. Eventually, I settled on both of those parts residing almost beside each other, never being able to fully bury all the shit I'd done and seen. Instead, I developed the skill of keeping that bit of me hidden unless I was willing to allow someone to glimpse it.

Ever since Mercer called, the tentative balance inside me was tumultuous. Turning what had become a sanctuary in the mountains, a place where the outside world didn't really have to intrude, into a place that could withstand the kind of people I used to kill… Let's just say it was encouraging the icy me to push down the parts I'd had to work really hard not to lose.

When I slept, visions of my past haunted me. Screams and gunfire filled my dreams. Sometimes Sabrina was at the center of the grim war dreams. Instead of a faceless, unknown woman, it would be Brina being tortured and abused.

As a result, this place was jacked with more security than it needed. The honest truth was I didn't need much in the way of protection because my hands were the deadliest thing in this house.

However, with Liam holding down the fort at work, I was stuck in this place with Sabrina day and night. I had to keep my hands busy. If I didn't, I was going to do something I shouldn't. Something I wanted to do really, really fucking bad.

Sexual tension and impending-danger tension did *not* mix well.

I stood at the large triangular window and watched as the van drove slowly away. I waited until it was long gone and then went to do a perimeter check around the property to verify nothing was amiss.

It wasn't, and I knew it would be that way, but I checked anyway. Those contractors were in my sight the entire time they'd been here, but I wasn't about to let some stupid rookie move be my downfall.

The muscles between my shoulder blades bunched a little when I went down the hall and opened the bedroom door. Sabrina glanced up from the center of my bed, a scowl written across her expressive and annoyingly beautiful face. It aggravated the shit out of her that I never knocked.

Too bad.

"You can come out now," I told her, smirking.

She tossed the fashion magazine on the mattress with a huff. "I'm glad this is so amusing for you."

I watched with shuttered eyes as she slid down over the side of my bed and stood. She was wearing those damn jeans again with a long-sleeved black T-shirt she'd tied into a knot at her hip.

When she moved past, she made sure not to brush against me, which pissed me off. I hadn't touched her since the night at The Tavern. Since then, we'd just danced around each other. I'd feel her eyes when I wasn't looking, and I knew she felt mine when she wasn't.

I was starting to go stir crazy.

I followed her out into the main room, seeing her standing at the window, staring.

"What's wrong?"

"It looks exactly the same," she remarked, pointing.

"You thought it would look different?"

She shrugged. "For all the noise those men made putting it in, I guess I expected something else."

I smiled. "You mean like a giant sign across the center declaring it's bulletproof?"

She made a rude sound. "Don't you think that's going a little too far?"

I echoed her impolite noise. "Considering that just last year, Bellamy was attacked in her own home by a man who shot through the window because there was no other way to get inside? No."

She gasped and spun, her eyes wide. "Are you serious?"

"Unfortunately."

"I had no idea! How scary!"

"That's not even the half of it."

Her eyes widened even more, seeming to take over half her face. They looked more gold today, matching some of the foliage outside on the mountains. "What happened?"

"Uh-uh," I said, moving into the kitchen. "You don't need to hear about all that. You're already scared enough without me adding more freakish scenarios to your head."

"I'm not scared!" she declared, storming into the kitchen behind me.

I looked up from the interior of the fridge. I wasn't even hungry, and it was too early for beer. "So the other night at The Tavern, when Beau was talking to you, you weren't having a mini panic attack about being in a room full of potential killers?"

Her breath caught. "How'd you know that?"

"I read you very well."

"Do not!"

Slamming the fridge door, I stalked toward her, my booted feet not making a sound. I watched her visibly swallow and tuck her hair behind her ears. She didn't back down, not at all, just stood there and watched me with that twenty-four-karat gaze.

We'd been avoiding each other like the plague, but in that moment, I didn't give a shit. The strain between us was getting on my nerves, and I wanted to feel something more. Curling my hand around her hip made her body jolt, making a predatory roar fill my head.

I watched her reaction as I forced her backward, keeping my palm anchored on her, feeling the sizzle of the touch. When her back came up against the kitchen counter, I planted my hands on either side of her and leaned in. We didn't touch, but we were so close our energy did.

"So right now you aren't anticipating my kiss? You aren't standing there telling yourself you don't want it when we both know you want it so damn bad."

"I could ask the same thing of you."

I smiled. I liked that she didn't deny it. And that she didn't try to run away from me either. It was satisfying to know that being in this house, which I'd never thought of as small until recently, with me was affecting her just as much.

I leaned closer, so close if I moved another inch, our lips would brush together. Her breathing stopped, and her stare dropped to my mouth.

"How about we get out of here for a while?"

Her eyes lifted. Confusion clouded them. "Wh-what?"

I pulled back and smiled. Yeah, okay, it was probably an arrogant grin. "Let's get out of here." Reaching between us, I offered my hand.

Sabrina looked between me and my hand, then smacked it away before bolting around me.

I laughed.

She went toward the door where her tall brown boots sat and jammed her feet inside. Next, she picked up a plaid yellow, orange, red, and black scarf to drape around her neck. I still didn't understand how that ended up being in a stack of "basics" she bought for while she was here.

I had to admit, though, she looked damned fine wearing it.

"Well?" she demanded gesturing toward the door.

I lifted an eyebrow. "Don't you wanna know where we're going?"

She snorted. "Like I care. Anywhere but here and with people other than you sounds pretty amazing right about now."

I chuckled and picked up my keys.

"Can I drive?" she asked.

"If I say no, will you just go hotwire it?"

She shrugged as if she were actually considering it.

"Fine, but if you wreck it, I'm going to paddle your ass."

"Promises, promises," she sang.

I blanched, and white-hot need slammed through me.

Sabrina sauntered over, plucking the keys right from my palm. "What's the matter, Alex? Cat got your tongue?"

My eyes narrowed.

It was her turn to laugh knowingly. "I can play the same games you can," she quipped before stepping out of the house.

Damn.

Sabrina

The wintry mountain town of Caribou, Colorado, was charming and something I'd only seen before in places like Pinterest and cute holiday movies that played on TV.

The streets were narrow but lit up, and I could only imagine how majestic it would be when it snowed, because even in the fall, it was stunning. The main street was packed with shops lining the sidewalks. There were small trees every few feet with string lights in them that made me want to stay here until it was past dark and I could see them twinkle.

Dry, curled leaves and other more colorful fresh ones littered the concrete and scattered across the road where cars drove slowly, drivers seeming to wave at everyone they passed.

The air here smelled alive, like earth and sun and damp leaves. The bite in the breeze caressed my cheeks, making them sting just a bit, and the tip of my nose was cold. A few shops had large baskets of orange pumpkins sitting outside, and almost every store window was draped in foliage and set up with scarecrows or some other festive decoration.

Ducking a little deeper into the scarf I'd bought at the resort, I hid a small smile. I loved it here. I loved the energy in the air, the feeling of new beginnings, and the urge to rush into the closest place that sold cider or cocoa to warm my hands against the cup.

Living in California, I never experienced this kind of weather. Sure, we all got excited for fall and had the seasonal drinks and bought fall clothes that it never quite got cold enough to wear. Here, though, you could live it. You could *feel* it.

"This is pretty much the heartbeat of Caribou," Alex said as we walked. "We don't have any of those big chain stores. Those are all in the next town over. Everyone comes here for anything they need, and most tourists who come to ski never even have to leave the resort because we have everything up there." As he spoke, I followed his gaze above the town toward the impressive mountain view and then to BearPaw Resort, which seemed to reside over the town, lit up like some kind of castle.

When I didn't say anything, he cleared his throat. "It's not much."

I gasped, offended he would say that. "It is! It's everything."

He looked over at me. "You like it?"

"It's something out of a storybook."

He chuckled. "Yeah, well, most locals wouldn't say that. Especially after back-to-back blizzards and shorter-than-short summers."

"I think I've had enough summer to last me a lifetime," I murmured, gazing at a storefront just two windows down. I gasped again, throwing out a hand to grab his arm. "Look! They have cider!"

He chuckled. "They have cider in Cali, too, kitten."

My insides warmed a little at the easy affection in his voice. I became acutely aware that I was still griping his arm but pretended I didn't notice because I wasn't ready to let go yet. Instead, I made a scoffing sound. "Yeah, but we never actually have the kind of weather to enjoy it!"

I started to tow him forward. "C'mon!"

He laughed under his breath and followed dutifully.

"They have pumpkins, too! Wouldn't those look so cute on your deck?"

"You want to put pumpkins on my deck?"

I glanced around at him, surprised at the surprise in his voice. "Haven't you ever?"

His lips pursed. I couldn't help but think of when he'd kissed me in Liam's office and just how sinful those lips had felt. "Can't say that I have."

I made a rude sound. "You've got to be kidding. You live in a place like this and you've never decorated with pumpkins? Or carved them?"

He shrugged.

"I don't know why I'm surprised. You don't even have lights on the window."

His feet stuttered, and his voice was bemused. "Lights on the window?"

I turned to face him, throwing up my hands in the process. "You have that adorable triangular window with a seat crying out for pillows and blankets that would look so inviting draped in lights, and how do you decorate?" I screwed up my nose. "By putting in bulletproof glass."

I mean, frankly, it was a crime. And lame.

Alex's expression grew curious. "You've been mind-decorating my house?"

I blinked, faltering. "What? No."

A slow smile spread over his face. "You've totally been walking around my place, redecorating it in your head."

I felt shy suddenly. Shy and insecure, as if those piercing eyes of his could see past all the layers and walls I'd purposely built to keep out perceptive men like him. Yeah, okay, maybe I had been imagining what his house could look like with some homey touches here and there… Who cares?

"There isn't anything else to do while I sit around waiting for someone to kill me," I muttered and turned away.

Alex moved like lightning, his hand shooting out to curl around the place just above my elbow and yanking. I spun back, stumbling a bit, colliding with his firm chest. I started to pull back instantly, my body on high alert because wayyyy too much of me was touching wayyyy too much of him.

He wouldn't let me go.

Instead, the grip he had on my arm slipped down to my lower back and pressed so I had to stand there and feel him against me.

"Sabrina." He commanded my attention, manipulating my eyes and body to betray me.

I looked up, finding him already staring at me intently. His eyes were icy and pale compared to all the autumn hues around us. I breathed in deeply, a hint of apple and cinnamon from the nearby shop mixing with his unique scent, and my body melted just a bit farther into his.

The hand at my back curled closer, holding me tighter.

"No one is going to kill you." He spoke low, still holding my stare. The resolve there was unparalleled, almost hypnotic. Someone could literally have a gun to my head that second and be ready to pull the trigger, yet I would still be calm because Alex said no one was going to hurt me.

"You hear me?" he asked when I didn't indicate I'd heard.

I nodded.

His hand rubbed over the spot he was holding, dragging away to briefly rest on my hip. "I'm not gonna let anyone hurt you."

"I know." My head was swimming. I couldn't think when he touched me. When he looked at me as if I were all he saw and we weren't standing on the street, but rather somewhere he could have me undressed in seconds.

Someone walked by and called out a greeting to Alex, and he nodded in reply.

Thank God for that. It snapped me out of whatever he was doing to me.

I wrenched away, adjusting my scarf. "You made a promise to my brother. I know you will keep it."

His eyes narrowed. "Your brother isn't the reason I made that promise."

The bottom fell out of my stomach. I felt it land right at my cute booted feet.

"Alex!" someone called. Actually, she didn't "call" his name at all. She purred it. A tall blonde with an ass that probably inspired the peach emoji sauntered over, inserting herself effortlessly between me and Alex. She was dressed in a pair of skin-tight black pants, high-heeled boots, and a bright-red fleece vest over a black and white-striped shirt. Her hair was curled to look effortless, but I knew for a fact it probably took an hour to get that tousled feel.

She barely flicked a glanced toward me with her perfectly made-up eyes and winged black eyeliner before focusing completely on Alex.

"It's been a while since I've seen you," she said, leaning into him. Her claws—excuse me—her hand curled around his arm just as mine had minutes before.

I could take her out. In two seconds flat. My brother taught me things… things she probably didn't even know existed.

"You know how it is," Alex replied smoothly with a smile. "I've been keeping busy up at the resort."

"Well, as part owner, I'd expect nothing less."

"Part owner?" I said, unable to keep the words in. He *owned* part of BearPaw?

The blonde didn't even acknowledge I'd spoken. Instead, she ran her claw—excuse me—finger down the center of his chest. "So when are you going to take me out again? Maybe we can double this weekend with Liam and Bellamy."

He was *dating* her? Oh, gross. Queasiness made me press a hand to my stomach and turn away.

What the hell was I doing? Standing here completely charmed by this little town, decorating his house in my head, and being hypnotized by his eyes.

No. No, no, no. I was stupid. Just like last time.

Ahead, someone stepped out of the shop I'd been dragging Alex toward, carrying a white paper cup with a red lid. The scent of cinnamon wafted close, and the person glanced at me and smiled.

I forced myself to smile back, though I was still trying to swallow back vomit. The glowing lights of the interior of the shop beckoned me like a safe haven, like the bright light offering reprieve from death.

God. That was what this felt like right now. Seeing Alex with some woman, a woman who clearly knew him well. Who'd hung out with him and Liam. It felt like a piece of me was dying.

I took off, rushing into the store, catching the glass door before it even closed behind the person who'd left. I heard Alex call my name, but I kept going.

I nearly vaulted inside, making a few people nearby, as well as the woman behind the counter, glance up. The second they saw me, everyone smiled, and I felt the embarrassing rush of tears at the backs of my eyes. I couldn't do kindness right now. No. Right now I needed someone to give me an attitude so I could pull out mine and not feel so vulnerable.

"Hiya!" the woman said. "Did you come in for some cider? It's the perfect afternoon for it."

I blinked and took a breath. Forcing a smile, I nodded. "I could smell it all the way outside, and I just had to come in."

"It's a family recipe, a secret family recipe."

"Don't even bother asking what the secret is," a man at the counter turned to tell me. "'Cause this one won't give it up for nothing."

The woman behind the counter laughed. "He's right."

"I'm sure it's delicious," I said, feeling much more at ease. I came farther into the store, glancing into the glass case. Inside, the most divine-looking pastries were artfully arranged, including a stack of apple cider donuts.

"Here we go," the lady said, placing a paper cup with the familiar red lid on the counter in front of me. "I added a cinnamon stick just for fun."

Immediately, I wrapped my palms around the cup, sighing when the warmth from the liquid seeped into my pores.

The door behind me chimed, and I knew it was Alex. I kept my back turned and sipped at the drink. The woman watched me, so I knew I would have too ooh and ahh, even if it tasted like crap.

It didn't. In fact, it was so good it made me sigh and roll my eyes toward the sky. "Oh goodness, this is the best cider I have ever had."

The woman clapped. "I'm so thrilled you love it."

I took another sip and nodded.

"Alex!" the woman called out, glancing up.

My back stiffened, and still, I refused to look in his direction.

I felt hurt, and I was angry I did. He made me feel out of control inside my own body, and I hated it.

"Donna." He charmed. "Looking as beautiful as always."

She giggled. I wanted to choke. "Oh, you," she cooed.

Alex stepped up beside me, his palm pressing to my lower back. "I see you've met Sabrina."

The woman's eyes rounded as she took in the way he stood close and touched me so casually. "Are you two...?"

"No!" I burst out.

The woman jolted and looked at me. I felt Alex vibrate with unreleased laughter. I wondered how he'd like a face full of the cider I was holding.

"We're just friends," I said, trying to lessen my previous outburst.

She pursed her lips and busied herself behind the counter, bending down to get something.

I stepped away from Alex and glared. He smirked.

"You can't have my famous cider without some donuts to go with it," Donna said, placing a stack of the donuts into a paper bag.

"I'm sure they are just as amazing as this," I told her, reaching to take the offered treats. "Thank you."

"Of course."

"How much do I owe you?"

The woman waved her hand. "For a friend of Alex? It's on the house."

"Oh, I couldn't," I said, reaching for my bag.

"I insist."

"Thanks Donna," Alex said, giving me a gentle push toward the door. "You're my favorite girl."

Donna giggled again. Good Lord. Were all women reduced to piles of hormones when he smiled at them?

As we passed the register, Alex produced a ten-dollar bill and stuffed it into the tip jar sitting nearby.

"Save me some of those pumpkins," he called out as he pushed the door open for me to go ahead. "I think we'll be coming back to pick up a few for my deck."

"Tell your parents I said hi!" she called as the door was closing behind us.

Out on the sidewalk, I glared.

"Damn, girl. If looks could kill," he quipped.

"You'd be dead."

"This about that bunny earlier?"

"Bunny?" I asked, blank.

He gestured to where I'd left him before. "That girl."

"You call her bunny?" I didn't know why, but that made me feel one hundred times worse. Like I couldn't even be pissed because the hurt was too sharp.

Did he have a cute nickname for every girl he dated?

He drew back. "What? No." Then his eyes widened and stupid realization dawned there.

I hated that look. The look that said he knew exactly what was going on. A look that proved my walls weren't working in keeping him out.

He stepped forward, and I held out a palm, warding him off.

He came closer anyway, disregarding my desire for physical space. "That's what we call the girls up here. The ones who are regulars at the resort. Snow bunnies. Well, actually, I call the tourists at the resort that, too. It's easier than remembering their names, and they all feel special when…"

He must have realized his explanation was only making things worse, because he stopped talking.

"*Shit.*" He scolded himself beneath his breath. "It doesn't mean anything." He backtracked. "It's just something stupid I say."

"Like kitten." I shut my eyes the second the words tumbled out. *Way to be even more obvious, Sabrina!*

Ladies and gentlemen, the winner of this year's dumbass award: me.

"No!" he hurried to say, stepping even closer and bending so we were nearer to eye level. Despite his effort to look at me directly, I avoided his gaze. "That is not at all the same thing."

Anger rose in me again, and I welcomed the way it scorched some of the pain. I met his eyes. "Did you sleep with her?"

He glanced away.

And the anger was gone again. I clutched the cup and bag like a shield.

"That's not fair," he murmured.

Maybe it wasn't. But neither was the way he affected me.

"Can we go?"

His shoulders lifted and then settled. "No."

My eyes flew to his. "No?" I echoed, dumbfounded.

"We haven't done what I brought you down here for."

"You mean you didn't bring me down here so I could see the parade of women you've slept with?" I snapped.

He sighed dramatically. "I brought you down here so you could meet my parents."

"What?" I squeaked.

"Their candy shop is right down there." He pointed down the street. "I wanted to show you The Confectionary."

I gazed down the street to the shop he pointed out. "Your parents are there?"

"Well, they own the place."

My gaze fell on his once more, and damn if I didn't feel a little of that hypnotic pull. I pushed at it, though, forcing it back.

"What do you say, Kit—" He stopped speaking when I glared. Clearing his throat, he started again. "What to meet the 'rents? My mom will give you a shit ton of free chocolate."

"Well, who am I to say no to free chocolate?"

He smiled, relief in his eyes. He moved to slip his hand against the small of my back again, almost as if he thought that was where it belonged. I side-stepped so he couldn't, and his hand fell back to his side.

"I gotta warn you," he said as we walked along the pavement. "My mom is gonna fawn all over you, probably ask you a thousand questions, and then tell you you're too skinny and try to force chocolate down your throat."

I laughed at the picture he painted. "I don't think she's going to have to force any candy on me."

He made a rude sound. "Say that after you've already eaten a pound of it."

I laughed, sipping at the cider. It had the perfect amount of spice and the perfect amount of sweet. We approached a shop with ornate wooden trim around the door and the words THE CONFECTIONARY in gold overhead. The trim was all dark brown, but the large wooden door in the center was a pale robin's egg blue. In the middle hung a wreath made of white pumpkins that looked like they were dunked in chocolate.

Out on the sidewalk with the door closed, I could already smell rich chocolate, and my mouth watered.

Over to the right of the door and trim was a lit-up window with an elaborate display of truffles and boxes of candy.

Before Alex opened the door, he touched my arm briefly, drawing my attention. "I'm serious, Brina. She's probably going to ask a million questions."

My brow wrinkled. "Why?"

"Because I've never brought a girl in here before."

A light, dizzy feeling came over me. As did a sense of giddiness. I held all of that back, though, refusing to let him see. Instead, I rolled my eyes. "Yeah right."

"For reals. The only other girl I brought here was Bellamy, but she's Liam's." Honesty and something even more convincing rang in his voice. Nervousness. He was nervous about this.

"Well," I remarked, "I promise I won't tell her what a pain in the ass you are."

He laughed. "She'd never believe you anyways."

I made a face, and he reached for the handle, pride enveloping his features. "Welcome to The Confectionary."

Alex

My parents' love of candy started in the kitchen of our simple three-bedroom house and the fact that winters here stretched on forever, forcing people who weren't into snow sports to find something to do indoors.

My mom was a bomb-ass cook, making the kind of dishes that should be featured in magazines and on TV. But she never wanted any of that. All she wanted was a quiet life in the small town of Caribou, her husband, and two kids.

She started crafting chocolates out of our kitchen, sharing them with friends and neighbors until the demand for them grew to the point her and my father pooled everything they had, took a leap of faith, and opened the store I ushered Sabrina in today.

They'd built this place from nothing, creating a chocolate world in the middle of a snow-white town. It was one of the most popular shops in Caribou, so popular that they now also ran an online store that sold almost more than they did in house. My sister, Zoe, ran that because my parents knew everything about chocolate and candy but nothing about technology.

I was proud of them. Not just for everything they'd accomplished, but of the people they were. I knew for a fact if they hadn't been the people to raise me, then the ice inside me would have swallowed me whole and I'd be a completely different version of the man I was today.

The bell on the door jingled overhead as we stepped in, the familiar smells of chocolate, sugar, and vanilla tinting the air.

Dad was at the register, ringing up someone, and looked up.

"Hey!" he called out. "There's my boy!"

My face split into a grin. "Hey, Dad."

Beside me, Sabrina was quiet, but I could feel her soaking it all in like a sponge, taking in detail upon detail.

The man at the register turned with a large box of chocolates in his hand, wrapped in a red bow. "Sam," I greeted.

"Alex, good to see you."

"Hope Alice enjoys those."

The man chuckled. "You know she will. Bringing my wife candy from this place every week is a tradition." He turned toward my father. "Thanks, Reggie. See ya next week!"

My father called out a good-bye, but his eyes were already fixed on Sabrina. "Linda! Come see what the cat dragged in!" he called toward the back room.

The room in the back was bigger than this front one because that's where my mother made all the chocolate. By hand.

"So," I said, glancing down at Sabrina. "What do you think?"

Her eyes wandered everywhere, taking in the ornate wooden trim, old-style cabinetry, and long display counters on each side, encased in glass. Everything in here was light and bright. Cream-colored walls and trim, pale-blue accents, splashes of pale yellow here and there, and long, gleaming white marble counters.

The cash register was old school, looking like something you'd find in an antique shop, but it was in pristine working order. Like I said, my parents didn't do technology. They much preferred pushing buttons and hearing the *ding* of the register every time it opened. Customers seemed to be enchanted by it, too.

"I feel like I've just stepped into another world," Sabrina whispered, gazing up at the painted tin ceiling and large chandeliers my mom had insisted on.

"That's what Bellamy said, too."

"Well, she was right. This place is amazing. It's old world meets small town with a level of sophisticated gourmet."

My chest swelled a little hearing her talk about this place like that, seeing that she thought it was just as amazing as I did.

"Well, with a description like that, you're my new favorite customer!" my mom announced.

We both turned. I'd actually forgotten we weren't alone.

"Alex," Mom cooed and came forward to hug me as she always did.

"Hey, Mom."

She didn't spend much more time with my greeting, practically pushing me aside so she could turn both eyes to Sabrina.

"Hi," Sabrina said, her cheeks turning pink under the direct attention.

"Mom, this is Sabrina." I introduced them. "Sabrina, this is my mom, Linda, and my dad, Reggie."

Sabrina held out her hand, but I knew what was coming. I grabbed the cup and bag from her grip just before my mother yanked her in for one of her over-the-top hugs. "It's so nice to meet you!" Mom pulled back, still holding on to her so she could look her over. "What a gorgeous thing you are. Isn't she gorgeous, Reggie?"

"Not nearly as beautiful as you, dear," Dad replied, winking at Sabrina behind Mom's back.

I rolled my eyes.

Mom giggled. "He's a handful, that one."

I was worried how Sabrina would take them. She didn't have any family that I knew of, just her brother, and he definitely was not like my parents. My parents were... over the top.

"I see where Alex gets it from," she quipped, making Mom laugh.

Mom put her arm around Sabrina and ushered her into the store. "Now you're going to have to try one of everything... I'll want to know what your favorite— Oh!" She interrupted herself. "You can taste test the new flavor I'm developing for the resort. Tell me which one you like best."

"Me?" Sabrina questioned.

My heart turned over watching her stare at my mother with wide, shy eyes. She hadn't been expecting this kind of welcome, and I could tell she was overwhelmed.

"I hope you warned that poor girl," Dad said, stepping into my line of sight and cutting off the image of Sabrina. "Your mother is already planning your wedding."

I groaned. "We aren't dating, Dad."

"Mm-hmm," he hummed.

"Reggie!" Mom called. "Come over here and help us. We have a guest. You can talk to Alex anytime."

"Geez, Mom. I'm just your firstborn."

A customer walked in, and Mom told me to take care of them.

Chopped liver. I'd become second rate in my own family within three seconds of Mom laying eyes on Sabrina. *God.* She probably was planning the wedding. Surprisingly, the thought didn't make me break out into a cold sweat like it normally would.

If anything, I found myself gazing across the rectangular space at Brina and wondering what she would look like in a wedding gown with flowers in her hair.

"That will be everything," the woman said.

I snapped back to the present and wrapped up the truffles, then rang her up. When the woman was gone, Mom waved me over to the hot chocolate bar.

"Come make your sweetie some hot cocoa, Alex."

"We aren't dating, Mom," I said for the second time.

"Well, good heavens, why not?"

Sabrina nearly choked on the truffle Mom was feeding her.

I plastered a pathetic look on my face. "She won't have me."

"What!" Mom gasped, turning to stare at Sabrina.

"That's not true." Sabrina tried to assure her.

"So you do want to date my son?" Mom pressed.

"No. I mean, yes… I mean…" Sabrina stuttered, flustered and cute as hell.

Mom turned to me, hands on her round hips. "Alexander Hamilton Carter, what did you do to this poor girl to make her not want to date you?"

"Why would you think it's my fault?" I demanded.

"Hamilton?" Sabrina noted, lifting an eyebrow.

"Don't even think about it," I growled.

A slow smile spread over her evil little mouth.

"Alex!" Mom gasped and turned back to Sabrina. "You'll have to make allowances for him. He's just like his father. Kinda rough around the edges."

Sabrina laughed.

For the love of—

"So how did you two meet?" Mom went on.

I glanced at Dad for some help, but he gave me a *you're on your own* look. "Sabrina's brother was in the army with me. He had to deploy for an extended amount of time and didn't want her to be alone, so she's staying with me for a while."

"You're living together!" Mom exclaimed, excited.

I groaned.

"Well, honey, I hope you can convince him to do something with his place. It's in need of some decoration. Zoe and I tried to spruce it up, but he wouldn't hear of it."

"You wanted to put pine tree wallpaper in the bathroom," I said through gritted teeth.

"We live in the mountains," she said, as if that were explanation enough.

"Let the boy keep his house the way he wants, Linda." Dad finally chimed in.

Gee, thanks, Dad.

"I wanted to get some pumpkins for the deck," Sabrina said, peaking at me.

In that moment, I would have bought every pumpkin in Caribou if she looked at me like that again.

"Oh, that would be adorable!" Mom agreed. "Alex! The cocoa."

Stepping close, I crowded Sabrina's back, knowing she wouldn't move away with my mother standing right beside her. I took advantage, reaching around her, making sure to brush against her arm and shoulder as I pulled a pale-blue paper cup off the stack.

I placed the cup in front of her, then repeated the same action to fetch a napkin. Sabrina shivered slightly the second time I touched her, and I felt a jolt of satisfaction.

Mom, being the eagle-eye stalker she was, noticed. "Heavens! Are you cold, dear?"

"Oh, no—"

"Alex, be a gentleman and give her your coat."

"That's not really necessary."

"Posh." Mom quieted Sabrina and gestured toward me.

The red fleece I had on slid over my arms, and once again, I stepped close behind her to drape it over her shoulders. Sabrina glanced over her shoulder out of the corner of her eye, and I had a sudden overwhelming urge to kiss her temple.

I resisted, instead whispering in her ear, "Better put it on."

She sighed low and pushed her arms through the jacket. Just because I knew she wouldn't say anything, I put both arms around her, stepping so close her back brushed my chest under the guise of pulling the coat all the way around her.

"Better?" Mom asked, beaming.

"Yes, thank you," Sabrina mumbled, slightly breathless.

"This is the most famous hot chocolate in all of Caribou," my dad said, thankfully drawing the attention away from the tension that seemed to crackle between me and Brina. "We got the idea from a place in Germany we read about many moons ago."

Instead of stepping back, as I knew Brina wanted, I grabbed up the steel decanter of warm milk and poured it into the cup in front of her. Dad set a square of chocolate on the end of a wooden stick, sprinkled with flaked salt and a drizzle of caramel, in front of her.

Sabrina glanced at me, having to look over her shoulder again to do so.

Unable to stop myself, I reached around her, caging her body against mine, and unwrapped the chocolate. Holding it in front of her, I spoke into her ear. "You stir this into the hot cream, and when it melts, it makes the cocoa."

"It's divine!" Mom added.

"I'm pretty sure it's why I can't ever lose the twenty extra pounds I carry," Dad added.

"You're perfect the way you are, Reggie," Mom told him.

Sabrina's fingers brushed mine as she took the stick and dunked it into the milk. Instantly, the chocolate started to melt, the mixture turning a rich shade.

I moved back, and as I did, I caught the scent of me on her. I knew it was because she was wearing my jacket, but oh, the primal roar that erupted inside me. I liked having my scent on her.

Like she was marked.

Like she was claimed.

"I think this is even better than the cider from down the street," Brina declared, smiling at Mom. "But don't tell her I said that!"

Mom beamed and hugged her again, nearly sloshing the drink over the rim. Deftly, I took it and snapped a lid on the cup.

"So tell me your favorite part of Caribou so far," Mom prompted. "What all has Alex already showed you?"

"Oh, um…" Sabrina paused. "We haven't had the chance to see much yet. But the drive here from the resort was just beautiful. I've never seen so many colors in the trees before."

Mom glanced to me. "You haven't showed her around yet?"

Well, I was a little busy trying to keep her alive. But I couldn't say that. "The resort's been keeping me busy. It's almost time for the first ski of the season," I said instead.

"Come on. I'll show you the back," Mom said, gesturing for Sabrina to follow. "That's where I make everything. I'll show you some secrets, and you can test some of the flavors I'm working on. Did Alex tell you we're opening a storefront at the resort? It was Liam's idea. That boy, he's just as ornery as my Alex."

Sabrina cast me a glance as she followed along behind Mom. I thought I might see a plea for help in its depths, but all I saw was amusement and… joy.

I still loved her. After all these years, I was still in love with Sabrina.

I watched her even after she looked back to Mom. I stared at the spot she left even after she'd turned the corner.

I didn't even glance away when I felt Dad pat me on the back and chuckle. "You got it bad, son."

He was right.

20

Sabrina

Is this what it's like to have parents?

Like parents who were present and acted like people who cared about the children they had? Did they ask a thousand too-personal questions, talk over you, and look at you like you hung the moon and stars?

Wow.

When I was younger, I'd considered many times what it would be like to have parents to love me and care for me, but then I got older and those thoughts seemed more like dreams or wishful thinking. Reality had a way of railroading over those thoughts. And I'd always had Daniel, who filled in so many gaps our absent father and uncaring mother left behind. After a while, I stopped thinking about what it would be like to have parents in my life.

Until today. Today, I was overwhelmed by the welcoming scents of chocolate and charmed by the penny candy bins Linda insisted I raid before we left. There was a sense of home inside The Confectionary that caught me off guard, and the all-encompassing warmth of his mother nearly railroaded me.

Before we walked in there, I'd been so incredibly pissed and hurt by Alex. Seeing him with that "bunny" on the street and listening to him try to explain her away caused pain inside me I never wanted to feel again. Pain I'd promised myself I would avoid at all costs.

Now here I was, sitting in the passenger seat of his Hummer, contemplating family and love and what it would be like to be part of his world.

He made me feel lonely.

I worked my whole life to not feel that way, but here I was. Lonelier than ever before.

"Was that too much?"

I glanced across the interior of his truck. His eyes were on the road heading out of Caribou and leading back up the mountain to the resort.

"What?" I asked almost as an afterthought once I realized he'd asked me a question and I hadn't just been drawn to look his way.

He tossed a glance toward me before turning back to the road. "My parents. I know they are over the top, and my mom was definitely on her game today." He smiled fondly at her behavior, and my chest tightened. "I should have told them I was bringing you by and to not to be so in your face. I shouldn't have sprung it on you either."

"Would they have listened?" I asked, amused that he was rambling like he was nervous. It was incredibly cute, and Alex was often everything *but* cute.

He barked a laugh. "Fuck no."

I smiled.

I felt him glance at me again. "But I would have at least told them."

"I like them," I confessed. "You're really lucky to have such great parents. Maybe next time I can meet your sister." Zoe, his mom explained, was out of town on Confectionary business.

He must have heard something in my voice. I should have known he would pick up on it. There wasn't much he missed when it came to me.

"Kitten…"

"Don't call me that."

His giant hands tightened on the steering wheel. "Why the hell not?"

"You know why," I intoned darkly.

Alex sighed heavily. "Sabrina."

"I miss my brother," I blurted out. It was the truth. I did miss him. More than anything. And I would much rather confess that than any other feelings I might have.

"Fuck."

Startled, I looked around. "What?"

"I should have thought about how that family time back there at the shop would have made you feel. I—" His voice cut off abruptly, and the heinous, horribly loud sound of groaning metal splinted through what had been a relatively quiet moment.

The sudden jarring of the large Hummer made me scream, and the flash of extremely bright lights blinded me before my center of gravity vanished.

I felt like a ragdoll being tossed into the air. My hair flew out around me in slow motion, and I knew I would have been in worse shape if the seat belt hadn't tightened so taut across me that I screamed again.

Shattering glass burst inward. I felt the prickly shards sting my skin as it was sliced open. Dull pain throbbed in me, but I couldn't figure out where it was coming from. Everything was upside down. Nausea rolled over me, and I felt myself gag.

Silence ensued as I blinked, trying center myself, trying to understand what just happened and why I felt so... unbalanced.

My head felt like it was in a vise. Unbearable pressure closed in around me, and I fought against it. Finally, I was able to focus, but everything was dark— no, my hair was in my face, falling all around my head like a drape.

I pushed at it, noting the way everything pulled me down.

I was upside down. Holy crap! The entire Hummer was upside down. I was only held in the seat because of the crushing tightness of the seatbelt. I groaned, swiping back my hair again, feeling the pressure I now knew was because all my blood was rushing to my head.

"Alex," I croaked, trying to lift my head to see him. "Alex…"

He didn't answer.

Grappling with the belt across my chest, I fought, trying to pull it free of my neck. "Hey," I rasped, lifting my head to look in his direction. Dizziness washed over me again, but I refocused and stared across the seats.

He was still in the car, held in place by his seat belt. But he appeared unconscious and… hurt.

"Alex," I whimpered, reaching for him. "Alex, wake up. Please. Please wake up."

Please be okay.

His arms were cut from the glass, dark rivulets of blood streaming down his forearms.

Tears blurred my vision, and a metallic taste washed over my tongue.

What happened? What caused this accident? One minute, he was driving along and I thought we were alone on the road, and the next... the next, I was begging him to wake up and watching him bleed.

A sob broke out of my throat, and I reached for him again, straining against the belt.

"Wake up," I pleaded. My fingers were almost there...

The groaning of metal made me flinch, and the rush of cold night air swarmed inside the Hummer behind me. I gasped and turned to see what was happening.

A pair of jean-clad legs and booted feet stood there.

"Help!" I cried. "Help us! Call 9-1-1!"

More glass crunched under the man's boots as he crouched closer and reached into the car for me. "Not me!" I said, trying to push his hands away. "The driver, you need to get the driver."

The man grunted, and seconds later, I felt him release the latch on my belt. I braced for the fall but wasn't ready for it regardless. I landed in a heap on the roof of the Hummer, crying out when more broken glass cut into my cheek and forehead.

A strong, rough hand latched around my ankle, gripping so hard I felt it through my thick boot.

"Hey!" I cried.

My body began to move or, rather, be dragged through the banged-up Hummer, across the glass and frame of the window.

I rolled onto my belly and grabbed ahold of the seat belt, hanging on for dear life. "No!" I yelled. "Stop!"

This man wasn't here to help us. This man wasn't here for any good at all.

"Alex!" I screamed, looking up at him still dangling in the seat, his chin lulling on his chest.

My chin smacked into the road when the man yanked me free and hauled me away from the yellow truck. Instinct kicked in, and I twisted, rolling onto my back and kicking out with my free leg. The man grunted when I kicked his knee, but he didn't let go.

I kicked him again and then did a sit-up from the waist to grab his hand where he held me. Clawing at his fingers, I demanded he let me go.

He laughed. "I own you now. Better resign yourself to that fact."

I lay back, spent, and sucked in a few breaths. Gravel scraped against my back, and I knew if I hadn't still been wearing the fleece coat of Alex's, my shirt would have already ripped.

The thought of Alex gave me a renewed sense of fight, and with a roar, I kicked out again, hitting the sweet spot in the man's knee.

He groaned and stumbled. Quickly, I wrenched my leg away and bounded to my feet. He was bent at the waist, but when I stood, he began to as well. I kicked him in the face as he moved, making him stumble again.

He was wearing a loose flannel, and not the cute kind, so I lunged forward and pulled the ends up over his head, making it impossible for him to see.

"Hey!" he yelled, fighting against the fabric. I kicked him again and then took off running back to the Hummer.

"Alex!" I screamed as I ran and dropped to my knees beside the driver's window. He was still there, and from this angle, I could see that his head was gashed open and bleeding.

I had to find his cell. It was probably in his pocket…

I started to climb into the window, half in, half out, scrambling desperately to find the phone. My instincts were screaming at me to run, run like hell, but there was no way I would leave him here like this.

Just as I was reaching for his pocket, rough hands grabbed me by the waist and hauled me backward.

I kicked and fought and scraped over his hands like a hellion on crack. If I was going down, then this fucker was coming with me.

"Get off me!" I screamed, trying to punch his junk. He avoided the hit with a grunt.

"We're going to have fun breaking you," the man growled and threw me onto the ground.

I didn't stay down, instead springing back up, bringing my fists up for a fight.

He laughed, and I cold-cocked him, snapping his head back. I put all my strength into that hit, but unfortunately, it was only enough to piss him off.

As he wiped the blood from his lip, his nostrils flared, and I bounced on my feet, ready to hit him again.

"You little bitch," he spat, then punched me in the face.

I crumpled to the ground. The last thing I saw before the world went black was the dented and mangled side of the Hummer.

Alex

The large truck with the plow on the front had been sitting on some barely used side road, just waiting for us to come by.

It was unexpected. I'd give them that.

Plowing into the driver's side as I drove past would have been a good idea, *if* it worked.

How unfortunate for the dick-for-brains who did this because he didn't know who he was dealing with.

It would take a hell of a lot more than a head injury, superficial cuts, and sore muscles to keep me down. Actually, the only thing that would keep me down enough for this douche canoe to kidnap Sabrina right out from under me was death.

I wasn't dead.

But this fool was about to be.

Somewhere in the fog of my brain, I heard her pleading with me. I struggled at first to push through it and find the exit, but I remained calm, icy calm, because I knew I would be getting out of here.

Awareness washed over me first, though I kept my body prone and relaxed. Using my senses, I evaluated the situation and grew more pissed by the second. I heard Sabrina and someone fighting. Because she refused to run off and leave me here, my little hellion was taking on some man who wanted to make her his slave.

Then her body dropped to the pavement nearby. I watched her eyelids flutter and all consciousness fade away.

Like a robot, I went on autopilot, banking the extreme emotion threatening to surge my adrenaline. I reached for the knife I knew was strapped to my visor, pulled it out, and, with one deft swipe, cut through the belt holding me. I landed on my hands and knees, ignoring the crunch of glass and any pain.

Lithely, I unfolded from the busted-out window and uncurled from the ground.

The man had Sabrina, dragging her backward to his truck, when he noticed me. His footsteps paused, and an unfiltered look passed behind his beady eyes.

I spit the blood pooling in my mouth, tossed the knife from one hand to the other, and smiled.

He began walking faster, dragging my girl over the ground and overall pissing me off even more.

I stepped forward, walking as though I were on a Sunday stroll, and the man cursed low and tried to pick up Brina to toss over his shoulder.

"I wouldn't if I were you."

He glanced up, a deer in the headlights. Her upper body thumped onto the ground, and she groaned when he started to run.

I let him go and crouched beside Sabrina, putting a hand to her face. "Stay down, kitten. Keep your eyes closed."

"Alex?" she whispered, turning toward my voice.

"Yeah, sweetheart. I'll be right back."

The truck engine roared to life, and I strode forward. The man behind the wheel started moving quickly, trying to leave. I knocked on the window, and he looked at me, smirking, and pointed to the lock.

I shoved my fist through the window, shattering the glass.

He gurgled and his eyes nearly bulged out of his head as I grabbed him by the throat and pulled him through the open window to drop him at my feet.

"How many of you are here?" I demanded.

He spit at me.

When I reached down and grabbed him, he struggled. His attempts to get free were weak and useless.

"You never should have come here," I intoned, and then I snapped his neck.

His body went limp in my hands, and I dropped him, disgusted I had to compromise myself for the likes of him. But it had to be done.

Anyone who touched Sabrina the way he had would get the same.

I stepped over his body and turned off the truck, pocketed the keys, and went back to where Sabrina was lying. She heard me coming and sat up, skittering back a little until she realized it was just me. Her body sagged toward the pavement, and I hustled to catch her, lifting her in my arms.

"Easy now," I murmured, taking in the cuts on her face, cracked-open cheek, and wild look in her eye.

"You're hurt." She noticed, reaching up toward my head.

I pulled back. "I'm fine."

"You're bleeding," she wailed.

"I've had worse."

Carrying her away from the man's body, I walked around the front of the Hummer. Shifting her weight into one arm, I dug out my phone with the other.

He answered on the first ring. "Yo!"

"I need you to meet me. Leave Bellamy and the baby at home."

I felt him snap to attention instantly.

"What happened?"

I quickly told Liam where I was and then reiterated to not bring Bellamy and to make sure she was under lock and key.

His voice was sober when he replied. "I'll be there in under ten."

I disconnected the call and glanced back to the truck and body. I didn't want to put Sabrina down, but I had to.

Crouching low, I set her gently in front of the Hummer, leaning her against the tire. "I'll be right back."

She grabbed my shirt, her eyes wide. "Don't leave me here."

I covered her hand with mine, gently rubbing over her knuckles. "I would never leave you."

"You did before," she said, her lashes sweeping down toward her cheeks.

"Hey," I demanded. "Look at me." Cupping her cheeks, I lifted her face. "Did you hit your head?"

"I don't think so."

Slipping my hands gently upward, I nudged around her scalp, searching for any bumps or broken skin. There wasn't any that I could find, but she still seemed a little woozy.

Refocusing, my gaze fell on the giant bruise already forming on her cheek. Using the pad of my thumb, I brushed over it lightly. She sucked in a breath and moved her face away from my touch.

"What happened here?" I murmured. "You hit it in the car?"

"He punched me," she replied, then suddenly seemed to realize there was someone here trying to hurt her.

Gasping, she jerked up, nearly toppling over as she tried to lunge to her feet. I went with her, and when she wobbled, I lifted her off her feet once more.

"We have to go! Someone was here. He was trying to force me into his car. He dragged me out of the Hummer—" Her voice caught, and her chin wobbled.

"Shh." I soothed, pushing her head into my chest. "He's gone. You don't have to worry about him. I have you now."

"You were unconscious. I thought you were dead." She started crying then. And no, I wasn't any kind of pleased she only started to really cry when it came to me.

I glanced over my shoulder to where the dead man lay. I should have made him suffer a little more.

"Alex?" Sabrina lifted her cheek off my chest and looked up with streaked cheeks and wet lashes.

"What, kitten?"

"Are you mad at me?"

I drew back. "Why would I be mad at you?"

"You just… All of a sudden, you just seemed so… cold."

"I was thinking about the man who tried to hurt you."

Her face burrowed back into my shoulder, hair falling over her cheek and clinging to her tears, partly disguising the wound inflicted upon her. "Please don't leave me. Not again."

It was if she reached into my chest and ripped my heart in half. Both pieces still lay inside me… both of them only beating for her.

I decided then. When I looked back later, I would realize the decision was much bigger than I knew in that moment.

I left the body there on the side of the road, beside the truck… right there out in the open. I needed to dump it in the bed or at least put it somewhere less visible. Anyone could turn down this road. Anyone could happen by at any moment. They would see everything, and I would go down for murder… And me going down meant Sabrina unprotected.

I couldn't put her down, though. She clung to me with trembling fingers, her cuts still oozing blood and a welt on her face from another man's fist.

She asked me not to go. I wasn't going anywhere.

A few moments later, the distinct sound of Liam's engine cut through the night. I stiffened even though I knew it was him because I was still very concerned someone else would also arrive.

The second he came around the bend, I breathed a little easier because there weren't any other cars behind him. He pulled close to where I stood on the side of the road, still cradling Sabrina in my arms.

He killed the bright headlights but left the engine running and leapt out of the cab, not even bothering to shut his door.

"Jesus, Alex! What the fuck happened?" he demanded, rushing over.

"Can you hold her a second?" I asked, keeping calm.

I shifted Sabrina into Liam's arms. She made a sound of protest and grabbed at my shirt. "I'm still here, kitten. Hang on."

"I'll be right back," I said quietly to Liam, gesturing over my shoulder. He followed my lead, and his mouth thinned when he saw the body.

He turned away, effectively blocking what I was about to do from Sabrina's eyes. I heard him ask her how she was but didn't hang around to hear her reply.

Quickly, I tossed the body into the back of the truck, climbed in, and backed it down the side street no one ever used so it would be out of sight from the main road.

The second I was within arm's distance of Sabrina, I held out my hands, and Liam transferred her back over. A thousand questions burned in his eyes, and I knew he wanted every detail, but he also knew this really wasn't the time or place.

"You think the wench on your truck is strong enough to flip the Hummer back over?"

"It's going to have to be."

I stood back while he maneuvered the Xtreme in position and got out to try and configure the best way to right my truck.

While he did that, I carried Sabrina to the passenger seat and set her down gently, reaching over to turn the heat up and adjust the vents to point to her.

"I tried to fight him off," Sabrina said, sounding a little clearer than before.

"You did a damn good job."

"You should go help Liam."

I dragged a hand down the side of her head. "I'll be right back."

It took a few tries and a hell of a lot of dirty cussing from the both of us, but finally, we got the Hummer back on four wheels. She started right up and the tires weren't damaged, so I could drive it back home.

The minute I could, I pulled it down that dark side street and parked near the trees. I was pretty fucking thankful in that moment that the guy decided to hit us on the side of a mountain where there wasn't much traffic and there was a lot of trees and empty roads that led nowhere.

It would make cleanup a hell of a lot easier.

Once the Hummer was out of sight, I jogged back to the truck. Liam was behind the wheel, and Sabrina was sitting on the passenger seat, staring out the windshield.

"Can you take her back to your place?" I asked him.

"Of course."

"I'll be behind you as fast as I can."

"I can take her home and come back to meet you," he offered.

"No." I cut that off instantly. This was my mess, my weight to bear, and it was already too much that I had to call him here at all. "I got this. But thanks."

Liam nodded.

"Keep the place on lockdown."

"Already done."

I turned my attention to Sabrina, reaching for her hand tucked into her lap. Her fingers were mostly concealed by my jacket sleeves, but what little I could see was smeared with red.

"There's something I have to do," I told her, praying she would understand.

Her eyes shifted to mine and offered a small smile. "Go. Do what needs to be done."

Because I wanted to so many times earlier, because she was sitting there bleeding but still the most beautiful woman I'd ever seen, I leaned in, pressing a kiss to her temple.

"See you soon," I whispered, then slipped into the trees out of sight. I stood there and waited until I couldn't hear Liam's engine anymore and until I was sure no one else might happen by.

Then I went to work.

Sabrina

He got rid of the body. A body I knew he was trying to hide from me or just plain hoping I was too freaked out to see.

I saw.

Dead bodies aren't exactly things to be missed.

I wasn't shocked or even disgusted Alex killed that man. In reality, what else was he supposed to do? Normal people might say call the police. Call for help. Let the man run away.

Those weren't options for a man like Alex. Not in this situation anyway. Calling the police would result in a lot of questions he couldn't answer, and it would put my brother in more trouble than he was already in.

This had to be dealt with quietly and quickly. Letting that dirtbag run away would never happen. Alex wasn't built that way.

And me?

I was glad he was dead. He would have done far worse if he'd stayed alive.

Population control. That's what Daniel would have called this. I couldn't say I was that jaded and hard, but I wasn't so innocent to think that men like that dead guy were men that could be saved.

Liam didn't ask any questions on the way to his house. He didn't try for silly small talk that would fail at distracting me. Instead, he drove quietly until we pulled up to a large home in the side of the mountain. The land around it was cleared and planted with grass, but then the yard gave way to trees, buffering the home from the outside world.

I saw now why Alex called it a mansion. The place was incredible.

I knew it was majorly impressive because it actually drew my attention, which was no easy feat given what just happened. Glancing away from the wood and stone home, I looked out the back window, hoping I'd see Alex's Hummer coming up the long driveway.

"He'll be here as soon as he can," Liam said, speaking for the first time.

"I know."

Liam hit a button, and a large garage door started to open. He waited until it was all the way up before pulling inside, his eyes watchful and never resting in one place too long.

He shut off the truck as the garage door lowered. I moved to get out, but his hand flew out to stop me. "Wait 'til the door is closed all the way."

I leaned back, feeling some aches and pains throughout my body.

When the door was closed, Liam glanced at me again. "I'll come around."

I didn't say anything as he jumped out of the truck and prowled around the massive garage, looking for anything out of the ordinary. When he was done, he checked some kind of monitor on the wall before backtracking to where I was.

When he offered his hand to help me down, I took it.

"I kinda feel bad for thinking of you as just some inflated athlete," I told him, slightly sheepish.

He barked a laugh, and it echoed beside my ear. "Here I thought you liked me."

"I do," I said, moving back just slightly so I could meet his stare. His eyes were gray and stormy… definitely the eyes of a man who didn't always have it easy. "I just meant you're a lot more like Alex than I realized."

A sound rumbled out of him. "This isn't my first rodeo full of people coming for my family."

"I know you have a wife and son to protect. I can wait out here, away from them—"

"I was talking about you." He interrupted.

My brow wrinkled as I tried to understand. "But—"

"You're my family now, just as much as the people inside."

Alex said that before. He called me family. Until now, I hadn't really believed that Liam felt that way, too. "You barely know me." I wasn't trying to sound bratty or ungrateful. I was just pointing out the obvious.

"Alex loves you. That's all I need."

I started to shake my head, but the look in Liam's eyes stopped the action. "We both know," he said, gesturing between us, "that you two are in love with each other. You don't have to admit it to each other, but there's no use in trying to deny it for me."

"What if I'm a horrible person?" I challenged, lifting my chin. "Would you still accept Alex loving me?"

Liam chuckled. "He needs someone like you to bust his balls on the daily." His eyes twinkled, and the man I saw before, the cautious protector, was gone. "Promise me you'll do it in front of me as much as you can. That shit is funny."

"That wasn't even an answer," I said, my lips twitching. If the situation hadn't been what it was, I would have been laughing.

He glanced over his shoulder as he led me toward the door leading inside the house. "If you were a horrible person, Alex wouldn't have let you into his house."

I fell silent. There was no arguing with this one. Not about this anyway. Besides, I was beyond exhausted, and dizziness made everything in front of me sort of slosh together. I pressed a hand to my stomach and swallowed, trying to push back the nausea I wasn't interested in feeling.

Where is he right now? Is he safe?

Liam pushed some buttons on the keypad on the wall near the monitors he'd been checking earlier, and the sound of some locks unlatching on the other side of the steel door echoed. Once the door was ajar, Liam gestured for me to go ahead of him, so I did.

I stepped into a mudroom that was large and much less tactical than the security in the garage, the locks on the doors, and the overall feeling I'd had as we pulled inside. The slate tile on the floor was rich in hues of the earth, and the large wooden cabinets lining the wall looked like high-end lockers you might find in some exclusive private school. There was a braided rug in the center of the floor and a large wire basket with various sports balls and a jump rope inside. Beside it was a large piece of sidewalk chalk, having fallen out of the box it lay beside.

A large iron chandelier hung from the ceiling, filling the space with warm light, and over on the far wall was a washing station for who I assumed was Charlie, along with a deep sink and a few other cabinets for storage.

Liam kicked off his boots and slung the jacket he was wearing into one of the lockers. When he was done, he reached for Alex's red jacket, and I flinched away.

He held out his hand like he meant no harm. "Just trying to help."

"I want to wear it," I said, unable to bear the thought of taking off the only piece of Alex I had with me.

He nodded and went to another door, one that was also closed and locked. I assumed that one led into the house. Once the locks were disengaged, he pulled it open, looking back at me.

I hobbled forward. The more time I spent on my feet, the sorer and stiffer I became. Another rush of dizziness came over me, and I swayed. Liam gasped a little and rushed forward, slipping his arm around my waist for support.

"Easy now," he murmured.

I leaned into him, and together we walked into a kitchen that was so big it probably should have felt cold. It didn't. It was warm and enveloping. Safe. Tears sprang to my eyes, and I blinked them back.

Bellamy rushed into the room from beneath a wide archway leading in from another room and gasped. "My God, Sabrina! What happened?"

"Had a bit of an accident," I said as Liam guided me into a high-backed chair at the bar.

"Where's Alex?" Bellamy asked, glancing around us.

"He'll be here in a bit," Liam answered, closing and locking the door to the mudroom.

"Is he hurt?" Bellamy pressed.

I nodded, and the tears I was holding back fell over my cheeks. Bellamy rushed forward and hugged me gingerly, and I sniffled into her sweatshirt.

"Where's the baby?" Liam asked.

"He's in bed," Bellamy said over my head.

I heard Liam move across the room. I pulled back and swiped at the tears on my face and watched him opening a cabinet door to reveal more monitors. After a few taps on the screen, he brought up the image of Shaw's room. Liam studied the monitor a few moments, and when he seemed satisfied his son was okay, he turned back to us.

"What's going on, Liam?" Bellamy asked.

"Someone ran us off the road," I answered.

"On purpose?"

"This house stays on lockdown until I say otherwise," Liam ordered. "You and Shaw are not to leave. You either, Brina."

"I'd tell you he's only bossy like this when he's worried, but that would be a lie," Bellamy said, glancing down. She gasped. "My God, you're bleeding!"

"In more than one place," I said, pushing my hands free of the coat and showing her all the cuts on my palms and arms. One of my wrists was an ugly shade of purple. No wonder it hurt so much.

"She needs a doctor, Liam," Bellamy declared. "Did you see her face? She probably has a concussion."

I couldn't even take offense because I was sure I looked worse than hell.

Liam dug his phone out of his pocket and hit the screen. A few moments later, he began talking into the line.

I sagged against the back of the chair, not even listening to his call. My eyes grew heavy, and all I could think about was Alex.

"Brina!" Bellamy snapped. I jolted up and blinked. "Don't go to sleep."

"Doc will be here in a few," Liam announced.

"You have a doctor coming here?" I asked.

"It's safer here than the clinic at the resort."

"He's a good doctor." Bellamy promised. "He knows how to keep a secret."

"Should we call Alex?" I asked, even though I already knew the answer was no.

"He'll be here as soon as he can," Liam said, patient.

I nodded miserably.

"Let's get you cleaned up some while we wait for the doctor," Bellamy offered kindly.

More tears slid over my cheeks, burning the cuts and scrapes on my face. As she led me out of the kitchen, I stopped and turned back toward Liam. "You're right, you know. I do love him. I didn't want to, and I certainly didn't want to admit it. But now… after tonight…" My voice wobbled as I pictured the way Alex had looked passed out and bleeding in his Hummer. As I glanced around this house where he wasn't. "But now I'm afraid I won't even get the chance to tell him."

Liam's face softened. "You'll get your chance, Brina. I promise."

"C'mon," Bellamy said, and I went with her, clinging to the certainty in Liam's voice.

Alex

"Where is she?" I asked, striding through the door into Liam's kitchen. I paused only long enough to make sure the locks were engaged before turning an impatient eye to my best friend who was leaning against the counter with a bottle of Jack and a shot glass beside him.

"Upstairs with the doc."

I muttered a curse and started for the door.

"Hey," Liam called.

I looked back as he poured the shot of whiskey.

I backtracked, tossed the alcohol down my throat, and slammed the glass on the counter. "I'll fill you in after I see her."

He didn't try to stop me again. He knew better. He knew I wouldn't be able to focus on shit until I'd seen for myself how she was.

I jogged up the stairs and into the master bedroom where I heard low voices.

"Sabrina," I said before I was even fully through the door.

"Alex!" She gasped, lurching to her feet and instantly swaying.

"Whoa," the doctor said, reaching for her, but I rushed in, nearly knocking him aside to pick her up.

"Not looking so hot, kitten," I said, eyes eating up every inch of her battered, pale face.

She relaxed into my arms and gave a deep sigh of relief. "What took you so long?" she demanded.

I sat on the large upholstered bench at the end of Liam and Bellamy's massive bed, holding her in my lap.

"Good heavens, Alex! Your head!" Bellamy fussed.

She reached out for me, and I drew back, shaking my head. "I'm fine."

"You are not!" both women declared at once.

I rolled my eyes and looked at the doc for a man's opinion. "I'm going to have to agree. I think you need stitches."

"I knew it!" Sabrina gasped, reaching up to finger the side of my head. "You're still bleeding."

I didn't give a rat's ass about my head. "How is she?" I asked.

"Concussion, sprained wrist, a few contusions, abrasions, and two stitches in her cheek."

With every new injury he listed, I grew colder and colder inside. I started to go numb when he said stitches, and callous indifference began to fill me. I might have already killed the man who did this to her, but I knew there were more. I would kill them, too.

"Alex," Sabrina whispered, and her warm hands seared my face when she touched me. I snapped back, letting the warmth from her palms seep into my skin. "I'm fine. It's all just superficial."

The fuck it was.

"Alex." She beckoned again.

When I looked down, she leaned up. Her lips caught mine, melting the worst of the freeze inside me.

I made a sound and moved against her lips, tasting salt from the tears I hadn't been here to wipe away. Not caring about the audience, not giving two shits about anything but her, I licked over her lips, lapping up whatever was left of the sorrow she cried and soothing away whatever pain I could.

Doc cleared his throat, and I lifted my head, but not before brushing against her one last time.

"Perhaps now that Alex is here, you will consider taking off the coat so I can check your arms and back?"

I stiffened. "You haven't done that already?" I glared at the doctor. "What the fuck have you been doing?"

"Don't yell at him!" Brina gasped. "He's been checking the rest of me!"

I glanced at the doctor, waiting for an explanation. This shit was unacceptable. I was going to have to fire him for this negligence. I couldn't have a doctor at the resort that clearly had no sense of urgency.

Doc cleared his throat. "She refused to take off the jacket."

I felt my eyes narrow. "You do something to make her uncomfortable?" The menace in my tone was unmasked.

The doctor blanched and alarm spilled over his features. "Of course not! Mrs. Mattison was here the entire—"

"I wouldn't take it off because it's yours," Brina said, cutting off the doctor. My eyes snapped to her, and she sighed. "He didn't do anything wrong, Alex. I just refused to take it off."

Oh. Well. That was okay, then.

More than okay, actually.

I stood, lifting Brina with me. "I apologize, doc. I, ah… It's been a long night."

"He has a head injury." Bellamy came to my defense.

"He's just being a jerk," Brina declared.

Through the monitor on the bedside table, the baby fussed. Bellamy started for the door. "I'll be right back."

Gingerly, I set Sabrina on her feet, making sure she was steady before reaching for the zipper on the jacket. It definitely had seen better days. The back was scuffed and beat up from her being dragged across the road, and the collar was dirty. Around the wrists were dark stains of blood, but Brina's raw-looking fingertips clung to the edges of the sleeves as if it were her lifeline.

All because it is my jacket.

My heart thudded heavily as I reached for the zipper and pulled it down. I wished we weren't standing here with a doctor. I wished we were in my bedroom and not Liam's. I wished that beneath this jacket she was completely naked and mine for the taking.

She moved stiff and slow when I peeled it off her. My jaw clenched because I could tell she was in a lot of pain. Her wrist was wrapped already, and a few bandages covered her other wrist and hands.

"I want that back," she told me when I tossed it aside.

"You can have anything you want, kitten. My entire closet."

"The sweater?" the doc asked, glancing at me and not her.

My back teeth gnashed together, but I knew him seeing her in her bra was pretty necessary. She could be injured and none of us know it.

Gently, I pulled her around so she was facing me and reached for the hem of her sweater. Our eyes locked, and for long moments, I forgot the circumstances of this moment and it became just me and her as I peeled off her clothing.

"Seems to be nothing more than road rash. Just use some of the cream I gave you for the other cuts. It should work fine," the doctor said, ruining the moment.

I made a sound, acknowledging him, and snuck a glance at her cleavage.

The way her chest rose and fell told me she was all too aware of where I was looking. My fingers ached to touch her. My lips taunted them because they'd already had a taste.

"It's your turn," Sabrina said, drawing my eyes. On the way up, I caught the large scrape beneath her chin, grabbed her face, and lifted so I could see it further.

It was raw, red, and already starting to bruise. I made an unhappy sound, and she grabbed the front of my shirt, fisting it over my abs. "I'm okay."

I kissed beside her lips, because I could, and enjoyed the way her fingers tightened farther into my shirt.

"I really think I should take a look at your head. It appears you've lost quite a bit of blood."

Sabrina snapped out of it, straightened, and spun to the doctor. "Yes, please."

I turned her back, glancing down at her chest. I got the doc needed to check her over, but enough was enough. Picking the red jacket back up, I draped it around her and pulled it closed to cover her skin.

Brina said nothing as she pushed her arms through and gestured for me to sit. I did but pulled her down to sit close beside me. My hand sought hers, and I linked our fingers tight.

I ended up with seven stitches, the diagnosis of a concussion, and whatever else he went on and on about.

I was fine. I'd sustained far worse injuries overseas and never had any kind of medical care. The only reason I sat still long enough and let the doc poke me with a needle and thread was because it was what Sabrina wanted. And maybe I wanted to stop the blood from dripping into my eye. It was annoying.

The doc was finishing up when Bellamy and Liam entered the room, Liam carrying a very awake Shaw.

"We woke him. I'm sorry." Sabrina apologized.

Bellamy smiled. "You didn't wake him. Liam did."

"I can't help that when he hears my voice, he wants me," Liam said, not bothered at all. He was wrapped so far around that boy's finger it was a wonder he could piss straight.

Bellamy looked at Sabrina. "When I put him to bed, Liam wasn't here. He wanted to say good night."

As if he understood everything, Shaw leaned against Liam's shoulder, hugging him close. Liam made a soft sound and rubbed his hand over the baby's back.

Shaw looked just like Liam, with gray eyes, light-brown hair, and the same face shape. I never really figured Liam as the kid type, but dude, he was totally a kid type. Or maybe he was a Bellamy's kid type.

I glanced over at Sabrina and suddenly understood. I was never a kid guy. Hell, I never thought I'd have any. I wasn't the fatherly type, even though my dad had been the best. I didn't even like kids 'til my nephew came around. I'd do anything for that boy, and now, sitting here with Brina's hand tucked in mine, I knew without a doubt I would be a kid person if my kids were hers.

"Well, since you both have concussions, I advise you to stay awake for twelve to twenty-four hours," the doctor instructed. "I know that's a cautious way of handling this, given you are both responsive and able to hold a conversation, but in my experience, it's better safe than sorry." He went down a list of even more directives, but I ignored him. I wanted to be alone with Sabrina. I wanted to make sure she was okay, and I wanted to make sure she hadn't seen me kill that man.

I was largely confident she hadn't. After all, she was tucked against me like I was her safe haven, something I wasn't sure she would be doing if she'd just witnessed me snap someone's neck.

You're no good for her, man. You're only making it worse.

"Thank you for coming, doc," Liam was saying when I snapped out of it. "I really appreciate the house call and your discretion."

"Of course, of course. If there is anything else I can do to help, please don't hesitate to call."

Liam shook hands with the man, who then turned toward Bellamy. "How are you feeling, Mrs. Mattison? Do you need anything?"

"Oh, I'm fine, thank you," she said, her cheeks growing a bit pink. I felt my eyes narrow on her, and she very obviously avoided my stare.

"Call if you need a refill," the doctor told her. She was quick to agree and even quicker to volunteer to see him out.

Before he left, I made sure to thank him personally and shake his hand. "Thank you for taking care of Sabrina. I appreciate it."

"Of course, Mr. Carter."

When he was gone, the four of us met in the living room. Bellamy clicked on a large wrought-iron lamp, and I gazed at her. "You pregnant?"

Liam chuckled, and the sleeping baby against his chest stirred. He rubbed a hand over his back and shushed him before lowering into a large chair and pulling a blanket over the child.

Bellamy nodded, sheepish.

I let go of Sabrina for the first time and made a whoop sound before swooping in to grab her around the waist and spin her around.

"Watch it," Liam growled, sitting up like he was going to take me on.

Bellamy blanched, and I pulled her back to study her face. "You're just as sick with this one as you were with Shaw."

"Unfortunately," she croaked.

"My bad," I said, gingerly placing her on her feet.

Then, because I was so happy, I ruffled her hair and gave her another hug. "Congratulations, Bells."

When I pulled back, I offered a hand to Liam. "Bro."

"Thanks, man."

"Why didn't you say anything?" I demanded.

Liam glanced at his wife, and she sighed. "You have enough going on."

"Oh, I don't like that," I told her, pursing my lips. "That's some dirty shit right there."

"Give her a break, man. She's been puking up her guts most of the day." Liam admonished.

"Congratulations," Sabrina said from a few feet away. I heard it in her voice, even though it wasn't really obvious. I felt it, regardless. She felt like an outsider just then. Something she wasn't and never would be. Even if she went back home tomorrow and I never saw her again, that girl would always be my family, and no one would ever take her place in my heart.

I backtracked, slipped an arm around her waist, and palmed her hip. I made a point of drawing her into the discussion.

"Thank you," Bellamy said. "We just found out last week."

"A whole damn week," I muttered.

"Next time, I'll tell you before Liam." Bells promised, cheeky. There definitely would be a next time. Liam seemed determined to make a football team.

"The hell you will!" Liam erupted.

Shaw made a sound, sat up, and looked at his daddy with wide eyes.

"Aww, little man, I'm sorry," he crooned. "Daddy's sorry."

The baby fell back into his chest and stuck his thumb in his mouth. Liam glared at me over the baby's head but didn't say anything more.

I grinned and then grinned wider because he couldn't say shit.

"I'm so sorry to have brought all this here tonight," Sabrina told Bellamy. "You really should be resting, not dealing with my problems."

Bellamy shook her head emphatically. "Oh, please, no. I'm fine, and you're family. I'm just glad we could be here for you both."

Sabrina yawned and leaned into my side. I glanced at her, concerned. "You doing okay?"

She nodded.

"How about I put some coffee on?" Bellamy offered. "Then we can talk."

"Caffeine is good." Sabrina agreed.

Bellamy nodded. "I'll just put the baby down, then make some." When she reached for the baby, he made a sound and clutched at Liam.

"He just likes me better, sweetheart," Liam drawled, winking at Bellamy.

"Well, then you can get up with him at three a.m.," Bellamy retorted without much heat.

"Anything for you, Bells," Liam said, standing and leaning in to kiss her on the forehead. "Go make the coffee. I'll put him down."

Bellamy brushed her hand over Shaw's head and then went into the kitchen. Liam disappeared up the stairs, and finally, if only for a moment, we were blissfully alone.

Sabrina

"Thank God you're okay." I wasn't able to hide the shaky worry in my voice. I was nearly consumed with it. If it weren't for the pain in my cheek and wrist, I might have succumbed to it completely.

The second I said the words, I nearly fell into him, clutching his waist as tight as I could.

"Hey now, kitten. I told you I'm fine." His voice was gentle but solid. The tone was soft, almost cajoling. Just a couple hours ago, the thought of him calling me kitten was gross, but now, the thought of never hearing him say it again was unbearable.

"You were unconscious, Alex. You have seven stitches in your head. I don't even know how you're walking around." He made a rough sound, but I pushed in closer to him. "I don't know what I would do if I lost you again."

His body clenched, but he didn't pull away. Instead, he walked backward, bringing me with him to sit on the couch and pull me into his lap.

I curled against his chest, letting my feet rest on the cushions beside his leg, cradled my injured wrist into my chest, and tucked my face against his neck.

He dragged a few fingers through the length of my hair, and I felt his lips brush my hairline. "You won't ever lose me."

I started to tremble. The night was beginning to catch up to me now that I finally felt like I could let some of my guard down. Now that Alex was so close I could touch and see him, some of the adrenaline keeping me vigilant was draining away.

"That man wasn't going to kill me. He was trying to kidnap me," I whispered.

Alex closed both arms around me in a bold protective gesture. "I know, kitten."

"He was going to do horrifying things—"

"Stop," he commanded. "Stop right there. It's not going to happen. I don't even want you thinking about it."

How could I not think about it? How could I not imagine grim scenario after grim scenario? Good Lord, these were the men after my brother!

"Sabrina."

I lifted my face. I could be standing in the center of a category-five hurricane, about to be blown miles away, and I would still react to the way he said my name. No one, not anyone, ever had the ability to compel me the way Alex did.

His shoulders hunched forward, his head lowering to claim my lips. I gasped at the sudden assault but recovered almost instantly to slide a hand up his neck and grip the back of his head. I strained upward, wanting closer. Alex pulled my body up and held me there without breaking the kiss.

I purred into his mouth, feeling his tongue stroke over mine and his body surround me. If any part of me had died tonight while being attacked, Alex just revived it.

For a man who so easily took a life, he also so easily gave it.

His chest vibrated against mine as he pulled back slightly. The startling shade of his eyes gazed down when his lashes lifted.

It took a moment to register anything beyond his closeness, and even then, my mind didn't get much further than him. "You've been kissing me a lot today."

"I guess I'm pretty tired of holding back."

My heart skipped a beat, and a warm, fuzzy sensation bloomed in my chest. "Alex, I wanted to tell—"

As I spoke, his head tilted up, as though he could hear something I couldn't.

"Are you eavesdropping?" he asked, slightly chuffed.

A second later, Liam appeared over the railing toward the bottom of the stairs. "What can I say? This shit is riveting."

Alex rolled his eyes, but a smile played at the corner of his lips. Lips I sincerely wanted back on mine.

I started to sit up, but even though I thought his attention was diverted elsewhere, he proved to me it wasn't. The hold he had on me was tightened, my place in his lap secured. With a very brief yet meaningful glance, he let me know I was exactly where he wanted.

"Payback's a bitch and all that, yeah, yeah," he muttered, looking over the back of the sofa at Liam.

Liam winked at me and laughed.

"I don't get it," I said, blank.

"This one here"—Liam pointed to Alex—"is a professional eavesdropper. He heard more private conversations between me and Bells than I care to admit."

"Just looking out for ya, bro," Alex quipped.

"Same."

Abruptly, Alex stood. I squeaked in surprise, and he glanced down, his eyes narrowing. "What hurts?" The tone of his voice was a promise that whatever it was, he would slay instantly.

"Nothing," I replied. "I just wasn't expecting you to stand up."

He made a sound but made no movement to put me down. "We're gonna head out."

Liam's face lifted. "Now?"

"Yeah, it's late."

"We still need to talk." Liam reminded him.

"I know. Tomorrow."

Bellamy came back from the kitchen. "Coffee's ready." She saw Alex standing there holding me and frowned. "What's going on?"

"It's all good." Alex assured her. "We're heading out. We'll come back tomorrow."

Bellamy gasped. "You can't leave! We don't even know what's going on. It could be dangerous!"

"Yeah, it could be," Alex muttered, dark. "And the last thing I'm gonna do is put you and that baby you're growing in any kinda danger. Not to mention my nephew upstairs."

I sucked in a breath, realizing he was right.

"This place is locked down." Liam reminded him.

"Keep it that way, at least until the sun comes up."

"What about you two?" Bellamy worried.

"My house is secure. I made sure of it."

Liam came the rest of the way around the couch. "If you need anything, call. Anytime."

"I will. Thanks."

"You're just going to let them leave?" Bellamy accused.

Liam smiled and put an arm around her to draw her close. "Now, sweetheart. Alex and Brina have some talking to do."

A knowing look dawned over Bellamy.

I felt myself begin to blush. My goodness! They thought we were rushing off to have sex.

Alex's chuckle was low and smooth. It made me feel all kinds of liquid inside.

Oh Lord… *Are we?* Surely not.

Butterflies, thousands upon thousands of them, fluttered around in my belly, and none of them were very skilled at flying. They seemed to bounce around in there, making me feel unstable. It made me grateful Alex was still holding me, because I worried my knees would give out.

As if he sensed it, Alex leaned against my ear to whisper, "I can see you blushing."

My only answer was to duck my cheek into his chest and hide.

"Take the baby maker up to bed so she can get some rest," Alex told Liam, humor in his voice.

"Only if you promise to come back in the morning," Bellamy argued.

"We'll be back tomorrow." He allowed, not agreeing to any time in particular.

In the kitchen, Liam pulled a set of keys off a rack in the cabinet with the monitors and tossed them to Alex. He snatched them out of the air without jostling me at all. "Thanks."

Bellamy was beside the island, looking unsure about us leaving. Alex stepped over and kissed her on top of her head. "See ya tomorrow, girl who got away."

"Bye."

I waved to them over Alex's shoulder as he stepped into the garage.

"I can walk, you know."

"I know," he said but didn't bother to put me down.

I didn't argue because I liked where I was.

He walked through the garage to the last stall, where a large, dark SUV was parked. Going around, he deftly deposited me into the passenger seat, gingerly pulling the seat belt across my chest.

After the audible click of the belt, he didn't pull away. Instead, he stood there for long seconds, staring down at the latch before lifting his penetrating eyes toward me. "You scared me tonight, kitten."

I gently caressed the side of his smooth face and didn't say anything.

His eyes closed briefly at the touch as he reached up, grasping my wrapped wrist lightly so he could pull back and press feathery kisses against the bandages.

My stomach was still in my throat when he climbed into the driver's seat and hit the button to lift the door. We sat in the driveway, waiting for the garage door to lower completely, before he scanned the driveway, then drove off.

Before we even made it to the main road, he reached into my lap.

We held hands the entire way home.

Alex

Things were different now.

Death always had a way of altering things. Especially when I was the one creating the dead. Three years ago, death changed the course of my life, turning my future into something else entirely.

Tonight, death changed it again.

Last time, death pushed us apart, but this time, it seemed to pull us closer. Something new shimmered in the air. The wall separating us had crumbled; we stood face to face, an unobstructed path between us.

Except it wasn't that simple. It never was.

After tonight, though, I didn't really care.

My blood pulsed with the need to be alone with her. My body thumped with desire, and an instinctual need to claim her completely roared so loud inside me it drowned out all of my doubts.

"Stay put," I told her when I pulled the SUV as close to my deck as I could. After a quick check of the house, I went back and opened her door.

Pleasure filled me when I noticed she hadn't removed her seat belt and I could reach across, fill up her personal space, and do it. She didn't protest when I lifted her out of the car, kicked the door shut, and carried her into the house.

The lights were already on, and I placed her on the sofa and moved off to start a fire in the fireplace. I felt her eyes the entire time I worked. Every muscle beneath my skin knotted and bunched until the tension in this small cabin could have lit the fire for me.

When it was finally crackling, I turned toward her, struck suddenly by how fragile she looked huddled into the cushions with her feet tucked under her and my dirty red coat cuddled close.

She didn't seem to notice her own vulnerability. Something I found both endearing and maddening.

"I think I'm going to take a shower," she said, sitting up. "I feel gross." When she pushed off the cushions, a grimace contorted her face, and her body locked up rigidly.

"Easy now," I said, hurrying over.

"I'm fine," she protested, using the arm of the sofa as leverage to help pull herself to her feet.

I cursed low and slipped an arm around her waist. "Maybe you should just sit down."

"I'm stiff and sore. Moving around will be good for me. So will the warm water."

I didn't argue. Instead, I helped her down the hallway, retrieving a fresh towel and putting it on the bathroom counter. Sabrina was standing at the mirror, grimacing at the sight of her battered face, when I stepped back into the small room.

"You're still gorgeous," I told her sincerely.

She jolted, seeing me behind her, and turned. Immediately, her eyes went to the flannel I had clutched in my hand. "Thought you might want to put this on when you're done."

"Your favorite one?" she asked.

"Did you want my least favorite instead?" I asked, cheeky.

She snorted, reached for it, and our fingers brushed together. The brief, innocent contact spiked my heart rate and sent a shiver of awareness through my body.

"Thank you," she said, draping the shirt on the counter, not realizing at all the way she affected me.

When she turned back, we stared at each other awkwardly for a long time, until she shifted and I realized she was waiting for me to leave so she could continue. The door shut softly behind me, and I sank down right there against the wood to wait.

A few light sounds were muffled by the door, and I couldn't stop thinking about the fact that she was probably naked in there right now.

So close...

I surged upright, about to barge in because I couldn't take it another second. Before I could, the door swung in.

A sound of alarm squeaked from Sabrina when she saw me standing there on the threshold. Pressing a hand to her chest, she gasped. "What are you doing?"

"Guarding the door," I said as if it should have been obvious.

Her brows lowered over her light-brown eyes. "I thought you said the house was secure."

"It is." I assured her. "But I'm not taking any chances with you."

The look on her face made me want to kiss the shit out of her. So much so that I reached out.

"Can you help me?" she asked, shifting like she was embarrassed.

My attention shifted to her wrist, which she thrust between us.

"I need to take off this wrap so I don't get it wet. The fastener is underneath here," she said, rotating her arm for me to see. "I could probably get it, but my fingers are raw."

Reluctantly, she held up the other hand, and sure enough, her fingers were all raw and red. Some cuts from all the broken glass were covered, but others weren't.

A sound ripped out of me, and I cradled the hand in mine. "Ah, baby." I bent and kissed her fingers, then palmed her waist and lifted. Her butt hit the bathroom counter, knocking over some of the products sitting between the sinks, but I ignored it and focused completely on her.

Shifting so my body fit between her knees, I lifted the sprained wrist between us and slowly undid the wrapping. "You sure you should take this off?"

"He said it was okay as long as I put it back on right after."

When the bandage was pulled away, anger rushed up from my toes, making my fist clench. "Jesus," I whispered, gazing down at the mottled, gross bruises on her normally blemish-free flesh.

"How bad does it hurt?" I whispered, gently cupping her wrist and hand.

"Not terribly," she replied and grinned conspiratorially. "He gave me a pretty good pain pill."

I found myself drowning in her eyes, getting lost and never wanting to find my way out again.

"Which is another reason I need to shower now." She went on, unknowingly pulling me back. "I want to do this before that pill wears off."

I frowned. I knew she was hurting a lot worse than she was saying. Hell, she had stitches in her face.

"How are you going to wash yourself with one hand and keep your face out of the water?"

"I like a challenge," she countered.

Even after everything, she still had the kind of spirit that took everything in stride.

Making a sudden decision, I reached in and turned on the shower. Next, I pulled off my shirt, tossed it on the floor, and kicked off my shoes.

"What are you doing?" she asked, alarmed.

"You need help."

"No!" She gasped, shaking her head for extra denial. "No. I'm perfectly capable of taking a shower."

"You couldn't even take off your bandage," I pointed out.

She gave an insufferable sigh and hopped off the counter. I didn't bother pointing out that motion made her grimace in pain.

Folding my arms over my chest, I stood there and watched her. "You're moving like a ninety-year-old woman with a bad hip."

"Am not!" she tossed out.

With her back turned, she reached for the button on her jeans, and through the mirror, I saw her contort in pain when her raw fingers fought with it.

I growled and moved around, brushing her hand away, deftly undid the button, and slid down the zipper. She gasped as though I'd accosted her and stared accusingly.

I rolled my eyes. "I'll leave my jeans on." Gesturing toward her, I added, "You can leave on your underwear."

"No!" she asserted and shoved me out of the bathroom, shutting the door in my face.

I couldn't help it. I grinned at the wood like it was the funniest thing I'd ever seen.

God, she was adorable.

I stood outside the door, grinning, until I heard her swearing and fumbling around a few minutes later. Enough was enough.

Pushing open the door, I was just in time to see her struggling to pull off the snug jeans using one raw hand and then toppling over toward the floor.

"Whoa." I rushed forward and caught her around the waist, lifted her with one arm, and peeled the jeans off her with the other while her feet dangled over the tiles.

"Alex!"

"One concussion is enough for tonight," I said, tossing the jeans on the floor. When she was back on her feet, she scowled at me. I ignored it and reached for the zipper on the red coat.

Her hand covered mine, stopping me from pulling it down, and our eyes met.

"You're safe with me, Brina. You know that."

"Define safe," she whispered.

Need slammed through me, but I shoved it back. "I just want to help you. Okay?" Then, because I thought it would help, I added, "You can help me, too. I need to wash off this blood and can't get my stitches wet either."

Concern filled her eyes, and the hand covering mine fell away.

I slid the zipper down, and the coat fell in puddle at her feet.

Steam filled the bathroom, clouding up the mirror and making the air feel balmy. She turned and stepped into the glass enclosure, glancing back at me with uncertain eyes.

Leaving my jeans on, I stepped in behind her and shut the door.

The only sound in the room was the spray of the shower and the water drops hitting the tile floor. Brina tilted her head back, and I used my hands to guide it and wet her hair, taking care to make sure her cheek with the stitches didn't get wet.

I tried not to notice how immediately her bra and panties got saturated and molded to her body like a second skin. The bra was black, so it wasn't see-through, but it only had a strap on one shoulder, leaving the other one very bare. Despite the warm temperature of the water, her nipples were erect and so stiff I could see them through the material.

Clearing my throat, I asked, "Are you warm enough?"

She nodded but said nothing else.

When she reached for the body wash, I pushed her hand away and washed her myself. Touching her as if this had been literally a dream up until now.

I would have reveled in it a little more if while I washed her, I didn't become acutely acquainted with all the injuries all over her body. She was bruised everywhere. Road rash covered her back, her legs, and even parts of her arms.

I washed gingerly, barely touching her with the soapy cloth, afraid even the slightest of touch would cause her extra pain.

"You doing okay?" I asked, lowering to wash her feet.

When she said nothing, I straightened. She was looking away, long strands of wet hair clinging to her shoulders and chest.

"Brina," I said, touching her shoulder.

When she turned, I saw the tears on her cheeks and the way she was biting her lip to keep from making a sound.

"Baby, did I hurt you?" I worried, dropping the cloth onto the floor and wrapping my hands around her waist.

She shook her head.

"Then what is it? Tell me what's wrong." I cajoled, reaching up to derail a tear from falling onto the bandage on her cheek.

"I've just—" She began but then stopped and shook her head.

I drew back, searching her face. The pain in her eyes made me think she was lying and I really had hurt her.

Drawing in a shaky breath, she looked at me, away, then whispered, "I've imagined this a thousand times."

My chest felt tight. The emotion rolling off her was making it hard to breath. So I did what I always did when I didn't know what else to do. Made a joke. Smirking, I asked, "You've imagined me taking a shower in my jeans a thousand times?"

The corner of her mouth lifted, but the humor didn't reach her eyes. When she looked at me, the pain from earlier was there, and I realized it wasn't physical. It was heartbreak.

"You. Me. Us. Taking care of each other like this."

Beneath my ribs, my heart somersaulted. I turned us so my back was against the spray and she was out of it completely. Careful of her raw chin, I cupped her face. "I've imagined it, too."

Tears clung to her lashes, creating a frame for the anticipation flaring in her eyes. "Really?"

Heat burned through me. All that want and need pulsing inside me before came rushing back like a double shot of adrenaline.

Moving closer, my wet, jean-clad legs brushed against her bare ones. Our feet were so close her toes bumped mine. Her chest rose and fell with a deep breath, and at her waist, my fingertips pressed deeper into her skin.

I watched her intently. The distance between us closed. Our gazes held until our lips touched and sight gave way to feeling. Looking at each other was no longer necessary; the way she felt against me, the way she felt inside me was so much more profound than anything I would ever find just looking at her.

My skin hummed as we kissed, my mouth slanted over hers like the water slanting over my back. I'd kissed her since she arrived here at BearPaw. I'd kissed her many times three years ago.

Standing here half clothed in the shower, with scrapes and bruises covering both of us—this kiss felt different.

It felt new.

It was the combination of the unwavering passion between us, stark, indescribable need, and a note of something I hadn't tasted on her lips before.

This kiss promised something, something we never had before.

Endurance.

As our lips met again and again, as my tongue made love to her mouth, confidence filled me. This time we could endure.

Three years ago, I kissed her for the last time.

Tonight was our first kiss to forever.

26

Sabrina

His tongue was warmer than the steamy air. His fingers glided over my bare skin more skillfully than the water.

I'd wanted him to touch me this way for so long. This moment became surreal, almost like a dream. So much so that a weighted veil fell over me, muting everything beyond him, including all the aches and pains in my body.

My fingers trembled when I dragged them over his chest and let them skim down his pecs and over his washboard abs. My thumb circled his belly button, making his muscles contract, and his hip muscles flexed, creating an even deeper V, disappearing below the waistband of his jeans.

Skirting around to his back, I followed his spine up the center until his teeth nipped at my lower lip and my fingertips dug in, clinging to his solid frame as he sucked my lower lip between his.

One hand curled around my hip so he could palm my ass and push my body fully against his. The full contact made me gasp. My lip popped out of his mouth, and my head fell back. Gazing up at him through hazy eyes, I watched his cool gaze rake over me before he claimed my mouth again.

I shivered when his fingertips grazed my side, flirting over my rib cage and then caressing the side of my breast. An ache began to throb inside my panties as he repeated the movement, teasing my breast with a barely there touch.

Alex's hand worked around to the center of my back where the clasp on my bra rested. He plucked at it, making me pant, but didn't unhook it. I squirmed closer to him, arching into his slick, bare chest, and pulled my mouth away. Tenderly, he pressed a kiss against my forehead at the same moment he freed the clasp.

The ends of the bra fell open, and he rubbed over my back with his wide, skilled hand before moving back just enough to peel the black fabric away.

I leaned against the shower wall, my hips jutting out, my breasts now fully exposed. My skin was wet and taut, my nipples puckered and begging. The bra made a slapping sound against the shower floor, but neither of us noticed. His stare latched onto my chest, and his teeth sank into his lower lip.

He made a sound, hovering his hands over them but leaving enough space that he wasn't touching me. *Oh*, I wanted him to touch me. I wanted to feel the weight of his hands, the sensation of his skin on mine.

Finally, he made contact, settling both palms over me and massaging just enough to make my eyes flutter closed. The back of my head fell against the tile, and I gave myself up to the way he kneaded and teased my aching flesh. Little tingles of pain shot into my core, making my inner muscles clench.

I jolted a bit when, unexpectedly, his lips brushed over mine, pulled away, then brushed over me again.

I opened to see him watching. The shocking lightness of his eyes penetrated me, making me feel he was already inside me even though we both still had on clothes.

He held my eyes as he sank to his knees, still holding both breasts in his palms. My stomach fell to my feet when he leaned in, flicking a tongue over a hard nipple, and I moaned. My eyes slid closed when his lips latched on, sucking and teasing the sensitive flesh until I began to pant.

I grabbed his head, either to push him away or pull him in tighter, but I never got to see which I would do because my thumb brushed over the bandage on his forehead, and a little reality snuck back in.

Picking up a cloth, I held it beneath the spray before using it to clean Alex. An appreciative sound filled the shower. He tilted his head back and remained on his knees while I gently cleaned his face and head, taking great care not to disturb the bandage or his stitches.

When I was done, he rose but stayed close enough that our bodies still touched. I reached for the button on his jeans. After fumbling with it, he half smiled and kissed me while he undid the pants himself. Once they were gone, he washed the rest of him quickly while I watched with passion-drunk eyes.

The water shut off abruptly, and he reached for me. I didn't know where I found the strength in my wobbly limbs to climb up his body, but I did, locking my thighs around his waist. Alex held me like I was weightless, confidently stepping out of the shower, and maneuvered through the bathroom with ease. He snagged a large, fluffy towel off the rack to drape over me before reaching for the door handle.

Before pulling the door open, his eyes met mine. "Tell me yes, kitten."

Oh God, his voice was velvety and dark. The pure seduction in those words and the way his hard body felt against mine was impossible to deny.

"Yes."

The air in the bedroom felt cold when he strode through, so I pushed closer to him as he walked toward the bed. Once there, he stood me on my feet and deftly but gently towel-dried my body before quickly doing the same for himself.

His body was incredible, muscular but not perfect. The body of a man, not a god. The scars he wore were from battles fought and survived. They were permanent reminders he'd seen things most people couldn't even fathom.

"Hey," he murmured, crouching so our eyes were on the same level. "You sure you're up for this tonight?"

I half smiled, suddenly feeling a little sassy. "'Course. I have a concussion. I have to do something to pass the time until I can go to sleep."

Alex threw back his head and laughed. His white teeth flashed in the dim bedroom, and renewed want swept over me again.

Not wanting to lose the private world we tumbled into, I slipped my fingers beneath the waistband of his boxers and tugged him close once more. "I've wanted you for so long, Alex," I whispered.

His eyes deepened, and a rough sound echoed through the room. He picked me up again, my bare breasts rubbing against his chest. The sensation of his hard chest against my swollen nipples made me rub against him for more.

The blankets on the bed were cold against my back, but it was merely a passing realization because Alex settled over me and everything else fell away.

We kissed and stroked each other until our bodies demanded more, and he rose between my legs to pull the boxers from his body. My toes curled against the sheets when I got my first look at his impressive length. Anticipation made my knees shake as I watched it jerk beneath my stare.

The second my panties were gone, Alex pushed my thighs wide and settled between them, making me sigh. I wiggled, wanting our bodies to meet, but he chuckled and kissed the side of my lips, moving so it wasn't his cock that touched me, but this hand.

I groaned when he slipped one finger and then a second inside me. My hips arched up, granting better access, and his lips latched onto my breast.

I writhed beneath him as his fingers slid in and out and his tongue stroked boldly over my erect nipples. I was gasping when he slowly slid out of me, planting a hand on either side of my head.

I tried to watch him as he entered, but my God, he felt so incredibly good my eyes wouldn't stay open. I melted against the mattress like ice cream on a hot day. A languid purr vibrated my throat as I grabbed at his hips to pull him deeper.

His throaty laugh only made me want him more, and I made an impatient sound, telling him exactly what I craved.

Alex slid the rest of the way in a single stroke, and my eyes went wide when his swollen head boldly brushed against my inner walls.

Watching me, he rocked his hips, stroking that spot again and again until all I did was moan. Just when I thought I couldn't take any more, he pulled out, leaving me feeling empty, and then surged back in with a single thrust.

I whimpered his name, and he began to move. He set a punishing pace that overran my body with sensation after sensation, and all I could do was feel. Bliss rolled over me in a continuous wave until I rose higher and higher, ready to plunge over the edge.

I thrust up, and he ground against me, shattering me into a million pieces.

I called out his name over and over as the orgasm flowed over me, until I sagged against the mattress, completely satiated and spent.

Using his arms, he lowered until his chest hovered just above mine, and he kissed me, long and deep, somehow drawing out the desire for more. Rising above me again, he filled my entire sight, becoming quite easily my entire world. His body stiffened, and I felt him begin to pulse inside me. I lifted, taking him just a little deeper, and a rough cry filled the room. He pulsed and quaked over me, spilling every ounce of pleasure he had inside me. My body drank him in, satisfying every part of me in a bone-deep way.

When he finally rolled to the side, it was because his arm muscles quivered from supporting his weight over me for so long. As he moved, he pulled me with him, draping my body over his chest and locking both arms around me.

We stayed like that for a long time.

27

Alex

I sensed him overhead, sort of like a bat senses vibration. It wasn't vibration, though, that made his presence known to me. It was disgust.

I didn't look up until after I fired my weapon. The bullet hit the target I still couldn't see. I heard him cry out. I fired again.

He didn't cry out this time because this bullet rendered him instantly dead.

Like a ragdoll, the terrorist dropped off the roof of the shack, landing close by. The sand underfoot muffled some of the sound he made, the bloodbath around us muted the rest.

On my way into the shack, I stepped over the other man I'd just killed and glanced at the one who'd been perched on the roof. The first bullet hit him in the shoulder. Actually, no, the collarbone. I bet that hurt like a bitch.

The second bullet went right between his eyes, creating a neat little hole in his forehead. His eyes were blank and stared at me accusingly. I spit out the sand in my mouth and kept walking, but not before I noticed the mess the back of his head had made on the sand around him.

The door to the shack collapsed when I kicked it. Whatever it was constructed of flung in every direction as I lunged into the room.

"Ice!" Wells yelled. "Behind you!"

Forgoing the gun strapped to my chest, I unleashed a blade I kept in my sleeve. My arm sliced through the air behind me, jamming the blade deep into the body of the man trying to grab me from behind.

The little bit of grip he'd gotten on me went slack, and blood gurgled in his throat.

As I turned to look at the criminal, I lifted the gun with my other hand and fired a few shots high, knowing Wells would be low.

A bullet whizzed past my head, so close I felt the tear of skin across my cheek and smelled the burning of my skin.

I kept moving, ignoring the almost fatal hit, and turned to stare at the man trying to hit me from behind. "Real men don't sneak up on other men," I said, twisting the blade and making the man's eyes go black with pain.

Roughly, I jerked it out, and the man fell to my feet, convulsing and bleeding out.

Spinning back toward my comrade, Wells, I searched the darkness for him. "Wells!" I said, rough, wanting to be sure he was still okay. I'd thought he was dead when I burst in here. I thought I was recovering a body, not rescuing a friend.

He made a sound, causing me to step forward.

"I wouldn't if I were you." A heavily accented voice rang out.

The sound of a match dragging against something rough was accentuated by the bright burst of a flame. A pathetic excuse for a human being stood there holding it, illuminating the shack with an orange glow. Shadows flickered, and the man grinned as though this were some kind of twisted haunted house and not a battle zone.

Wells was lying at the man's feet, hogtied and beaten. But he was breathing. He was alive.

That was the only thing that mattered.

"Good to see you, buddy." No, technically, I shouldn't show any emotion at all. Emotion was weakness, and the man holding the match would like that, but I didn't give a flying fuck.

The man with the match reared back and kicked Wells in the back. He coughed and curled inward, but otherwise didn't make a sound.

What happened next was done in a matter of two seconds, but my God, it felt like ten minutes. In every single nuance of those seconds, I felt everything and saw everything tenfold.

The man who kicked him looked at me and smiled, laughter bubbling out between his lips. A bullet from my gun burst out, barreling straight through the space between us. The man wasn't surprised. A knowing, almost arrogant look crossed behind his eyes, and in that nanosecond, I realized my mistake.

"No!" I roared, the word dragging out and echoing around me like I was under a ton of water.

Instead of running backward to the door, I went forward toward my brother, but it was too late.

The bullet slammed into the asshole, and the match in his hand fell, landing on Wells, who immediately burst into flames.

Oh God, he screamed. The sound of my friend shrieking as his entire body whooshed into a gigantic flame was blood curdling.

I hovered near him, scooping up sand from the floor and tossing it on him as if that would somehow put out the flames.

The terrorist I killed lay nearby, eyes open, looking at me with a smile still etched on his dead face.

This is your fault. *His eyes laughed.* You shot me, and now your friend burns.

"Wells!" I screamed.

The wails of my friend distorted, his voice becoming someone else's entirely.

"Alex!" Sabrina screamed. "Alex, it hurts. It hurts so bad. Please help me!"

Newfound horror burned through me, and I bellowed like a beast in the middle of a kill. "Sabrina!" I lunged toward her as she burned. I could see her face perfectly, begging me for help.

I leapt onto the body, flame singeing me and melting my skin. I used my body to try and put out the flames swallowing her alive.

The pain... Dear mother of mercy, the pain.

"Alex!"

* * *

A knee slammed up into my nuts, making my body recoil. The pain brought out reality, something I very quickly discovered was much worse than the dream I'd just been suffering through.

I was in bed, Sabrina beneath me, sporting a wild look in her eyes. The gasps and uneven way she dragged in air was like ice-cold water over my head.

"Jesus!" I swore, horrified. My hands were around her neck, my large body pinning her down.

I was attacking her. A woman I'd die to protect, a woman who so trustingly gave herself to me just a little while ago…

I could have killed her.

Launching off the bed, I fell onto the ground, landing with a thud against the floor. Leaping onto my feet in one swift, fluid movement, I hovered near the bed, but at a distance.

I could have killed her.

"Sabrina. Sabrina, baby," I prayed roughly. "How bad is it?" I paced, rubbing a hand over my head. "How bad did I hurt you?"

She was sitting up now, her knees drawn in to her chest, arms wrapped around them. She wasn't crying, but there were tears on her face. Her breathing was still ragged, and I was so fucking scared.

"I'm calling an ambulance." I decided and rushed around the bed to where my cell lay on the nightstand.

"No," she said, her voice hoarse.

I ignored her and lit up the phone.

"Alex, no," she said, a little more audible this time.

"You can't breathe, for fuck sake!" I roared. "I probably crushed your windpipe." I made a desperate sound. If she wasn't okay, I wouldn't be able to live with myself.

Sabrina rose onto her knees and swiped the phone from my hand. "I'm fine," she said, moving back onto the bed, keeping the phone.

"No, you aren't." I paced away, this time pinning both hands around the back of my neck. "I was having a nightmare, shit from my past…"

"I know."

I stopped pacing and looked at her. "What did I say to you? Oh, baby, I'm so sorry."

"It's okay. I know it was a dream. You would never hurt me." Her voice was still hoarse. I bet her neck was going to be bruised.

A tortured sound ripped out of me, and I rushed to flip on the lamp. Both of us recoiled when light flooded the dark room, but I blinked and forced my eyes to adjust.

She was shielding her eyes with her hand, and her hair was over her shoulders.

I stayed back, my hands shaking. "Let me see."

"What?"

"Let me see what I did to you!" I yelled.

"Alex." Her voice was soft and forgiving. I hated it. I didn't deserve that tone.

I didn't deserve to have her in my bed. This was exactly why Mercer didn't want me anywhere near her. This was exactly why I left without a good-bye three years ago.

I was damaged goods. So filled with ice any trigger sent me subzero.

I might want her. My God, how I wanted her, but it didn't matter. What I needed was exactly what I had before she showed up here. I needed to live alone in the mountains with my family and nothing else. I couldn't handle the kind of love I felt for her. It made me volatile. It made me dangerous.

I was better off alone, having one-night stands with snow bunnies who meant nothing to me. I couldn't hurt those women. I couldn't kill them.

I shouldn't have slept with her. I shouldn't have let the emotion from earlier tonight prey on the soft spot I felt for her.

Hell. It wasn't just a soft spot. My entire heart was a giant sinkhole that gave way to her.

I loved her with every fiber of my being. Which was exactly why I should have known better than this.

The endurance I felt in that kiss before was just a wish. Just a trick my heart was playing to get me to surrender. And I did.

Now just fucking look what I'd done.

We couldn't endure this. Sabrina could not endure me.

Sabrina

Watching him skitter away from the bed, deeper into the shadows of the bedroom, nearly broke my heart.

This was bad.

Bad for him. I mean, yes, it sort of scared the shit out of me when I tried to wake him and he tackled me. Some definite alarm skittered over my spine when his hands slipped around my throat to squeeze and the look on his face was unrecognizable.

Even still, I trusted him.

You know why?

Because though I was scared in those few moments, I wasn't scared of *him*. I knew what Alex was capable of. It was the same thing Daniel was capable of. They were hardwired different. Trained to react before they thought.

I knew Alex wouldn't admit it, but he probably had some PTSD going on from everything he experienced. There were many nights I'd heard my brother scream out in his sleep. There were also many nights I'd heard him pace the floor because his demons kept him awake.

These men—Alex—had seen and done things that most men never would. I would be far *more* afraid of him if those things *didn't* affect him as they did now.

I might not have ever lived it, and I might not have those haunting nightmares that never fully allowed my past to rest, but I could still try and understand. And maybe it was that non-experience I spoke of that made it easier for me to forgive him than he could himself.

The fear for me had been instant, the same anyone would feel when being physically pinned down and threatened. But that fear abated quickly. I called his name, and when that didn't work, I kneed him in the nuts. As soon as he realized what he was doing, he stopped. It wasn't as if he knew exactly what he was doing and continued.

Daniel warned me about this kind of thing many years ago. When he started to notice the looks his military friends would give me, and I guess when he started to realize I was becoming more woman than kid sister.

He was adamant I not become involved with anyone in his field of work, but even so, he used every opportunity he had to tell me what to expect (or more likely try to scare me) if I did. Dreams like this weren't uncommon. How could they be?

These men were trained so acutely their bodies reacted the instant they felt or saw any kind of hairy situation. Sometimes their minds couldn't distinguish between wake and sleep.

I actually was grateful for that kind of reaction. I knew it had kept my brother alive more than once. Sometimes the threat wasn't always a dream. Sometimes these men almost died by attack in their sleep.

Regardless, I knew better than to move over Alex and try to wake and soothe him. I should have gotten out of bed and woken him from a distance. It was one of the reasons Daniel slept with a lock on his bedroom door.

I didn't get out of bed. I reacted with my heart before my head had a chance to get involved. I regretted it now, only because Alex would torture himself for this maybe forever.

"I mean it, Sabrina. I want to see your neck. I want to see the bruises," he intoned, bleakness and danger warring within his tone.

I sighed, pushed aside the covers, and slipped out of the bed. The indrawn breath across the room reminded me I was naked. My hand closed around his flannel, and I tugged it on, buttoning it as I went.

"What are you doing?" he asked, watching me. I could feel the tension in his body, feel the wariness waft off him as I walked across the room.

He moved back a step, and my heart hurt a little, but I continued, knowing this wasn't something I could just hug away. The bathroom light flipped on, and I blinked against it. The tile was cold against my bare feet, but I held in the grimace because I worried he would think it was from pain he caused.

Going to the mirror, I snatched a hair tie off the counter and pulled my hair up into a loose, lopsided bun on the top of my head. When that was done, I grabbed the collar of the flannel and spread it out, revealing my neck.

"See," I told him. "No bruises."

"What?" he asked, stepping into the doorway.

Gazing at him through the bathroom mirror, I nodded. "You didn't leave any bruises, Alex. You let go almost as fast as you grabbed on."

"Turn around."

I did as he requested, rotating so I could look at him through my own eyes and not the mirror. He gestured for me to lift my chin, so I did, holding the collar wide so he could see.

He came closer, walking tentatively. Still, the distance between us was at least arm's length, and I wanted to tell him to come closer.

"See?" I whispered. "It's okay."

"Your skin is red," he replied, harsh.

"I'm fine." I insisted, trying for a smile. "Hell, your nuts probably hurt worse than my neck."

He didn't think it was funny. Not even a little.

"You think it's funny you had to knee me in the sack to get me off you?" He spoke low. The dead calm in his voice and filling his eyes made me shiver. "I could have killed you."

I gasped and lunged forward. "No!"

He moved back, eluding my touch.

"Alex! You would never do that."

He laughed, and it was unlike any laugh I'd heard from him before. I felt like, for the first time ever, I was seeing a glimpse of the man my brother and his friends called Ice.

"You have no idea what I'm capable of."

I swallowed. "I'm not afraid of you."

His eyes moved over me from my head all the way to my toes. "We fell asleep," he said, a muscle ticking in his jaw. "Not that it really matters. How's your head?"

Who gave a rat's ass about my head? "It's fine." I allowed. "How's yours?"

He didn't even answer, as if he thought the state of his health was so trivial it didn't require a response. "I never should have let this happen."

"My head injury is not your fault. That dream was—"

"This!" he yelled, gesturing between us and then at his shirt on my body. "I never should have slept with you. It was wrong. *So* fucking wrong."

My spine stiffened. He regretted sleeping with me? Well, that hurt. Having his hands on my neck didn't. But those words? Those hurt most of all.

"Don't say that," I replied, sounding weak and defeated.

"I'm going out on the couch. Stay back here." He started away, then stopped but didn't turn back.

He was leaving, just like that?

"I know you killed that man earlier tonight," I burst out, making his feet stop again. I wanted him to see, to realize I knew who he was.

I loved him anyway.

Even from across the room, his back to me, I heard his intake of breath. "You saw?"

"I didn't see you do it, but I know what happened when you went over there. I know you sent me with Liam so you could get rid of the body and the truck."

He spun, his eyes flaring with anger and life. Seeing those emotions made me feel one hundred times better because that frigid, hollow look he'd been sporting before was gone.

"Then what are you doing on my bed right now?" His arms flung out into the air. "What are you thinking, letting me touch you?"

Well. Maybe telling him I didn't care he killed that man wasn't such a good idea. My shoulders slumped. I had to get through to him. This time couldn't be like three years ago.

"I'm not thinking right now, Alex. I'm feeling." I pressed my palm flat against my chest, trying to quell the ache there. Hoping to God he might feel it, too. "Thinking is hardly an option when you're in the same room with me. All I can do is *feel*. All I can do is want."

The anger was gone from his voice when he finally spoke. "You're too good for me."

It wasn't just my emotions I was feeling right then. It was his, too. He wanted me. He wanted me so much it was palpable, but he was trying to do what he thought was right.

"If that was true, you would have taken my virginity three years ago and told my brother to go to hell."

He groaned. "You have no idea how much it tortures me that I wasn't your first. Your only."

"You are my only." I promised. "What we did over there…" I pointed to the bed. "I've never felt that with anyone else. Ever."

"That can't happen again." He turned and left the room, walking so silently and leaving the room so empty if I was any less of a woman, I would have thought the room had always been empty.

I went after him, the bottom of my bare feet slapping against the floor, making a ruckus so he would be sure I was still there.

He was standing near the window, looking out into the dark, empty yard.

"You regret sleeping with me?" I couldn't keep the hurt from my voice.

Alex's large hand hit the wall in front of him, and all his weight seemed to be suspended against that one arm. His head hung low. I pictured him gazing at his feet as he stood.

"I could never regret any moment I've spent with you," he answered, making my heart flutter then beat a little bit stronger.

Unfortunately, he kept talking.

"That doesn't change anything. Your brother was right about me, Brina. I'm toxic to you. He asked me to protect you, and that's what I'm going to do. From everything and anyone who could hurt you. Including me."

"No." I denied, stepping farther into the room. The comforting crackle of the fireplace wasn't so comforting in the moment. "I know you, Alex. I know you could never hurt me like that."

"I already have."

"Why are you doing this?" I yelled, feeling him getting further and further away. "After everything that happened, after tonight…" I was getting angry, and I welcomed the anger. It was a hell of a lot better than the splintering hurt.

He spun, regarding me with a stranger's eyes. "You think you know me? You don't have a clue."

"No?" I challenged, taking a step closer. "Tell me."

"The last time I killed, the time before tonight, it wasn't just one bad guy. Or even two bad guys. It was a massacre. I killed an entire village. I did it without any hesitation." He stared at me as he spoke, that pale, emotionless look dropping like a veil over his already piercing eyes. "There's a switch inside me I can flip… I do it so easily it's terrifying. One minute I'm just me, Alex. And the next? He's completely gone, immune to any kind of humanity at all."

"Ice," I whispered.

Slowly, he nodded. "Ice. It's how I got my name."

He continued, his voice hoarse but steady. "That night, the switch in me flipped automatically. I went on autopilot. They killed my brother, and then they laughed right in my face. That was the last sound I heard until the silence around me was so loud everything came back into focus."

"What happened?" I asked, fingering my throat as my stomach twisted and I readied for his reply.

"Blood was everywhere. It stained the ground, the rocks around the fire. The makeshift walls of the shacks were splattered, and my boots stood in a puddle. I glanced behind me at my team, who all stood stoic and pale in the dark. They stared at me like I was a stranger, like we hadn't just spent the last few years shoved up each other's asses. They were shocked, and at first, it didn't really penetrate. We'd been in these situations before, where missions turned into bloodbaths, where we had to make decisions no one else could have made."

He paused and glanced at his hands. Lifting them in front of his face, looking at the front and then the backs as if he were seeing them not as they were right now, but as they had been that night.

"I was covered in blood, too. My hands were slick with it. So was my gun. My uniform was stained and saturated... Then I realized I could see myself too well for the middle of the night and in a place with no electricity."

Alex walked to the fireplace, taking care to give me a wide berth. Both his hands hit the mantle, and he leaned down, his head dropping low, and gazed into the crackling fire. "The entire village was burning. The crappy buildings, the little belongings they all had..." He sucked in a breath and straightened. "A wooden toy truck."

How horrible. How life altering. I was wrong before. I didn't understand. Yes, I tried, but I would never know what his eyes had seen. I went to him, speeding across the space with full intent to comfort him.

"Don't touch me."

His warning stopped me in my tracks. The way he spoke was low and hard. It wasn't a request. It was a demand.

"Alex…" I wanted to badly to reach out. I knew I couldn't comfort him, but oh, how I longed to try.

"I don't deserve your comfort, Sabrina. I deserve to live with what I did. With how I acted."

"That was an extreme situation." I asserted. "A situation that no human should ever have to be in. You can't know—"

"I killed kids! Women!" he yelled, spinning around to stare at me. His face was a mask. A mix of the Alex I knew and the man he was describing right now. "I killed families." I watched him swallow, and some of the chill left his eyes. He became more recognizable. "I killed kids whose only crime was being connected to the scum who lived there."

He expected me to be horrified and ashamed. Maybe he hoped I would be. He hoped I'd be so disgusted I'd never touch him again.

He might hope it, but that wasn't what Alex wanted.

His chest was still heaving when I started to move again. His eyes flashed in warning, and he took a step back. I ignored the look and his movement, instead quickening my steps.

He didn't shove me away when I slipped my arms around his waist or pillowed my cheek in the middle of his chest. Pressing close, I wrapped my arms around him so tight I had room to rest my forearms up his back and press both palms against the backs of his shoulders.

"It's okay." I soothed.

His body was rigid. The way his heart hammered at my cheek almost hurt. He believed he didn't deserve any comfort, but he was hurting enough to not push me away.

"How can you touch me right now?"

It was simple. "I love you."

His heart literally skipped a beat. When it started up again, it was at a much slower thud than just a second ago. His body was still locked. Upon my confession, it stiffened even more.

"What?" His voice scraped from his throat, rough and low.

I lifted my head to meet his eyes. "I love you. You shattered my heart three years ago. And all that did was create a million pieces inside me to love you still. There is no limit to what I feel for you, so if you're telling me these things to try and scare me away, it won't work."

Emotion flooded his eyes at the same time he moved. My legs wrapped around his middle, and his hands cupped my ass.

He didn't kiss me. He kept his head back so our stares could meet. I kept the truth right there for him to see, proving it, not backing down from it. Loving him wasn't something I should be ashamed of, and it wasn't something I wanted him to be ashamed of either.

"I've killed so many people. So many it's not even hard anymore," he confessed, the words ripping out so jaggedly it tore through him and into me. "I'm not a good guy."

"You're not a bad guy either."

"Say it again."

"I love you."

"Again."

"Alex. I love you."

He turned and pressed me against the wall beside the fireplace. The stone facing was cold and rough against my back. His body pinned me so his hands could cup my face. Strands of hair fell around us, tangling in his grip and lying across my chin.

He stared another moment, and I let him look his fill. Finally, his eyes drifted down to my neck, still searching for a bruise he hadn't left. As if seeing a bruise would somehow justify everything he felt. He whispered, "I'm sorry. You'll never know how fucking sorry I am."

When he tried to look down, I lifted his face. "I'm not sorry. I want all of you, Alex. Even the parts that scare you to death."

"I am scared, kitten. I'm so afraid of not being the man you deserve."

"You already are."

A sound ripped out from somewhere inside him, and his head finally swooped in. The first touch seared me. The second touch melted me, and when his tongue swept into my mouth, taking command, I gave in completely.

Alex held my head, keeping me still while the assault of his kiss sent a frenzy of emotion through me. The way he pinned me, the way he owned every inch of our mouths as we moved together, left me feeling like a volcano filled with molten hot lava, ready to erupt.

But I would only erupt when he allowed it.

I succumbed. As strong and capable as I was, I gave up all control to Alex. At times, I loved fighting against him. I loved pushing back and getting a reaction.

But right now, I wanted him to feel just how much I trusted him. I wanted him to see that even if he was afraid, I was not.

I wanted to be owned right now. To be owned and commanded by him and his touch. There was nothing more I wanted as badly as I wanted him. And so I surrendered to every feeling he ever elicited in me. I gave in to the love I so desperately tried to deny.

My center pooled with desire, and twinges of pain sparked through my lower belly. My mouth ripped away, my head fell back, and a deep moan tumbled from my lips. Alex kissed across my jaw and down my neck. I lifted my chin, exposing more skin, and he took full advantage.

He held me prisoner against the stone, his hard body, soft lips, and I endured every single twinge of pain from my already damp entrance that nearly wept for him.

Alex pulled back, leaving me drunk and dizzy. "Tell me I don't have to stop."

"Please don't stop. Don't ever stop again."

Our lips fused again, and my body left the wall. He was clutching me against him, and I tightened my thighs as he walked down the short hall and kicked open the bedroom door.

My back hit the mattress, and Alex came over me, straddling my thighs. His cock strained against his sweats above my middle, and I reached out to brush my fingertips over the bulge.

Gently, Alex moved my hand aside and reached for the buttons on the flannel. With agonizingly slow, patient movements, he undid each button, one at a time.

I arched up when he was partway done, making the shirt fall open a little bit more, and his eyes caressed the exposed skin. When all the buttons were undone, he spread the shirt on either side of my body, fully revealing all of me to his heated gaze.

His hand hovered over my bare breasts, making my breath catch as I anticipated his palm on my delicate flesh. At the last minute, he drew back, instead brushing his fingers through my hair, spreading it across the blanket beneath me.

"You are so goddamn beautiful," he whispered, raking his eyes over me again. I was flushed and heated. He wasn't even touching me, yet I felt seared to the core.

"Like an angel." He went on. "When I was out there… when things were really bad, it was you I thought of."

"Me?"

He nodded. "You were always the purest thing in my world."

I whispered his name, sitting up and reaching for him. Our chests collided, my skin on his, and we tumbled back onto the bed with him falling between my legs.

Alex pushed in with one single stroke, and my body clutched him tightly as if vowing to never let him go. He groaned and pushed up, staring down. "I don't think I can walk away this time."

"Don't ever," I echoed. "Don't ever leave."

Leaning down, he kissed me deep as he thrust into my body passionately.

A little while later, I arched up into his body, my mouth falling soundlessly open. He grazed feather-light kisses over my neck, yet another apology for how he'd reacted to the dream.

My back hit the mattress once more. My eyes sought his, and our stares collided. "I love you," I told him. "That won't ever stop."

His eyes flared, and his hips bore down.

Both of us crested and fell together, finally dissolving into a heap in the center of the mattress, two bodies creating a single imprint.

Alex

"Do you want to know why I left?"

She sucked in a breath, and a little of that post-sex haze in her greenish-golden gaze lifted. A ribbon of pain passed over her features, almost like a ghost haunting an old house. "Because my brother told you to."

I moved, sliding off her supple, flushed body to fit myself right beside her. She shifted, too, and we ended up spooning against each other, my front against her warm, fine ass. "We'd only been back from that mission, the one I just told you about, for a couple weeks. We were all still raw. Still on edge."

"That's the one where Wells died." Her voice was solemn.

I nodded and rested my chin on her bare shoulder. "Such a waste of a good man."

Sabrina wiggled a little closer into me. Her presence affected me right down to the bottoms of my feet. The urge to bury myself into her so deep I didn't know where she ended and I began called to me. It tempted me. It didn't matter I'd just had her. I wanted her again. Talking about this kind of thing left me raw and essentially vulnerable. Her body was like the devil on my shoulder, whispering that I could forget everything the second she was under me.

I kept talking, telling the devil I knew he was a goddamn liar. We had to talk about this. It was beyond clear to me I couldn't walk away this time. I wanted us to endure.

The truth was endurance. She had to know everything, the darkest places I kept hidden. Only then would we have a fighting chance.

"You made me feel better… more human. You were the only one who still looked at me like I was just me and not some frozen-over ice block. I just wanted to be around you," I whispered in her ear. "You were all I could think about."

"The night my brother walked in and found us kissing…" She recalled softly, as if my words had taken her back to that night.

"We were more than kissing," I said, kind of rueful. "If he hadn't walked in, I wouldn't have stopped."

"I didn't want you to then. Just like I didn't want you to tonight."

"You have no idea how much it tortures me I wasn't your first. Your only."

Her body softened against mine, and she whispered, "You are my only."

"Maybe if I hadn't killed all those people. Maybe if I hadn't lost control."

"I don't understand."

Gazing over her shoulder and down her body at where our hands were clasped tightly together, I explained, "Mercer didn't want me around you. He'd just witnessed me slaughtering people without any kind of attachment. Yeah, the guys all knew I was icy. Hell, they already called me Ice. But this was a whole new level. I think some of them had actually been afraid of me that night."

"I'm not afraid of you," she said bravely, like a kitten with a giant roar. I loved she wasn't afraid of me, but I wanted her to look past any allusion she might have. I was only a man. A flawed one at that.

"Maybe you should be."

"My brother had no right to tell you to leave."

I kissed her shoulder. "He didn't."

She jolted, turning to gaze at me over her shoulder. "What?"

"He told me to stay away from you. He told me he'd kill me if I touched you again."

She hissed out a breath and turned back around, pushing my arms away and sitting up in the bed. "You should have fought for me!" she yelled, hurt raw in her eyes. Her fist collided with my chest, and then she hit me again.

I let her hit me. I deserved it.

She started weeping. Her fists fell away, and her head hung low. I wanted to reach for her. To curl my hands around her body and pull her back down.

I refrained.

"He was right," I whispered, reliving some of the misery I'd felt that day. Of all the fucked-up shit I'd seen and done in my lifetime, nothing compared to how miserable it was to hear from a witness how savage I'd been. Those images in my head coupled with my own spotty memories and recalling how my own brothers had stared at me that night convinced me. I had to leave.

Her eyes flashed with anger, but I wanted to make her understand.

"He painted a bloody and grim picture of what I did that night, filled in details my own mind omitted. Daniel said I couldn't be trusted around you. That switch inside me could flip anytime, and you would pay the price."

She swiped at her cheek deftly, then grabbed the ends of the open flannel still on her body and pulled it closed over her chest.

"I had to go. After what I'd done, who I thought I might become. I couldn't even stay with the team anymore. Wells was dead. I was a liability to their safety. To my own. If I couldn't be one hundred percent trustworthy, if those guys couldn't know without a shadow of a doubt that I would never turn on them, I couldn't stay. My contract was almost up, and around that time, I got word Liam had been injured." My mouth tipped up a little, remembering when I'd gotten to the hospital and saw Liam for the first time in almost a year. "He was more of a mess than I was."

"Seriously?" she asked, unbelieving.

I nodded. "In a fucked-up way, focusing on his problems helped me with my own. So I took leave, and when my contract expired, I refused to reenlist. They were shocked. They offered me a huge pile of cash as a signing bonus."

"You still said no."

"My place is here at home. With my family."

Her lower lip wobbled when I said it, and I knew it hurt her. I didn't want that, but it was my truth.

"I could have been your family, too."

"You are my family, always have been. You wouldn't be here right now if you weren't."

"You left anyway. You didn't even say good-bye."

"If I had tried to say good-bye to you, I never would have left."

"That's the lamest excuse I've ever heard."

I sat up, catching her by the shoulders. Giving her a gentle shake, forcing her to look into my eyes. "It's not lame. It's the truth. You would have asked me to stay, and I would have buckled. I would have gone to war with your brother, the guy you love most in this world. It would have ripped you apart, and you would have had to choose."

She looked away, knowing I was right.

"I was fucked up in the head, kitten. I felt like a walking timebomb. I wasn't about to go off in your vicinity."

"You would have stayed if I asked?"

A choked sound ripped from me. "I tell you how fucked up I was, how I massacred an entire village by myself and I was terrified I might go subzero again and hurt you—and *that's* what you say?"

Her eyes narrowed. "Well, would you?"

I laughed. "I fucking love you."

She froze.

I froze.

We both stared at each other.

Her throat began moving first, working and trying to swallow. Eventually, she dragged in a ragged breath, the sound making her sound asthmatic. "You love me?"

"I've loved you from almost the first moment I saw you sitting at that poker table, shuffling cards and purring like the kitten you are."

She sucked her lower lip into her mouth and released it. My still semi-hard dick jerked. "And still?"

Unable to stop, I dragged the pad of my thumb over her damp lip. "Always."

Her body folded into mine. She felt so right it physically hurt.

Sabrina sniffled, burrowing in a little closer, then wiped her nose and cheek on my shoulder before pulling back. "You're a stupid jerk."

I stroked the side of her head. "I know, kitten."

"I like when you call me that," she confessed like it was some kind of crime. Like I didn't already know.

Remembering how upset she was before the accident, before meeting my parents, I took the chance to tell her, "You're the only woman I've ever called that. The only one I ever will. You will always be my kitten in a world of lions and tigers."

Her forehead rested against my chest, and I didn't resist filling my arms with the rest of her.

"I had to go, Sabrina. I didn't trust myself enough to say good-bye. I never would have left."

"I didn't want you to go."

I didn't want to go either. "I know."

She sat up again, facing me. "We have another chance now."

I searched her eyes for long moments before asking, "Is that really what you want?"

Her eyes rolled heavenward. "Really?"

I chuckled. "I know it's hard to see past all this." I gestured to my naked body. She gave me a playful shove, and I fell back into the blankets.

Staying down, my gaze turned serious, and I held out a hand. She surrendered hers, and I linked our fingers together. "Seriously, though. Life with me wouldn't always be easy. I'm going to have skeletons and ghosts rattling around inside me for the rest of my life. I'm not in the army anymore, but I still have the capability to kill. That part of me isn't something to take lightly."

Sabrina lay beside me, both of us on our sides, staring into each other's face. "I want you. Us. As long as I have that, everything else is just details."

My chest squeezed with emotion. Fuck, I wanted her. *This.* I was still afraid I was doing the wrong thing here, that in the end, I might destroy her. Staring at her now, though, looking into her golden, sincere eyes after hearing her confess her love, *not* being with her didn't seem like the right thing either.

We can endure. I would make sure of it.

"I guess we're official, then." I decided, and despite my worries, a sense of peace I hadn't known since I was a kid washed over me.

A beautiful smile transformed Sabrina's face, drawing me forward for a kiss. Just as I was about to claim it, she pulled away abruptly. "No take backs."

Inside my chest, I felt the warmth of a summer sun. Gently, I brushed back the hair from her face. "Definitely, no take backs."

She lifted her hand between us, holding out her pinky like a challenge. "Promise?"

I gazed at her small finger dubiously. "Really?"

Her nod was swift and decisive. "Pinky promises are iron clad."

Chuckling, I lifted my finger and hooked it around hers. "Well, in that case, I promise."

It was hella adorable how satisfied a stupid pinky promise seemed to make her. Fighting back a giant smile, I asked, "We straight now?"

"Straight." She agreed.

Our pinkies were still hooked, so I pulled her into me. "Good, now come over here and give me some sugar."

She moved closer, and I captured her lips, not pulling back for a long, long time.

Sabrina

My yawns were yawning. I didn't even know that was possible, but here we were.

I didn't know how long we'd been awake, but it had to be close to twenty-four hours by now, didn't it?

When Alex stepped into the bedroom, I groaned, rolled, and pulled a pillow over my head. I could hear his chuckle even through the stuffing covering my head, and I considered kicking him. I didn't, though, because my legs were tired, too.

My entire body was tired. And sore.

"C'mon, up," Alex ordered.

I lifted the pillow to yell, "You're not the boss of me!" then promptly pulled it back over my face.

The mattress dipped with his weight, and my stupid body stirred in response. I was a sick, sick woman. Even as exhausted and sore as I was, I still got turned on because he sat on the bed beside me. Just the way my body automatically tilted toward him because his weight was that much greater than mine was enough for me.

The pillow over my head was tossed aside. "I brought you some coffee, kitten."

I cracked one eye open and gazed up at him. Sweet mercy, he was intoxicating to look at. The warm tone of his skin against the pale blue of his eyes was striking. And his skin was supple and pore-free. Every woman's dream, but of course, this kind of gift had been bestowed on a man who wouldn't even appreciate such a thing.

"Did you put creamer in it?" I croaked.

His full lips drew into a smile, and amusement sparked in his gaze. "Went all the way outside and milked a cow for it. Just for you."

I threw a pillow at him and sat up. "Ha. Ha," I muttered, thinking of the day I first got here.

Just thinking about it made my stomach drop and this hollow, almost anxious feeling grope me.

Alex sensed the change in me instantly, without me even saying a word. "What's wrong?"

"I miss Daniel," I confessed.

He cupped the side of my head with his palm. "I know, baby. He'll be back as soon as he can."

I nodded and reached for the coffee. The warm, sweet liquid slipped down my throat with ease, and I sighed appreciatively. "Thank you."

"Anything for my girl."

Oh, I liked that. "Say it again." I beckoned.

"You're my girl."

Invitation sparked in my eyes as I watched him over the rim of the mug. "Come back to bed."

His nostrils flared, but he shook his head. "Uh-uh. Stop tempting me, you vixen."

A little bit of hurt flared in me at the quick denial. I turned toward the drink, away from him.

"Hey, now," he murmured, reaching for my chin to pull me back to face him.

The second his fingers grazed my busted chin, I flinched. He made a sound and dropped his hand immediately. "See. This is exactly why I'm not crawling back into this bed with you. You're hurt and sore enough already. Going at you again will just make you more exhausted."

He was right. My body was sore from the wreck, and now it was sore in other places, too. Places that hadn't been used in quite a while. But just because he was right didn't mean I was going to admit it.

"Don't look at me like that." He scolded.

"Like what?" I asked innocently.

He made a rude noise. "C'mon. Get your cute ass outta bed. We're going to Liam's."

"You go. I'm going to sleep." I set the coffee on the bedside table and burrowed back into the covers.

Next thing I knew, the covers were gone and the cold air was assaulting my bare body.

"Ahh!" I screeched, reaching for the blankets.

"No, you don't," Alex said, picking me up off the bed. "You know you can't go to sleep. It hasn't been twelve hours."

"We already fell asleep," I pointed out. "You're the one who said it didn't even matter," I muttered.

"Just another reason I can't get back in that bed of sin with you until we can fall asleep."

I blinked. "Bed of sin?"

A slow smile spread over the lower half of his face. "You sure as hell felt sinful to me."

Gliding my hand up his bare bicep, I made a small purring sound.

"Naughty kitten," he drawled, carrying me away from the bed to gently place me on my feet. "But I won't be distracted. Liam's waiting. I need to talk to him. And we need to get out of this house before your wicked ways seduce me."

"You act like you're a saint and I'm trying to corrupt you," I muttered.

Alex's hand curled around my hip, sliding beneath the open flannel to curve around my bare ass and flirt with my crack. "Oh no, baby. I'm already good and corrupted. Later, I plan to show you just how much."

Swaying into him, I lifted my face so he could lick into my mouth. I moaned and surrendered to the kiss.

"Get dressed," he said, finally pulling away.

"Can I wear your shirt?" I bargained.

His eyebrow arched quite beautifully over his eye. "You even have to ask?"

I giggled and started forward to get a pair of leggings I could pull on beneath his flannel. His hand bunched in the fabric at my back and towed me back before I could get far.

"Kitten," he murmured.

I looked up.

Tenderly, he kissed me on the forehead.

The action made my heart drop, and even though I thought all of me already loved him, a piece I didn't even know was inside me fell hard. I stood there dazed and sort of dumbfounded until he patted me on the ass and smiled. "You can go now."

My feet seemed glued to the floor, though, and I ended up standing there watching him saunter away, the muscles in his back rippling as he went across the room to get some clothes.

Alex

We were holding hands when we walked into the house. Liam looked up from the island where he was sitting with coffee in front of him and Shaw in his lap.

He said nothing at first, instead glancing down to our clasped fingers. When his eyes lifted, there was a stupid knowing smirk on his face. "'Bout damn time," he quipped.

"What?" Bellamy asked from beside the sink, turning to see. Her eyes zeroed in on the exact same thing, almost as if the fact we were holding hands was some kind of miracle.

She smiled and hurried across the room to throw her arms around the both of us. "Finally!"

Sabrina blushed. "Have we been that obvious."

Liam laughed.

Bellamy gave him a stern look before turning back to Brina. "We're happy for you."

I leaned down and whispered beside her ear, "That's Bellamy's way of saying we were so obvious it exhausted her."

Bellamy smacked me in the stomach, and I pretended like it hurt, but not enough to make me pull my fingers from Sabrina's.

"How are you guys feeling?" Bellamy went across the kitchen again.

"Like we got hit by a truck," Brina muttered.

"Speak for yourself, woman." I denied but rotated to face only her. Her face was pretty battered. The cuts from all the broken glass looked angry and agitated. The purple smudges beneath her eyes created a hollow, gaunt look, and the bandage on her cheek covering the stitches made me want to punch something.

Instead of touching her chin to tip it up, I bent at the waist and looked up beneath it. The road burns were raw and painful looking, and I wished I'd brought some of that cream the doc gave her.

"Maybe we should do this later," I mentioned. I'd been in such a hurry to get out of the house before that, I really hadn't taken the time to think about how the activity would affect her. Perhaps I should have just let her go back to sleep and sat over her to make sure nothing went wrong.

It was easy to forget that I had a unique ability to push past pain and injury. Practice and training honed that skill scarily well. Brina wasn't like that, though, and after what happened last night, despite the way I rocked her world afterward, I knew she was probably barely holding on.

"I'm fine." She assured me. "I just look like shit."

The corners of my mouth pulled. Sweeping another lingering gaze over her face, I settled on her eyes and hoped she saw the sincerity in mine. "You could never."

"You can rest here," Bellamy offered, reminding me we had an audience. "Let's go out to the living room."

I gave Brina a questioning gaze, and she nodded once.

"Would you like some tea, Sabrina? Coffee? Hot chocolate?"

Brina looked away from me to where Bellamy was pouring hot water into a mug. I smiled, seeing her making that damn ginger tea she had to live on when she was pregnant with Shaw. For a while, it was all she could keep down.

"No, thank you."

Shaw waved to me from Liam's lap and smiled.

"Little man," I greeted, going forward to take him out of Liam's arms. "How's my favorite nephew?"

He made a sound and reached for the sunglasses I'd tucked into the neck of my shirt.

"You better take those." Bellamy warned. "You remember what happened the last time you let him play with your glasses."

I shrugged. "I'll just get another pair."

Shaw grinned up at me, clutching the glasses. Brina shifted, and his attention went to her. She smiled and leaned in to touch his belly and greet him.

He swayed toward her, holding out his arms. Brina seemed surprised, but she took him and tucked him close to her chest. "What have you got there?" she asked.

He held up the glasses, which were already covered in slobber.

"You want to put them on?" she asked, using her one free hand to take them and open the sides. A quick glance at me asked for help, so I moved in to help her put the glasses on the baby.

"Don't you look so cool!" Brina crooned. "So much better than your Uncle Alex."

I grunted in disagreement.

Shaw laughed and reached up to pull the glasses off his face and toss them toward the floor. Moving fast, I caught them before they could hit. Straightening, my chest brushed against Brina's arm, and I found myself gut punched by the sight right before me.

Standing so close.

Gazing at the baby in her arms.

My heart clutched, watching her, my mind filled with thoughts of what it would be like to have her standing there beside me with our child in her arms. For long moments, all I could do was stare, my dry tongue sticking to the roof of my mouth.

A heavy hand slapped me on the back, snapping me out of whatever trance I was in. "C'mon. Let's go sit." Liam urged.

"Dadadadada." Shaw rattled on and held out his arms.

"You miss me already?" Liam asked, reaching for his son. "I miss you, too, buddy."

All of us traipsed into the living room. Bellamy set the mug she was clutching on the coffee table and began lowering onto the floor on a blanket that was spread out and littered with toys.

Liam made a rough sound, reached down with his free arm, and wrapped it around his wife. "Go sit on the couch. Rest," he said, lifting her to her feet.

"I can play with—"

"I won't have it." Liam griped. "You're green as a pickle."

Bellamy blanched at the mention of a pickle.

Liam rolled his eyes. "See? Go sit, sweetheart. I can handle my son."

Bellamy settled into the corner of the loveseat with a sigh. After sitting the baby on the floor, Liam draped a blanket over Bellamy, handed her the tea, and kissed her on the top of her head.

"Thank you," she whispered quietly, lifting her eyes to where he towered over her.

"Anything for you, sweetheart," he replied.

Dropping on the couch, I ignored the protesting of my stiff muscles and propped my legs up on the coffee table. Across from us, the fireplace was going, but there was some kind of barricade set up in front of it so Shaw couldn't get too close.

Brina patted my leg so she could get by to sit beside me. "What's the magic word?" I drawled, not budging an inch.

"I will kick you?" she replied sweetly.

"Nope." I crossed my arms over my chest and leaned back even farther.

"Alexander Hamilton!" she insisted.

I sat forward, my feet hitting the rug. "Girl, don't even play me like that." Calling me by my middle name… making me sound like some old man. *Hells no.*

Her eyebrow arched, and a spark of life came into her tired eyes. "Hammy."

I snatched her off her feet so fast she squealed when she fell into my lap.

"Ow!" she said, curling onto her side against me.

Alarm filled me. "Kitten? Shit, I'm sorry. I was too rough. What hurts? What did I hit?"

She kept her face in my chest so I couldn't see her. Fuck, I probably made her cry. I went to grab her face to pull her back, but I was afraid I'd hurt her again.

A sound of frustration filled the room, and I stood abruptly, having no problem hauling her with me. "I'm taking her back to the doc."

"I'll drive," Liam said, his voice concerned.

I felt her tremble against me, and I glanced down. Her shoulders were shaking… My eyes narrowed.

"Sabrina," I commanded.

Her silent laughter turned audible.

"You little brat!" I roared. "You scared the shit outta me. I thought you were hurt."

Still in a fit of giggles, she lifted her head. "Gotcha."

"I oughtta paddle your ass." I fumed.

She made a face. "That's what you get for grabbing me like that."

"She got you," Bellamy sang, amused.

"That's enough outta you, too!" I told her.

"Fucking women," Liam said, returning to his seat on the floor.

"Watch your mouth around my son!" Bellamy scolded him.

Liam winced. "Don't be like Daddy, little man. Or else Mommy will get you."

Shaw laughed and hit a button on some toy that played an annoying sound. Liam sighed. "I'm bringing this one to your house next time we're over."

"Where's Charlie?" Sabrina asked, a smile on her face.

"Outside," Bellamy answered. "Liam won't let him in."

All eyes went to Liam. He grumbled, "He's fine."

"I miss him." Bellamy rested her head on the large arm of the loveseat.

Liam rolled his eyes. "He was so clumsy this morning he nearly knocked you on your ass. I ain't having it. You're already puking up your guts."

"He didn't mean it." Bellamy defended.

"I know that, sweetheart," Liam said, patient. "I'll let him in later."

"Poor Charlie," she whined.

Liam rolled his eyes and looked at me. "Damn dog is bigger than her, and she's pregnant."

"I'm on your side," I told him, and he looked smug.

Sabrina tried to crawl off my lap to the place beside me, but I tightened my arms. "You're good where you are," I told her quietly.

She didn't try to get away after that, instead settling back into me with her sock-covered feet on the cushions beside us.

"You gonna tell me what the hell happened last night?" Liam asked, effectively changing the topic.

"He was parked on a side road. Didn't see him until he was already plowing into the side of the Hummer," I answered.

Bellamy made a distressed sound, so I glanced at her with a soft smile, letting her know it was okay.

"Then what?" Liam pressed.

"Then the ass—"

Bellamy cleared her throat and looked at her son. I sighed.

"Then the bad man yanked Sabrina out of the car and tried to haul her off."

Liam sat up, forgetting the toy in his hand. Newfound alarm was written on his features. "He tried to kidnap her?"

I nodded, grim. Around Sabrina, I tightened my arms just a little. "It's not just a hit. Not this time."

"You mean they don't want to kill her?" Bellamy asked, puzzled.

I glanced down into my lap. Brina looked up, and our eyes met. I saw the fear there, the fear she always tried to keep under wraps. She only let me see it for a second before burying her face back into my shirt.

I kept my voice low when I answered, "Oh, they want to kill her. But they want other things first."

She shivered against me, and I stroked her hair.

"So what do you know about this guy? Who sent him?" Liam asked. I could see his mind already working to formulate some kind of plan.

"I don't know. I don't know much of anything right now, and I didn't have time to torture any info out of that douche."

"Did he run away?" Bellamy worried.

"No," I said.

"What happened to him?"

Liam and I shared a glance. Then I shifted my gaze over to Bells and dropped the wall I used to hide the cold inside me.

Realization dawned on her face. Silence filled the room.

Sabrina felt the change and perked up, turning to face Bellamy. "He did what he had to do."

My stomach somersaulted. Part of me was awed Sabrina loved me enough to not even blink an eye at what I'd done... The other part of me? It was horrified. What kind of man asked the woman he loved to accept he was a killer?

"I know," Bellamy told her softly, offering a smile. "Men like that don't deserve to live anyway."

Sabrina nodded, seeing Bellamy wasn't all that shocked, and sank into me again. One of her scraped-up hands curled around the back of my neck and stayed there.

"You don't know anything?" Liam pressed. "Nothing that could help us protect her?"

I didn't bother to point out that I was the one who would be protecting Sabrina. The last thing I wanted was for Liam and Bellamy to get caught in the crossfire.

Still, I had to keep him in the loop. Unfortunately, there might come a day that I was forced to call him. Just like last night.

"I have a theory," I said carefully.

Sabrina sat up in my lap, her eyes wide. "You do?"

I nodded. "Obviously, whoever we're dealing with has done their homework."

"How so?" Liam asked.

"Because they know the only way they're going to get to her is to take me out."

Brina gasped and shot up. "What?"

The distress in her voice made me pause, only momentarily. I would have preferred to keep this shit on the down low. On the down low = not telling her all the details. Unfortunately, this was one of those situations where protecting her from the truth might get her killed. It was better if she knew exactly what was happening.

Besides, Brina wasn't a damsel in distress. I might be tasked with protecting her, but it wasn't because she was weak.

"They plowed into the Hummer on the driver's side where I was. Then they pulled her out of the truck while I was unconscious. When I came to, the fucker was trying to stuff her into his truck."

"They know who you are," Liam replied, thoughtful, his face grim.

I nodded. "Enough to realize they won't get to her unless I'm dead."

Upset, Sabrina tried to scramble off my lap and nearly fell. Catching her around the waist, I pulled her back down. "You're gonna hurt yourself."

She was unfazed. "Because of me people, want to kill you now, too!"

"This isn't your fault."

"Oh, so you mean if I hadn't been in your Hummer last night, that guy would have come here, run into you, and made you unconscious!"

"It's gonna take a lot more than that to take me—"

A rough sound forced its way out of her, and with it came a sudden burst of strength that allowed her to propel herself off my lap. I reached for her, but she skirted back, out of arm's length.

"Don't you even say it!" she demanded. "Don't even insinuate something so terrible. I will not put your life in danger by being here."

Her words were punctuated with her retreat.

"Brina," I called.

She didn't stop or turn back.

I stood and glanced at Liam. "We'll talk later."

He nodded, understanding on his face.

I caught up with her in the mudroom as she was struggling to get the lock on the door unlatched. From behind, I wrapped my arms around her and pulled her into my body.

A sob broke out of her throat, and she pushed at my arms. "Let go, Alex. I'm leaving."

I didn't let go. I did turn toward a nearby keypad, entering the code so the locks would disengage.

When the door was open, she tried to run away from me again. I bent and lifted, swinging her up into my arms.

She opened her mouth to likely yell at me, but I growled and silenced her with a hard look. Her teeth sank into her lower lip, but her eyes were angry.

"If you're leaving," I told her, unaffected, "then I'm coming with you."

Sabrina

I've come to learn that war is gritty.

It's messy and there really are no winners… just survivors who pick up the pieces and embrace the life they fought so hard for.

Love is a lot like war.

If Alex thought I was the type of girl who would just roll over and accept his life was on the line because of me, he was wrong. He might think of me as a kitten, but when I really wanted something, I knew how to fight like a lion. My brother made sure of that.

Still, I was there. In his house. In his bed.

Why?

Two reasons:

1.) I made a promise to Daniel.

And…

2.) I asked Alex not to leave me again. How could I then turn around and do it to him?

It took forever to get here with him—the man I knew would be the love of my life. How the hell could I go?

How could I stay and put him in danger?

If you're leaving, then I'm coming with you, he said.

I'll go somewhere you can't find me! I'd hurled the words back.

His eyes flashed with promise. *There is nowhere on this earth you can hide that I won't find you.*

We spent the rest of the night going at each other between the sheets like one of us was going to prove who was the most dominant.

In the end, exhaustion beat us both, and we fell sleep tangled together, all naked limbs and sweat-dampened sheets.

As much as I wanted to run, I wasn't stupid. It would be useless. He could find me. He would. And while I was out running around, playing stupid games, he would be out in the open, risking himself even more.

At least here in his triangle house, he was familiar. He had a plan.

My only hope was Daniel would come back soon and all this would be over.

What then? What would happen when Daniel came home? Would I just go back to California and Alex stay here? Life was different now. Changed. I had no idea what anything would be like moving forward.

I was awake, pondering all this, when I heard a car approach the house. Alex slipped out of bed but left his gun where it was—a very telling act.

As soon as he was gone, I sat up in the middle of the twisted blankets to listen. All I heard was the soft sound of a door opening and, shortly after, closing.

His footsteps drew closer from the hall, and I dove back into the blankets and shut my eyes.

A few moments later, he spoke above me. "I know you're awake."

I pushed the blankets back from my face and stared at him, about to demand what he was up to.

The large, orange pumpkin in his arms stopped the words from forming.

"What is that?" I gasped.

He glanced down at it and then at me. "After all the noise you made about wanting to put these things all over my deck, you don't even know one when you see it?"

"I know it's a pumpkin." I grumped, sitting up. "What I don't know is why it's here." Cocking my head to the side, I considered something else. "Did you just have that delivered?"

Alex plopped the pumpkin in my lap. It had a tall, winding stem.

"It's your birthday present."

I gasped, clutching it. "My birthday?"

He chuckled. "Did you forget what day it was?"

I squinted, thinking.

When I didn't answer right away, he patted my head. "It's okay, kitten. It's been a rough few weeks for you."

"Today is my birthday?" I asked, dubious.

"I should get some points because I remembered and you didn't."

I scowled. "How can I think about my birthday when I have to worry about you being shot up because of me?"

He crossed his arms over his chest, regarding me. "Don't be so dramatic."

"It's true!"

"Well, good for you I've been *shot up* before, and it's not anything for you to worry about."

"Alex—" I began, wrapping my arms around the huge pumpkin and leaning over it toward him.

He stopped the words with his lips, kissing me sweetly with the giant orange surprise right between us. When he pulled back, I was dazed and a little confused. "No more worrying about this. Not today."

"Not today," I echoed.

Smiling, he kissed the tip of my nose. "Happy birthday, kitten."

I smiled, glancing down at the pumpkin. "You got me a pumpkin."

"There's a few more out in the kitchen."

I hugged it. "I love it!"

"Most girls want jewelry or fancy trips. You want something that grows in a field," he muttered as if he were confused.

"You're going to help me carve it, right?" I asked, trying to climb out of the bed with it.

He reached down and lifted it so I could stand. "Do I have to?"

"It's my birthday. You have to do whatever I want."

"Then I guess we're carving a pumpkin."

"I'll handle the knife. You can scoop out all the goop." I decided, picking up a sweatshirt off the dresser to pull over my head. It was his, but it was my birthday, so I was doing what I wanted.

"Like I'm giving you a knife," he argued.

I scoffed. "Please. I'm better at carving than you!"

"That so?" he drawled, turning from the doorway of the bedroom to look at me. "How many pumpkins have you carved, Miss California?"

"We have pumpkins in Cali," I refuted.

"How many?" He pushed.

"It's my birthday. Why are you arguing with me?"

He laughed. "All right, come on, then. Show me these mad pumpkin-carving skills you have."

I marched after him, making faces at his know-it-all back.

The second I stepped into the kitchen, the look fell from my face and I gasped. Alex turned, a small smile on his face.

"You did this?" I said, gazing around in awe.

The entire kitchen was filled with balloons. All of them, yellow, orange, and red, crowded the ceiling. Some of them were clear but filled with golden glitter, and the long golden strings attached to each one hung down from the ceiling like glittering rain.

A large bouquet of red roses sat in the center of the island with a few more pumpkins around it. If that wasn't enough, there was a box of apple cider donuts and cups of hot cider from Caribou sitting right beside them.

"When did you have time to do all this?" I asked, finally pulling my eyes away from everything to stare back at Alex.

He wasn't looking anywhere but at me. The large round pumpkin was still in his arms.

"I had some help." He half smiled. "I didn't want to leave you here alone."

"I can't believe you did all of this," I said, awed once more. Wandering into the center of the room, I lifted a hand to trail my fingers through the long strings. The balloons overhead bobbed and knocked into the ceiling.

Alex caught my hand and tugged me around. "This is nothing. This is all I could throw together last minute."

"This is more than anyone has ever done for me before," I confided. "Trust me when I tell you this… this is everything."

Alex lifted me, my legs snaking around his waist. Snatching a single balloon overhead, he tugged it down so it was beside us and offered me the string. "From now on, your birthday is a holiday in this house, got it?"

My heart squeezed so tight I had trouble breathing deep.

When his lips touched mine, it was like a whoosh of oxygen right into my lungs. The balloon I'd been holding hit the ceiling when I let go to reach around and grip the back of his head. When finally he lifted his head, my chest rose and fell rapidly as I gazed up at all the beautiful balloons.

"You like it?"

"I love it."

"What about me?"

I looked at him, at the way his eyes were playful and his head cocked to the side. I smiled. "You're okay, too."

He growled and dove into my neck, nipping at the skin and making me squeal.

"I love you, too!"

The smug smile on his face only made my heart swell further. "Breakfast, pumpkin carving, and then…"

"And then?"

"And then you'll probably need a shower from all those pumpkin guts I'm going to make you scoop."

"You're probably going to have to shower, too."

He wagged his eyebrows suggestively.

"Sounds like the perfect birthday." I sighed and glanced up at the ceiling again.

"You think that's all we're doing?"

"It isn't?" I asked, brow puzzling.

"Nope. The annual BearPaw Fall Fest is tonight. It's pretty much the last thing we have here before the first ski of the season."

"I love fall."

He chuckled. "I know. You're like a walking pumpkin head."

Smacking him playfully, I replied, "We don't get seasons in California. Not like this."

"Liam and Bellamy will be there, too. They want to wish you happy birthday."

I nodded.

Alex sat me down and reached for the pumpkin again. "All right, birthday girl, let's do this."

Alex

Even though it was technically off season at the resort, the BearPaw Fall Fest was a big draw. People came from Caribou for the yearly tradition, as well as guests from out of state. This year's turnout was impressive, with crowds forming everywhere.

There was an entire vendor row with different booths filled with food, games, and crafts. Local businesses from Caribou had setups, as well as a few businesses that traveled here as sponsors. The crisp air was filled with the scent of fried dough and cinnamon, baking apples, and pumpkin spice.

String lights hung everywhere, and a live band played from a stage. Kids were racing around, laughing, adults were smiling, and the ski lift was running for the crowds that wanted a spectacular view of the colorful mountains.

Leaves scattered the ground everywhere and blew in front of us as we made our way toward the heart of the festival.

"I don't think I will ever get enough of all these leaves. The scent and the sound of them underfoot," Sabrina said, dreamily gazing down at her booted feet shuffling through the multicolored foliage.

I leaned down beside her ear. "Wanna know a secret?"

She glanced at me from the corner of her eye, nodding. Unable to help myself, I reached up and tugged the end of the giant-ass scarf she draped around her neck. The long strands of her hair were tucked beneath it. "We have extra leaves brought in just for this."

She made a sound and smacked me. "Don't tell me such things! Let me believe this is all just natural."

I chuckled. "Whatever you say, birthday girl."

"Hey, what's that crowd up ahead? Must be some popular booth," she said, forgetting about our conversation.

I glanced up and smiled. "That's not a booth, kitten. That's Liam."

She sucked in a breath. "Liam?"

I laughed beneath my breath and snatched her hand to link our fingers. "Your forgetting again that Liam is a big deal. People literally line up to see him. Whenever we have events like this at the resort, some people come just to see him."

"How exhausting," she muttered.

"Lucky for us we have front-of-the-line privileges." I tugged her hand, angling my body slightly in front of hers as we moved through the crowd.

People parted naturally. Liam might be the celebrity in these parts, but I wasn't someone anyone ignored.

"Bro," Liam called out when he saw me. Pausing in the middle of signing an autograph, he held up his fist. I slammed mine against his and glanced down at the pic he was signing.

"Dude, that pic is not your best." I cackled.

From beside him, Bellamy giggled. "I think he looks handsome."

Pulling Brina up beside me, I said, "What do you think, kitten?"

She glanced at the picture and then at Liam. "Looks fine to me."

"Ha," Liam said and finished scrawling his name. After handing it back, he posed for a couple pictures and then started to move out of the crowd.

People still stared and whispered as he went, but he was used to it and barely noticed. Bellamy still wasn't quite used to the fascination with her husband and glanced back at all the people staring.

I caught her eye and winked, which made her blush and turn back around.

"Killer turnout this year," I called to Liam. "Everyone wants a glimpse at last year's winter games gold medalist."

"Exactly why we left Shaw at home," Bellamy said. "Too much ruckus."

"Does all the attention bother you?" Sabrina asked Bellamy.

"I'm getting used to it," she replied with a smile.

Liam hooked an arm around Bellamy and pulled her into his side. "She knows she's my favorite girl."

"Happy birthday!" Bellamy said, switching subjects. "We have a gift for you in the car."

Sabrina seemed surprised. "Oh, you didn't have to do that."

Bellamy made a sound. "We wanted to." She stepped closer to my girl. "So did you like your surprise this morning?"

"You know about it?" Sabrina asked, her brows lifting.

"Liam is the one who dropped off all the stuff," I explained.

"Oh." She turned to Liam. "Thank you."

"Minor," he quipped. He was approached again by a small group of people and moved off to speak with them, giving the rest of us a little space.

"So…" Bellamy cajoled Sabrina.

She smiled, her fingers tightening around mine. "Best birthday ever."

Bellamy beamed. "I'm so glad." She looked back at Liam, who was once again signing autographs. "This could go on all night," she mused. "Let's go get some cider."

"Better make that hot chocolate from my mom's booth. She'd kick my ass if she saw us walking around here with someone else's drink."

"Of course!" Bellamy said and linked her arm in Sabrina's. "Hey, tell me how it was when you met his parents. Aren't they something?"

Sabrina was tugged along, and eventually our linked hands separated. I trailed behind the two women as they gossiped and giggled like high schoolers and waved at people as we went.

After some time at The Confectionary's booth and the introduction of BearPaw Resort's exclusive new flavor Mom had created, we were shooed off to have some fun with cups of hot chocolate in our hands.

Sabrina grew noticeably quiet as we walked away.

I bumped into her with my shoulder. "What's wrong?"

Her eyes lifted. Tonight they were burnished gold, matching so many of the leaves cluttering the ground.

She held up a small gift bag with a bow on it. "I wasn't expecting a gift from your parents."

Ah. "You don't like it?"

Her eyes widened and her footsteps stuttered. Automatically, I reached up to cup her elbow, keeping her steady. Our feet stopped, and we stood in the center of the crowd, staring at each other.

"I love it." She promised. Her stare turned worried. "Did it seem like I was ungrateful?"

I shook my head. "Of course not. They know you were thankful."

"I just..." she said, her words falling away.

"You just aren't used to family and people doing shit for you."

"Just Daniel," she whispered, her eyes lowering to the ground. "We spent every birthday of mine together. Except for the times he was deployed, of course. He was the only one who ever celebrated."

I cupped her face and leaned close to her. "Not anymore."

She nodded, eyes still locked on mine.

"It's overwhelming to have a family. It's okay if you need time to get used to it. My parents are very… overbearing."

She giggled. "But I like them."

"They like you, too."

From ahead, Liam whistled. I glanced up, noticing how far they'd gotten from us. I lifted a hand to tell him we were coming.

"Now I have two scarves to wear for fall," she said, lifting the bag to indicate the gift my parents had given her.

I rolled my eyes. "You and those damn scarves."

"I wonder how they knew I liked them," she mused as we started to walk forward.

I shrugged, nonchalant. Truth was when Mom asked, that's what I told her. But I wasn't going to ruin any of the thoughtfulness of my parents' gift for my girl. She was so touched they'd given her something. I didn't want her to think I'd told them to gift her anything.

The minute we met up with Liam and Bellamy, Liam hitched his chin toward a nearby booth. "You up for the challenge."

I glanced at the row of large water guns with targets and scoreboards beside them. Overhead, stuffed toys and lights dangled. The man behind the counter was dressed like a barber with a red-and-white-striped tie and some old-school hat.

A slow grin spread over my face. "You're going down."

"Oh boy." Bellamy sighed. "Here we go."

Liam and I raced over to the booth, slapped down some cash, and started shooting. Behind us, Bellamy and Sabrina laughed and watched us compete.

The competition between us drew a crowd, and soon people were cheering and watching us battle it out with giant water guns.

"You should just give up now," I told Liam a little while later. "I wouldn't want to embarrass you in front of all these people."

Oohs and ahs went through the crowd, and I grinned.

"Final match," he suggested. "Winner takes all!"

Everyone around us cheered.

"How in the world did you two become some kind of attraction?" Bellamy asked from close by.

"It's a talent, sweetheart," Liam told her.

I glanced at Brina and winked.

"You two have fun with that. I'm going to get a candy apple over there," she informed me, pushing away from the counter.

"You mean you aren't going to stay here and watch me kick his ass?" I asked, offended.

"You've kicked his ass in almost every game you've played," she noted, pointing to the scoreboards.

"That's just cold," Liam told her.

I cackled. "When she's right, she's right."

"I'll be right back," she told me.

Before she could get far, I tugged her back and dropped a quick kiss to her lips.

"You ready?" Liam asked, taking aim.

I nodded, and we both looked at the guy manning the booth. People started cheering, and a little bell went off, signaling the beginning of the game.

We started "shooting," and everyone cheered, growing louder as both scores started to rise.

"I got you!" Liam cackled as he pulled ahead.

I laughed and stepped up my aim. We were neck and neck. I was about to pull ahead and take the win.

Then, over the crowd, I heard a familiar shout.

My head twisted around as she shouted again. The people crowded around started to pitch sideways and yell as someone shoved through.

"Alex!" Sabrina screamed, sheer terror in her voice. "Alex, get down!"

"What?" As I turned, water sprayed in a wide arc.

That's when I saw it.

A familiar red dot… one that was currently trained on the center of my chest.

The sound of a gunshot silenced all other noise around me, and every moment broke down into slow motion.

People nearby ducked, and out of the crumbling bodies, one materialized. She leapt forward, plowing into me, and both of us slammed into the ground.

Sabrina

Men were large children.

A fact currently being proven by the intense water gun match raging behind me.

I had to admit it was pretty entertaining. I could definitely see why everyone here at BearPaw was so taken with them. Both Liam and Alex had qualities that drew people toward them. They were both kind of mysterious but also two of the most powerful men in this town.

People were totally loving watching these guys go at it over a stupid water gun battle.

Myself included, but I was also totally entranced by this entire festival, and currently, my sights were set on the incredible display of candy apples ahead.

Smiling to myself because of the way Alex and Liam were carrying on behind me, I lifted my face into the autumn night and breathed deep. Some of the tension seemed to drain right out of me and be carried off with the leaves. Not all the tension I felt, of course, but enough to make me feel noticeably lighter.

By the time I made it to the candy apple stand, the last of the people in line had moved off, giving me an unblocked view of the setup. The sweet scent of apples lingered around me, almost overpowered by the aroma of rich caramel. I took my time gazing at all the different apples on display. Some had nuts and chocolate; others had sprinkles. There was a row of more traditional ones that didn't have caramel, but instead that red candy coating.

The woman in the booth came over to where I was looking, a warm smile on her face. "Happy harvest," she greeted.

I smiled, brushing some blowing strands of hair out of my face. "These apples look amazing!"

She beamed. "It's our specialty."

"If I could, I'd take one of each."

"Well, I'd sell them to ya, but don't come back complaining of a stomachache."

I laughed. "How about a caramel and chocolate one?" I pointed to one that looked absolutely sinful drizzled with white and dark ribbons of chocolate. "And that one over there with the pecans and cinnamon." I thought Alex would probably like that one.

The woman grabbed both apples, which were already wrapped in clear cellophane and topped with a red bow. After she put them in a small paper sack, I handed over some cash.

"Whoa!" people were exclaiming behind us.

"Get him, Liam!" someone else hollered.

"Those boys." The woman tsked while smiling. "They just never grew up."

"That's the truth." I agreed.

"They're good men, though, and everyone around here loves them."

More yelling and clapping erupted behind us, and I heard Alex yell out a challenge to Liam.

"Would you look at that?" The woman chuckled. "He's catching up."

I turned and pushed up to my tiptoes but couldn't see because of the crowd.

"Oh, come around here, honey." She invited, waving me into the booth. "It's higher up. You can see."

"Oh, that's okay,"

"Come on now. Don't you want to watch your beau win?"

I felt myself blush. "You know I'm here with Alex?"

"Oh, honey, everyone knows. You two are the talk of the resort. And Caribou. Alex was the most eligible bachelor here at BearPaw, next to Liam of course."

"Well, I like him better than Liam," I said, smiling. As I did, I stepped up into the booth.

The woman laughed. "Well, I should think Alex would be happy to hear that." Her eyes went back to the where everyone was cheering. "Look at them." She giggled.

I turned from her to glance over the crowd to where Alex was battling. The second I did, an overwhelming sensation of anxiety clutched my chest and stomach at the same time. My body heaved with the strength of it, and panic sparked inside me.

I swayed forward, gripping the counter. I heard the woman saying something to me, but my ears no longer worked.

I blinked, trying to focus on Alex, wondering why I was suddenly nearly immobile with panic.

Then I saw the red dot.

Small and round, it glowed like a single evil eye. I knew exactly what it was, thanks to having Daniel for a brother. I knew exactly what a single laser-made dot was for.

A target.

And currently, that target was moving across Alex's back to settled at the spot I knew his heart would be.

All the life drained out of me, and what went empty filled up with unfiltered adrenaline. Panicked, I swung my head around, searching for someone with a gun, only to see nothing but smiling faces and laughing people who had no clue what was about to happen.

Stupid! Guns like that can be used from a distance.

My eyes snapped back to Alex. The dot was there, centered… ready to take him out.

I didn't think about myself in that moment or the fact that whoever was out there only wanted to remove the threat of Alex to get to me. It didn't matter. If Alex got hurt, what happened to me was of no consequence.

"No!" I screamed. "Alex!"

"What in the heavens are you—" The woman beside me started.

He can't hear me. There are too many people. Too many cheers.

"No!" I screamed again and launched myself over the counter. Apples and display items scattered everywhere. The paper sack in my hand went flying. The woman behind me was yelling, but I didn't pause to listen.

I went fast, dropping over the counter and stumbling into the leaves. They clung to my feet as I ran, trying to drag me back, to slow me from reaching Alex.

"Watch out!" I screamed, pushing past people who were in my way.

"Alex! Alex!" I yelled.

People were turning to look at me. I kept shoving them aside, trying to fight through the crush of people.

"Alex, get down!"

Finally, the crowd began to part as others seemed to grasp there was some kind of emergency. I saw him, so close yet so freaking far away.

His eyes were searching the crowd, looking for me. "What?" he said, and as he moved, that stupid red laser beam moved with him.

Now that he was turned, it was in the center of his chest.

I heard the gunshot echo through the air, and the fear of that sound somehow pushed me faster. I leapt at the man I loved, the entire time praying to God the bullet would hit me and not him.

Alex

I felt the force of the bullet slamming into the body. I felt the power behind the slug, and for a moment, I was back in the center of a war zone.

Gunfire rained down on everything and everyone. The scent of smoke and ash filtered through the air. Sounds of people screaming, crying out in death, was almost louder than the weapons being used to kill them.

Reality snapped back in the form of chaos and yelling and the feel of dead weight pressing me into the ground.

Someone just tried to kill me. To snipe me in my own backyard.

Sabrina.

She'd been running. She somehow knew what was happening, but instead of running away, she'd been heading toward me…

"Sabrina!" I roared, rolling from beneath what pinned me down and standing in one fluid movement. "Sabrina!"

A small moan from below snapped all my focus downward. A cry ripped out of my throat, and I fell onto my knees beside her. She'd been the weight on top of me, the shield pushing me down.

"Oh fuck!" I yelled, pushing her hair out of her face and leaning down to look at her. She was on her stomach, unmoving. Her breathing sounded more like a wheeze.

Her eyes strayed upward as though she were trying to look behind her.

I sat up. A sound that could only be described as a roar ripped out of me. The people still left scrambling around stopped to stare.

There was a bullet hole in her jacket. There was a bullet hole in Sabrina. My girl had just been shot.

Liam's booted feet appeared beside me, and he dropped to his knees. "Alex!"

"She's shot," I told him, hollow, still staring at that damn hole. Blindly, I reached out and grabbed his shoulder to squeeze. "Someone fucking shot her!"

Sabrina moaned again and acted like she wanted to move.

I put my hands on her sides to still her movements. "Don't move, sweetheart. Hang on. I got you."

"Alex," she said, her voice strained.

"Call the fucking paramedics!" I roared to Liam, who was staring down at Sabrina.

"Alex."

"I said call the goddamn hospital!" I yelled again.

"Alex!" Liam's hand slapped over the back of my neck and squeezed. "Why isn't she bleeding?"

"What?" I snapped, but then the question penetrated and I remembered.

A keening sound tore out of me. Reaching for Sabrina, I hauled her up into my arms, flipping her around so I could look at her face. "It's okay. You're okay." I told her.

One of her hands moved to rest on my arm. "I thought getting shot would hurt a lot worse."

By now, instinct was kicking in, having been completely blown out of the water by seeing that bullet hole in my girl. I surged to my feet, bringing her with me, hunching myself around her body.

"Bellamy?" I asked Liam.

He moved behind the water gun booth and returned with her also in his arms.

"Let's go," I barked.

Instead of heading through the center of the festival where everyone was scattering and running in fear, we moved off into the trees, taking cover in the mountain we knew so well.

"We gotta get to a hospital," Liam said. "Sabrina, stay with us!"

"Is she shot?" Bellamy gasped, worry clear in her voice.

I glanced down at Brina as I moved quickly, her eyes focusing on me.

"What happened to me?"

"Hush," I told her. "Hang on."

Finally, we came to where Liam had parked, his orange truck pretty much a beacon in the parking lot. It almost made me turn for our SUV, but it was farther away, and these women needed concealment.

"Leave Bellamy," I ordered. "Pull the truck up as close to the trees as you can get."

Liam set his wife beside me, and I shifted so I was in front of her.

"Haul ass," I told him, and he took off.

Seconds later, the Xtreme roared over the road, up onto the landscape, and right beside the tree line.

I opened the back door and ushered Bellamy into the cab.

"Get down!" Liam and I both demanded at the same time, causing Bellamy to sink onto the floor. I put Sabrina onto the floor behind the passenger seat and pulled back.

"Alex?" she called out, reaching for me.

"Take them to the hospital," I instructed Liam and then went running back into the trees.

36

Sabrina

I took a bullet for that moron, and what does he do?

Run off in search of the man who tried to shoot him!

If I wasn't in so much pain right then, I'd be inventing new swear names I could call him. I was going to kill him for doing this!

If he makes it back.

That seemed to curtail every other thought and worry inside my mind. I whimpered at just the idea he might be out there right now, getting shot.

"Stop the truck." I gasped. "Stop the truck!"

The engine didn't slow. In fact, it seemed to rev.

"Liam," I said, mustering all the force I could into my voice. "We have to go back for him!"

"I'm getting you both out of danger right now." Liam denied the request. "Alex can handle himself."

"He almost just died!" I sobbed, feeling the surge of tears rush to my eyes. "I can't leave him!" I said, heaving up off the floor and then falling over against the seat.

"Sabrina!" Liam demanded. "Get down!"

"No!" I yelled. "I won't until you take me back to Alex!"

Tears were falling freely now, and as hard as it was to breathe before, it was even harder now. I gasped for breath, sucking in great gulps but only feeling like I was getting a tiny breath.

"Please," I cried, sinking toward the floorboards.

Bellamy reached her hand across the seat, her other arm wrapped around her middle, and another worry assailed me.

"The baby," I whispered. The truck sped up even more when I spoke.

"Bellamy!" Liam yelled.

"I'm fine." She assured us. "The baby is fine, too."

Our hands clasped together as another sob ripped out of me.

"He's fine." She tried to soothe me. "Alex will be fine,"

I was beyond being reasoned with. I was beyond thinking about his skills and knowing how capable he was at taking care of himself. He'd almost just been killed.

A bullet in the back didn't care about all his training. He'd been living his life, having fun with his friends, and all of it was almost taken away.

I cried harder, clinging to Bellamy's hand as my body ached.

Seconds later, the truck screeched to a stop, and bright lights shone through the windows. Liam lunged out of the driver's seat. I could hear him yelling and calling out. Moments later, the door where I was sitting was wrenched open, and hands reached in to grab me.

I started screaming and fighting, kicking at the unknown hands.

"Back off!" Liam yelled, pushing past the nurses. His eyes met mine. "I'm going to pick you up now."

I nodded, allowing him to pull me from the truck. Bellamy was already being ushered inside, and Liam strode with me in his arms under the metal awning and through the wide automatic doors.

"She's been shot," he said. "In the back."

The nurse grew alarmed and rushed to get a gurney. When it was close, Liam laid me on my side and gazed down with a worried expression on his face.

"Go find Bellamy," I told him.

His eyes gazed around, but he hesitated. He was torn between leaving me here and going to look for his wife.

I grabbed his hand and squeezed. "Go."

He rushed off, yelling over his shoulder that they needed to take care of me.

I was whisked into a cubical with curtains all around. A doctor and a few nurses rushed me, and I cringed, but they didn't stop. Instead, they began assessing me and cutting away my clothes.

One of the nurses made an odd sound. "This isn't cutting."

"What do you mean it's not cutting?" the doctor barked, slapping on a pair of gloves.

"I mean the scissors won't work."

The doctor came over, and I felt the nurse showing him.

"What the…?" the doctor said, and I felt him touch where I'd felt the bullet hit me.

I winced a little, but honestly, it didn't hurt as much as I thought it would. "Am I in shock?" I asked. "Why doesn't it hurt worse?"

There was a pregnant pause.

I lifted my head to look at the doctor. "How bad is it?" I asked, bracing myself.

The doctor looked at my face, then back to my shoulder. "Ma'am, you weren't aware you were wearing a bulletproof vest?"

"What?" I said, twisting around to try and look behind me. The movement hurt, but not enough to keep me from looking.

"Your coat appears to be bulletproof."

I shoved up, teetering a little as I moved to sit. One of the nurses helped me keep my balance, and I glanced down to the plain black quilted coat I wore.

A conversation with Alex from just a couple hours ago replayed in my mind.

"Here, wear this tonight."

I looked up to see a black, quilted coat gripped in his hands. "You bought me a coat?"

"It's cold here. Your California blood can't hack it."

"I bought a jacket." I reminded him. I cocked my head to the side. "When did you buy me a coat?"

"I ordered it the other week," he said, then scowled. "Can't a man get a coat for his girl? You should be happy I don't want you to freeze."

I got up from the table where I'd been sitting and admiring the jack-o-lantern we'd carved together and went toward him. "How did you know my size?"

He scoffed. "You're small. It's not that hard."

I rolled my eyes. "Let me see it, then."

He held it up like a gentleman in a movie. I turned, pushing my arms into the sleeves. He settled it around me and made a sound of approval.

I wrinkled my nose. "What is this thing made of?"

"Coat fabric."

I spun. "Coat fabric?" I scoffed. "What the hell is coat fabric?"

"You hate it." He frowned.

The hurt in his voice made me straighten. "Not at all! It's just heavier than I imagined."

"I want you to be warm." His cool-toned eyes met mine, sincerity in their depths. "I'm just trying to take care of my girl."

I smoothed my hands over the coat. It was heavy, and the material wasn't anything I would have chosen on my own. I couldn't say that to him. Not after he seemed so proud he'd bought me a coat.

"Thank you, Alex. I love it."

"You'll wear it, then?"

"Of course. Just because you gave it to me."

"That's why he was so insistent," I said, realizing exactly why he'd wanted me to wear this coat. It was *bulletproof.*

"Miss?" the doctor said.

I glanced up. "I, uh, I didn't know it was bulletproof."

He didn't seem to know what to make of that, but the bewilderment on my face must have convinced him. "Well, I still need to check you for injuries, make sure where the bullet hit the material, you aren't too badly injured."

I submitted to the exam, answering questions when spoken to, but not clearheaded enough to ask any of my own.

Had he known something like this was going to happen? Is that why he bought me that coat?

Someone snapped their fingers in front of my face, and I jolted. "Sorry," I said.

The doctor was standing there frowning. "I've completed my examination."

I nodded.

"You appear to be in good health, aside from the bruising and slight swelling on your lower right shoulder where the bullet hit the coat."

I nodded.

"You will likely have some soreness for a few days. Nothing an over-the-counter anti-inflammatory can't help."

"That's good," I said, still trying to process everything, still trying to make sense of it all.

"Your wrist," he said, glancing down.

I covered the bandage with my other hand. "That was a previous injury. It's just sprained."

"And the stitches in your cheek?" He pressed.

"From the same unrelated accident."

"Sabrina!" a man roared from out in the hallway.

I bolted upright. "Alex!"

"Sir!" someone out in the hall yelled. "Sir!"

The curtain separating me from the rest of the ER was pulled roughly back.

"I beg your pardon, sir!" The doctor bristled.

"Christ!" Alex heaved, relief making his shoulders sag. "I thought I was going to have to search every damn room in this place."

"They wouldn't let you back?" I worried.

"This is against policy," a nurse said, storming in behind him.

"Then call the police chief," Alex said softly, his eyes sweeping over me.

"It's fine!" I said, imploring the doctor. "He's with me. He's… important."

The doctor waved away the nurse threatening to throw him out and then glanced between us both. "Miss, I have to ask. All of these injuries you have… Do you feel safe at home?"

Alex laughed. Then he laughed again.

A quiet calm dropped over him, and then the laughter died away, leaving behind a cold silence that made my toes curl into the soles of my feet.

He swung around, fully facing the man who just dared to imply Alex was the reason I had so many injuries.

"It's hospital policy," the doctor said, taking a step away from Alex.

"I've had about enough of your hospital policy for one night," Alex remarked, utterly calm.

The doctor swallowed.

"Alex," I said, grabbing the back of his shirt. "Stop it."

"I would never, *not ever*, hurt her. In fact, I would kill anyone who tried." Alex went on. His voice was so cold, so utterly even that it was absolutely impossible to think he was lying. He glanced around to me, the look in his eyes melting. "The coat worked?"

I nodded. "It worked."

His entire body sagged. Reaching behind where I was gripping his shirt, he took my hand and threaded our fingers together.

He looked back at the doctor. "How's her injuries?"

"Minor."

Alex made a satisfied sound. "You can go now."

The doctor left, followed closely by the nurses standing there gaping.

"That was so mean." I admonished him.

His arms wrapped around me, pulling me into his chest, and a great, heavy sigh released into the air over my head. "For a minute there, I thought that coat didn't work."

I pulled back. "Why didn't you tell me this was a bulletproof coat?"

"I didn't want to scare you any more than you already were." His face darkened. "I didn't actually think it would be necessary."

"You didn't think it would be necessary," I repeated, a little unbelieving.

Alex's hands closed over my shoulders and squeezed. "What the fuck were you thinking tonight?"

"What?"

"You ran in front of a bullet," he bit out, his fingers digging into my skin.

"You were going to get shot!" I cried. "You almost died!"

"You don't ever get between me and a bullet. Me and anything, ever again!"

"Where's your bulletproof coat?" I yelled, shoving him back. "If you aren't going to wear one, then I damn well will jump in front of you!"

His eyes went icy. The flat, dead way he regarded me almost stole my breath. "You had no idea you were even wearing something that could protect you."

"Who cares?" I fumed, ignoring the stony way he spoke. "I will not ever stand by and let you get killed!"

"Yes! You will!" he roared.

The sudden burst of heat cut through me.

I drew backward, staring at him in shock.

A few choice curse words dropped out of his mouth, and he reached for the hem of his shirt. The second he lifted it, I saw the vest strapped to his chest.

The relief was so strong it made me dizzy. "You mean to tell me I almost had a heart attack right there in the middle of that crowd because I was so scared for you, and you were wearing that? This whole time!"

"I'm not a careless man, Sabrina," he informed me quietly. "When I said I would protect you, that meant protecting myself so I could keep my word."

A sob broke out of me, and I sank forward, crying. All the anger and fear drained right out of me as hoarse sobs wracked my body.

Alex came forward, scooping me into his chest and using gentle hands to stroke my back. "It's okay now, kitten. Everything's okay."

"Y-y-you sh-should have told me."

"Yeah." He agreed.

"I thought you were gonna die," I wailed.

He held me tighter. "I'm not gonna die. I'm right here. I'm right here with you."

I pulled back, sucking in a deep breath. "Where were you? Where did you run off to?"

He brushed a few tears off my cheeks before resting each palm on the bed on either side of my hips. Leaning close, he spoke quietly. "I went to track the man who shot you."

"Did you find him?"

A muscle in his jaw worked, his eyes flashing before he glanced away. "No. He was gone."

My eyes searched his. Anger and ice burned there… It was a frightening combination.

My voice wobbled. "I saw that red dot on your back, and I was so afraid I would be too late."

"You took a bullet for me."

I shook my head. "Sort of."

"Don't ever do something so reckless ever again," he bit out, this time keeping his anger in check.

My eyes narrowed, and frustration filled my voice. "You can do it for me, but I can't for you?"

"That's right."

"That makes no sense."

He grabbed my chin, forcing me to look into his frozen-over stare. "If you want to protect me at all, then it's yourself you need to guard."

"I don't understand," I whispered.

He drew back, his fingers caressing me before pulling completely away. "Saving my life means nothing if it costs yours, because my life would be over anyway."

My breath caught.

"Understand?"

I nodded once. The ferocity with which he spoke left me unable to say anything at all.

"Good," he remarked, satisfied. "C'mon now. We're going home."

Home.

Since my clothes were cut away, all I had on was a flimsy hospital gown. Alex pulled off his jacket and put it around me.

Before we stepped out of the cubical, I tugged his hand, making him turn back.

"Even though we almost died…" I began, making his eyes narrow with anger. "This was still the best birthday I've ever had."

His entire expression changed and softened, a small smile tugging at his lips. "It's not over yet."

Alex

Something shifty was going on. The fact that these men were so hell bent on making Mercer pay for whatever he'd done to piss them off by going after his sister was proof.

As ex-army elites, our identities were nearly impossible to find. Buried deep under government tape, firewalls, and false information. This included the identities of those in our lives who could be considered weaknesses. I'd known Merc a long time, and even though we'd parted ways on less-than-good terms, I still knew him.

I was certain, without a shadow of a doubt, that he wouldn't do anything that would lead the type of men we were now dealing with to Sabrina.

What's more? These men had figured out very quickly that the only way to get to Sabrina was by taking me out of the equation. That meant they not only knew about Sabrina's identity, but they knew about mine.

I should have been flattered they viewed me as so ruthless and intimidating the only way to get around me was to kill me outright.

I wasn't.

I was annoyed and growing more restless with each passing day.

Something niggled at the back of my mind. It felt like there was a loose thread hanging from the hem of my jeans and it continuously brushed against my foot, sort of like a phantom spider, yet every time I looked to see the cause, I never found it.

I wanted to make some calls, a few discreet inquiries, but I kept holding myself back. There was no one to trust. If there was, Merc wouldn't have showed up on my doorstep.

I needed information, but that info could come at the cost of Sabrina's life. That was a price I just wasn't willing to pay.

So here I was, in a holding pattern, feeling like a tiger in a triangle cage.

"Halloween is next week," Brina said, coming up behind me, wrapping her arms around my middle. "You gonna let me give out candy to trick-or-treaters?"

I gazed out across the yard. It was a cold day, the sky gray and overcast. More leaves lay on the ground now than clung to the trees.

"You know I can't let you do that, kitten," I said, trying to soften the answer with the pet name.

She made a sound. "Please?"

I looked down to where she grasped me. Her wrist was still wrapped, the cuts and scrapes on her hands almost healed.

"Next year." I promised.

"I feel like a prisoner," she muttered, pulling away to drop down on the couch.

We'd barely gone anywhere since her birthday. It was just too risky, and seeing her on the ground with that bullet hole in her back scared me more than I was willing to admit.

"Wanna watch a movie?" I offered, still scanning the yard.

"I'll make some popcorn," she announced and went into the kitchen.

A few minutes later, the sound of popping kernels filled the air, along with the unmistakable scent of the popcorn.

"You're stinking up my house!" I hollered.

"Get over it!" she hollered back.

I grinned and moved from the window.

I needed to figure out my next move. If Daniel couldn't get this job done, then I was going to have to step in. Blowing what little cover we had left might be the only way to do it.

Maybe I could send Sabrina away somewhere… until this was all finished. The thought made me feel itchy and raw. Instant denial poured through me, but the logical part of me, the one that lived at subzero, knew it might be the only way.

"Do you want a beer?" Sabrina called out.

Moving into the kitchen, I rested against the wall, watching as she tried to throw a piece of popcorn into the air and catch it with her mouth. She missed.

I laughed, and she glanced over at me. "Think you can do better?"

I made a rude noise, shoving off the wall, and grabbed up a piece of the white stuff. It landed dead center in my mouth on the first try. I grinned as I chewed, then winked.

"Showoff," she muttered.

Chuckling, I picked her up and planted her on the island, then held a piece of popcorn to her lips. "Here."

She took it and chewed. "Needs more butter."

"You doing okay, kitten?" I asked, touching the tip of her nose.

"Don't I look like I am?"

"You've been kinda restless the last few nights," I pointed out.

"You're restless, too."

I nodded. "Have you been having dreams?" I pressed. "You know, about what happened at the Fest."

Her eyes turned downcast. In her lap, her fingers fidgeted. "Maybe one or two."

"You can talk to—"

A sharp rapping on the back door made her jump and fall into me. Intuitively, I moved to block her, lifting her off the island and depositing her behind me.

"Is it Liam?" she whispered, her hand fisting in my shirt.

"Liam's at work."

"Then Bellamy?"

"Bellamy would have called first."

"Alex…"

"Stay here," I ordered and went to the back door. The gun resting in the waistband of my sweats was a comforting reminder that I had the upper hand.

"Who is it?" I called out from behind the door.

No one answered.

A few seconds later, I heard a truck start up and drive off. My body relented. I knew that was the sound of the mail truck.

Still being cautious, I opened the door and looked out. No one was there, the taillights of the large truck were disappearing, and there was a brown box on the porch.

Pulling the door open wide, I said, "It's just the mail."

"Did you order something?" she asked, coming across the room.

"Stay there," I commanded. Her footsteps faltered, and I glanced around. "I didn't order anything. Let me check the box."

Instead of bringing it in, I went outside with the package to inspect it. When I was certain it was just mail, I opened the door with it in my arms, nearly hitting Sabrina with the edge.

"I told you to stay inside, woman."

"I am!"

"That doesn't mean to be a stalker on the other side of the door. If this had been a bomb, you'd have blown up!"

Her eyes widened. "Is it a bomb?"

"No."

She rolled her eyes and reached for it. "What is it?"

I held it up out of her reach and pulled the pocket knife out of my sweats to cut open the top. "Let me look."

She waited while I did, lifting the lid to glance inside.

"It's for you," I said, stepping back from the package.

"Me?"

I nodded.

As anxious as she was to look before, now she hesitated.

"Looks to me like your brother remembered your birthday."

Her eyes grew twice their normal size, and she gasped. Rushing across the floor, she grabbed the box and ripped up the top. "He's never forgotten, not ever. Not even now... I miss him so much."

With a smile, she glanced down into the brown box. Then everything about her changed.

"Sabrina?" Concern washed over me as I watched her. Lips rolling inward, skin turning the color of ash, and the way her trembling fingers moved turtle slow toward what was inside.

"Brina," I said again.

She was lost it seemed. Lost to whatever was in that box. I knew the second her hand closed around it because a rough sound vibrated her throat. I started forward. She moved, pulling free what seemed to be upsetting her so much.

"No," she croaked, staring down at the gift in her hand. "Please, no."

I frowned, not quite understanding why something so innocent could get this sort of reaction. Her head fell forward, the hair swishing over her shoulders like a curtain, and beneath it, her body vibrated.

Both hands closed around the gift, squeezing until they were stark white.

"Noo," she crooned, emotion building in the room, making the hair on the back of my neck stand tall.

"Sabrina," I said, moving closer.

She flinched when I reached out to touch her, so I drew back.

"What's wrong?" I demanded. "I don't understand why you're so upset."

"This isn't a birthday gift." Her voice was so hoarse and throaty I had to replay the words over in my head a few times before I could even understand what she said.

Confusion cloaked me, but so did wariness. "Then what is it?"

Her hands clutched the soft fabric, digging into the brown fur of the teddy bear. Slowly, her eyes lifted, and I was struck by how hollow and empty she suddenly appeared.

After several attempts at swallowing and a single tear dripping from her eye and rolling down her cheek, she answered.

"It's good-bye."

Sabrina

I had one memory of my father.

In it, I couldn't see his face or even the color of his hair or hear the sound of his voice. Sometimes, the faint smell of coffee made me think of him, but even that was few and far between.

All I remembered was the day he left. At three years old, it was a wonder I even recalled that. Standing here now, clutching this teddy bear, I realized it wasn't really him I remembered, but the moment my then nine-year-old brother decided even if our father didn't want me, he did.

Reliving the memory now as an adult was much different from the eyes of a child. I comprehend now the enormity of what my brother did that day and the fact he kept to his vow even though he made it when he was so very young.

It was all the proof I would ever need to know that Daniel was probably the best man I would ever know.

Silent, pain-heavy tears tracked over my cheeks as I gazed through blurry eyes at the brown bear I hated but also wanted to clutch close.

The door to the bedroom stuck, which made it hard to open and impossible to close. The squeaking sound it made when it moved was ear piercing, so I often just squeezed in and out between the space it always seemed to settle.

I was wearing a pair of blue polyester shorts with rainbow stripes on the sides. I hated them because they made my skin itch, but I didn't change because they were clean and my other pair smelled.

Sitting in the center of my bed, my arms wrapped around the stuffed toy in my lap, I was sad. I didn't really understand what

Daddy told me a few moments ago, but I knew it was probably a big deal because he'd given me this present.

After that, I heard him and Mommy yelling. They screamed so loud I escaped onto the bed and hid beneath my covers.

A little while later, the yelling stopped, and the house was very quiet. I was still too scared to come out, so I sat in the middle of the bed, rocking back and forth.

Daniel slipped inside the door, not making a sound. The door never squeaked when he came in. He said he moved like a cat, and I believed him. His hands were in his pockets, his head low against his chest, when he stepped up beside the bed.

I glanced up, wiping the tears off my cheeks, and looked at him.

"Dad left," he said.

I nodded. "When is he coming back?"

"He's not."

"Not ever?"

"Not ever."

I started to cry again. "I don't like Mommy. She's mean!"

"Shh!" he hushed, reaching out and grabbing my arms.

I stared up at him, eyes wide.

"Shh, she's already drinking. Don't make it worse." Daniel let go of my arms and looked down at what was in my lap. "What's that?"

"Daddy gave it to me. He said it would take care of me now."

Anger bunched up Daniel's face, and he wrenched the bear from my arms.

"Mine!" I tried to snatch it back.

He threw it across the room, and I tried to climb off the bed to get it.

"No, Brin-Brin." He scolded me. "You don't need that bear to take care of you. You have me."

"You'll be my bear?" I asked him.

He nodded. "Forever and ever."

Every night after that, for months, he'd sit on the edge of my bed and hold my hand until I fell asleep.

"I have no idea what happened to that bear after that night. I never saw it again. I never looked for it. I didn't need to."

"Sabrina." Alex reached for me, but I backed out of arm's reach.

I'd already cried so many tears the neckline of my T-shirt was already soaked. My breathing was hitched, and my ears felt hot. Everything in my head was sluggish and thick…

"If he's sending me this now, it's because he knows he isn't ever coming back."

Even though I hated everything that bear represented, I clutched it against my chest with a sob so great it made my throat raw. "He can't be my bear anymore, so he sent this one instead."

More sobs forced their way out, and I slid down toward the floor until I was nothing but that three-year-old girl sitting on the floor, clutching a bear, and crying.

Dropping beside me, Alex moved so I was positioned between his legs and his body could surround mine. The warmth coming off his skin made me feel dead inside, which only made me cry harder.

"Kitten," he said, his voice pained and helpless.

I turned into him, holding the bear between us, and openly wept until my voice went hoarse and my eyes nearly swelled shut.

I was trembling like a frail leaf about to be defeated by the winter wind when Alex drew back. Instead of clutching at him, I clutched at the bear.

Is this all I have left of my brother?

Is he really not coming back?

Alex's hand felt especially large when it rubbed over my back in soothing motions. "Maybe it doesn't mean what you think."

"I know what this means," I insisted. "It means he couldn't find a way to end this, so he's taking the only other solution he thinks he has. His life for mine."

Alex was silent, his hand pausing in the center of my back.

Another sob ripped out of me because he knew I was right. It was exactly what my brother would do. There was nothing I could do to stop him.

The cold, hard fact was that it was probably already done.

The horror of that slapped me so hard I fell backward. Alex clutched at me, trying to keep me upright. Evading him, I scrambled to my feet, a wild, impatient feeling pummeling me. "When was this mailed?" I yelled. "I need to know how long ago he sent this!"

I rushed to the box, clutching the bear in one hand and grabbing the box with the other. It fell off the counter and banged on the floor with my jerky movements, and I started crying once more.

"Okay, hey." Gently, Alex grabbed my arm and pulled me into his chest. I melted there, begging him to tell me the date.

Still holding me, he picked up the box and checked the outside. "It's unmarked, sweetheart. No return address. No postmark. Nothing."

"That's impossible!" I denied, even though I knew it was entirely possible because my brother was involved.

"I have to know!" I fumed, pacing away from Alex. When he tried to grab me back, I used all my weight to shove him away.

My chest was heaving and my heart pounding when his quiet voice cut through my anguish.

"There's a note."

I spun so fast I tumbled over. Alex moved, grabbing me by the arm and keeping me on my feet.

"Let me see!" I snatched it out of his hand, staring down at the folded piece of paper.

It wasn't anything fancy. There wasn't even an envelope, and my name was scrawled across the front with a pen.

In that moment, it was the most prized possession I would ever have.

I unfolded the small sheet and stared down at the familiar handwriting. Fresh tears welled and rained over, making it impossible to read or see.

I held it out to Alex and begged, "Read it to me."

"Maybe we should wait a few—"

"Read it, goddammit!" I yelled, then dissolved once more into a fit of tears.

Alex took the letter and cleared his throat. His eyes skimming the words before he read it out loud. A dark aura settled around him, and sorrow etched into every expression on his face.

Please don't hate me for this. This is the only way I can keep the promise I made you.

I've always loved you more than anyone. Move on now and be happy.

—Daniel

"No!" I cried, lunging forward to rip the paper out of Alex's hand. I read the words over and over again until they were burned into my broken soul.

"Why would he do this to me?" I asked Alex. "Why?"

"Because he loves you."

"If this is love, then I don't want it!" I raged, slapping the note down on the counter and moving away.

"You're going to make yourself sick." Alex worried, coming over to me. "Calm down."

His arms tried to wrap around me and pull me close.

I turned and slammed my fists into his chest. "Calm down? My brother is dead because of me, and you want me to calm down!"

Alex let me pummel him. I hit him until the sides of my hands ached and my arms burned from exhaustion. Just before I slid into a puddle on the floor, he lifted me and cradled me against his chest.

Carrying me into the living room, he sat down on the couch, holding me in his lap.

A long time later, when I was so exhausted my eyes wouldn't even open, I found the strength to speak. "Do you think he's already dead?"

Alex didn't say anything for a long time.

Finally, he gave me the truth. "Yes."

I spent the rest of the night clutching the bear, while Alex clutched me.

Alex

Death isn't hard for the deceased, but for the ones they leave behind.

I knew if Daniel sacrificed himself for his sister, it was because there was no other way out. He did what he had to do to ensure no one else would be coming for Sabrina. With him gone, there was no need to use her as revenge or a pawn.

She was safe now.

But she was broken.

And because of that, I sat awake for many nights, holding her as she cried, remembering my friend, and feeling like his death was for nothing.

439

Sabrina

I couldn't sleep anymore. I'd slept so much it felt like a heavy weight now, like a suffocating Band-aid, not allowing a wound any kind of air.

I knew the air would burn. I knew waking up would hurt like hell and make me wish for sleep again. I couldn't succumb any longer. I had something I needed to do.

What I needed was a jolt of life. A jumpstart to my crumbling heart.

The only thing that would give me that was the man lying beside me.

I didn't know how long I'd been grieving. I didn't know how many pounds of tears I'd cried. I couldn't recall nights and days passing, but I did know, through it all, he'd been there.

His job of protecting me was over. The promise he'd made to my brother fulfilled. Still, I needed him. The spark only he could provide was the only thing that might keep me alive.

Beneath my cold hands, his skin was supple and warm. The contours of his body were still familiar, as were the sounds the sheets made when he turned toward me.

His hand cupped the side of my face, then brushed the unkempt hair away from my cheek.

"Hey," he whispered, his voice thick with sleep.

I didn't say anything, instead just gazing at his face through the dark.

"It's the middle of the night," he said. "What's wrong?"

"Make love to me," I whispered, my voice sounding foreign and raw to my own ears.

Alex didn't hesitate or try to tell me it was too soon. He trusted the fact I knew what I needed and didn't even blink when I told him it was him.

Sliding across the mattress, his nearly naked body met mine. The hand in my hair curled around the back of my neck, but he didn't pull me close. Instead, he came to me.

At first, he was the one kissing, grazing his lips over mine. When he started to pull back, my hand slapped over his wrist and squeezed until he lowered his head again.

The warm, slightly rough feeling of his tongue dragged over my dry lips and elicited a sound of pleasure that gave me hope. Gradually, I started to kiss him back, greedily drinking in everything he so willingly gave.

When his hand pushed against my shoulder, I rolled, my body flat against the mattress as he rose above me.

His eyes were like a night-light in the dark, offering direction, guiding the way back to life. Though he was between my legs, he didn't enter my body. Instead, he kissed across my jaw, down my neck, and over my collarbone.

My aching body relaxed, going boneless beneath him, and I surrendered everything I had left. Alex kissed and stroked my body, doing such a careful and thorough job that when the first sparks of golden light erupted inside me, I almost seized in shock.

His patience was unmatched, skill level undefeated. The passion inside him coated me like a shadow. I started moving beneath him, writhing a little with every stroke and kiss he gave. Want and desire blossomed inside me, proving not all was completely lost.

When at last he joined our bodies, pain wasn't far behind. Not because he was hurting me… but because he was proving to me I was still alive. That I could still feel deeply.

It was hard to accept life when someone you loved more than yourself was no longer living. It was hard to even fathom how you could move on when that meant you had to let go.

The sensation of him filling me up made me feel less empty. The rocking motion of his hips as he thrust deep soothed my roughest edges.

When I thought he might rise farther above me, he didn't. Sliding his arm under my body, he lifted me off the mattress, holding me against his chest, and pushed deep. There wasn't a part of us that wasn't touching, every inch of me against every inch of him.

Tilting his hips, his rigid length rubbed against a spot inside me, and pleasure bloomed over my body. I moaned as I felt it spreading like the sun on a new morning, the warmth and life of the orgasm diffusing the very worst of my pain.

We stayed linked for a long while after we'd both finished. Feeling his heart beating against mine was comforting and reminded me that I was still alive.

Finally, he rolled, taking me with him. I stayed in his arms until he drifted back to sleep.

Slowly, I slid out from under him, staring down at his handsome face.

"Thank you," I whispered, kissing my fingers, then gently holding them to his lips.

Slipping out of bed, I dressed in the dark, seeing clearly, as if I were standing in the light. After grabbing his keys off the kitchen counter, I stood at the back door, glancing back toward the bedroom.

I knew he would be angry when he woke up and found me gone, but this was something I needed to do. Something I *wanted* to do alone.

Alex

Golden rays of the morning sun peeked through the window, offering warmth to an otherwise cold room. The temperature outside was dropping daily. Soon, snow would fall and coat everything with white and our busiest season here at BearPaw would begin.

My body was languid this morning, a feeling I'd almost forgotten. Tension and worry had been so constant as of late it was foreign to feel it taking a back seat.

It was the first time she reached for me. The first time since news of Daniel arrived that she finally accepted any kind of comfort. The relief of that was so great I'd passed out with her in my arms, finally succumbing to the rest my body had been begging for but had been denied.

Feeling the cold draft, I shifted, too lazy to get out of bed and start a fire yet but more than willing to use our body heat to keep us warm.

The space where she normally lay was empty. Any warmth that might have lingered on the sheets from her body had long since turned cold.

Springing up, I glanced around the bedroom, calling out her name.

Silence was my only answer.

Kicking off the covers, I pushed open the bathroom door, expecting to hear her fuss about the fact that I never knocked.

She wasn't there either.

"Brina!" I hollered, snagging a hoodie off the dresser on my way through the room.

Curb your anger, man. She's probably in the kitchen, maybe finally willing to eat. Don't make her upset by acting like a caveman.

The interior warning was hard to yield to. In truth, panic seized my chest and tingled my limbs with the urge to rush. "Brina, honey, you finally feel up to eating?" I called out, keeping the edge out of my voice.

She wasn't in the kitchen.

Or the living room.

Sabrina wasn't anywhere inside this house.

"Sabrina!" I yelled out the back door, panic making my voice husky.

When she didn't answer, I slammed the door, making the entire wall shudder, and stomped back into the kitchen. The force of my movements sent a gust of air across the counter, and a note I hadn't seen before fluttered to the ground.

Snatching it up, I read.

I have to go. I'm sorry.

She had to go? Go where?

The paper collapsed under the pressure of my fist. Fuming, I paced the length of the kitchen and back again. "Stupid woman!" I roared, chest heaving.

How could she just walk out like that?

I rushed to the window over the sink and gazed out. The rental I was using while my Hummer was being fixed was gone.

Red-hot anger exploded within me, and a growl burst out of my throat. With the force of it, I swung my fist, punching the first thing it came into contact with.

The cardboard box that stupid bear came in went flying across the kitchen, hitting the wall, and smacked onto the ground.

Shame burned through me, and a little bit of reality rushed back in. Sabrina wanted that box. Even though it represented nothing but pain, she begged me to keep it. It was the last thing she would ever receive from her brother.

Cursing, I stalked forward and snatched the stupid thing off the ground. The force of my movements sent something flinging out from the inside. It made a small sound when it hit the floor and rolled all the way into the living room and beneath the sofa.

"What the fuck?" I muttered, setting the box carefully on the kitchen table.

Feeling around beneath the sofa, my hand closed over the object, and I picked it up. It seemed familiar to me even before I opened my fist to look at it. Straightening from the floor, I gazed down at the coin lying in the center of my palm.

Flashes of my army days hit me full force. Sights, sounds, and memories passed through my head like a movie.

Blinking, I gazed down at the special coin that was significant to our secret elite team. No one outside of us knew this coin even existed. They weren't sold like all the other collector military coins. These were only earned…

So few of us had one.

Clutching the cool metal in my palm, I turned back to look at the box. Why hadn't I seen this before? Snatching the box, I searched it over painstakingly to make sure there was nothing else I'd missed. Upon inspection, I was pretty sure the coin had been stuck between one of the flaps, and through the trauma of realizing what his gift and note meant, no one bothered looking for anything else.

I glanced back at the coin again, realization dawning.

This hadn't been a gift for Sabrina.

This coin was for me. It was a warning. Daniel was telling me that even though he was dead, this might not be completely over.

Every filthy curse I knew dropped out of my mouth like a bomb as fear unlike anything I'd felt before terrorized my heart.

Snatching my cell up, I dialed Sabrina, praying to God she would be smart and answer.

When the automated message came on, signaling her phone wasn't even powered on, I put my hand through the closest wall.

"Sabrina!" I screamed and ran back into the bedroom. Ignoring the blood dripping from my knuckles, I called Liam.

"Alex?"

"I need a car. I need a car right the fuck now."

Holy shit, please, God, don't let me be too late.

Sabrina

I had to get the landlord to let me into my apartment. The second I walked through the door, I felt like I was stepping into the home of a stranger.

These weren't my things anymore. This wasn't my safe haven or anywhere I wanted to be.

This place was now just four walls, an empty shell. All that existed here was memories from the past, things I no longer wanted or needed. I cried, walking through, mourning what would never be again and the girl I used to be.

The flight from Colorado had been long and restless. More than once, I caught the wary looks from the flight attendants and even other passengers. I ignored them, pretending instead to be asleep. Every once in a while, a tear would leak from beneath my lids, and I'd use the sleeve of the hoodie I'd stolen from Alex to soak it up.

He'd be awake by now. He'd tried to call. My phone rested, turned off, in my pocket because I knew if I heard it ring and saw Alex's name on the screen, I would have answered.

There would be time for me and Alex later.

Right now, this was Daniel's time.

I took a shower in my old bathroom, using familiar products that only reminded me they weren't familiar anymore. The jeans I pulled on from my closet were looser than they used to be, further proving the things here weren't mine anymore. Even though Alex's sweatshirt was too big and less than fresh from the plane ride, I put it back on anyway.

I moved, woodenly placing some belongings into a large bag. Mostly photos, gifts from Daniel, and the purse I'd left behind. The landlord could deal with the rest of this stuff. I didn't care where it went.

Once I was done, I left the final month's rent on the kitchen counter and walked out without looking back or locking the door.

Going to Daniel's apartment made me far more emotional than my own. The pain was so sharp it was hard to stand upright as it stabbed at me over and over again.

Everything I looked at reminded me of him. Even the scent still lingering in the air was his. In some ways, it was comforting because it was as if there were still a piece of him here with me. But then harsh reality would overcome that little bit of hope to remind me this was all just a giant scene of what would never be again.

Scents faded. This apartment would be rented to someone new. Memories would stick with me, but in the headspace I occupied right now, that wasn't comforting at all.

After wandering around aimlessly for a while, I went to the hall closet where my brother kept a bunch of empty boxes. He moved so often he stopped getting rid of them, instead just storing them for next time.

I thought you said you were staying here for a while, I said the day he moved in and placed them inside.

Don't you worry, Brin-Brin. I'll never go too far from you.

Tears dripped onto the cardboard when I lined them up on the table. I didn't want much from my apartment, but I wanted everything that had been Daniel's.

My stomach grumbled, a sound I was used to but growing tired of. My body felt weak, my eyes strained and grainy. Going into the kitchen, I put on some coffee and found a box of crackers in the cupboard.

I forced down the crackers and drank the coffee while I painstakingly packed up what was left of my brother's life.

I was so angry with him for doing this, for thinking my life was somehow more valuable than his. The anger that should have propelled me forward exhausted me, leaving me drained and unable to even feel pissed.

I just wanted him back.

The coffee and crackers didn't do a good enough job sustaining me, and I stumbled and nearly fainted, catching myself on a box and spilling everything I'd packed inside.

Defeated, I shuffled to the couch and lay down. I was drifting off to sleep when there was a knock on the front door. My first thought was of Alex, that maybe he'd somehow figured out where I went. Then I thought perhaps it was the landlord because someone notified him there was someone finally here.

I went to the door, legs wobbling and stomach jittery, not even considering how shitty I would appear to my brother's landlord. What did it matter anyway?

It wasn't the landlord. It wasn't Alex either.

I gasped a little when I saw the large man standing there on the threshold. "Rush," I said, surprise clear in my tone.

"Sabrina." The look in his eyes was tender and sorrowful. "As soon as I heard about Daniel, I had to come."

The grief in his tone reminded me of my own. My lower lip wobbled, and tears welled.

He made a pity-filled sound and came forward, wrapping me in a tight hug. Against my ear, he whispered, "Mercer was a damn fine man. It was an honor to be at his side during our time in the army. He wasn't just my friend. He was my brother."

I cried into my brother's friend's shoulder, clinging to his jacket for support. I hadn't seen Rush in almost a year, but the bond their elite team had was such that it didn't surprise me he came.

"Come on now," he murmured, lifting me off my feet and walking into the apartment to shut the door. After another brief hug, I pulled back, swiping at the tears on my cheeks.

"You look awful," he said, eyes moving over my face.

"Yeah, well, it's justified."

He reached out to grasp my hand. "What can I do for you? What do you need?"

I shook my head. "Unless you can bring my brother back to me, nothing."

"I'm so sorry, Sabrina."

"Did you want some coffee?" I asked, going ahead into the kitchen to get him some anyway. "I don't have cream, but I remember you drink it black anyway."

"You remembered," he said, coming into the doorway of the small galley-style kitchen.

"Of course." Back when the team was still together, I saw the three men my brother practically lived with often.

After pouring the brew, I handed the cup over, trying to ignore the way the liquid sloshed around in the mug beneath my shaking hand.

Rush accepted the cup and took a drink. His dark hair was much longer than it used to be. It fell around his face, waving to just below his chin. The back was even longer, the ends flipping up around the collar of his jacket.

His eyes were also dark, there was stubble on his usually shaven face, and there were dark circles beneath his eyes.

Even when they'd all just come home from a hell mission, Rush never looked this bad.

"How are you?" I asked.

Lowering the mug from his mouth, his lips pulled up slightly. "Guess I don't look much better than you, eh?" He sighed, setting aside the mug. "Mercer's death hit me pretty hard."

I swallowed.

"I always thought the four of us were invincible."

"Until Wells died," I whispered, remembering the fourth man on their team. His death was the beginning of the end for Mercer's team. Shortly after, Alex resigned, leaving behind just Daniel and Rush. Nothing was ever the same again.

Rush nodded glumly. "Now there's only two of us left."

Pain pierced my chest as I wondered where Alex was and how angry I'd made him.

"Have you seen Ice lately?" Rush asked, glancing around. "Is he here, too?"

Prickles of warning raised all the hairs on my neck and arms. "Why would Alex be here?"

Why would he ask me about Alex? No one knew I'd been staying with him all this time.

Rush shrugged nonchalantly. "Figured he would come, too. Pay his respects."

"He isn't here," I said, picking up the coffee I'd abandoned a while ago. It had since gone cold, so I dumped it out and got some fresh.

"How did you find out about Daniel's death?" I asked, keeping my voice conversational. I hadn't told anyone. As far as I knew, no one else would know that

Daniel was gone. Especially not a man that hadn't been around for at least a year.

"I got a call from someone in the chain of command. Someone we used to work with. He said a contracted job went bad, and Mercer…" He cleared his throat and shook his head. "I couldn't believe it. I thought that bastard would outlive us all." He smiled, but I didn't return it.

"It's not like the army to give out that kind of information."

Rush straightened. "Of course not. But he knew how close Merc and me were."

I nodded. His answer made sense. Still, something didn't feel right.

"Thank you for coming," I said, trying to move through the kitchen and out into the living room. Rush stepped in front of me, blocking my path. Swallowing back the sudden fear slamming against my ribcage, I forced myself to smile up to him. "Maybe you can help me carry some of these boxes down to my car."

Rush's eyes bounced between mine, searching for something… something I knew damn well not to let him see.

I held his gaze until he looked away first.

"Of course. Anything for Merc's sister."

I brushed past him, and this time he let me by. "So what have you been up to lately?" I asked. "Are you still doing contract work for the government?"

"I stepped away from that," he answered. "Too many rules to follow. Too much red tape."

My eyes snapped up, focusing on the wall across the room. *Get out. Get out of this house right now.*

Urgency screamed in my bones. Adrenaline poured through my limbs, making me even shakier than I already was.

"Oh well," I said, forcing lightness into my tone. "I hope whatever you're doing now is a better fit."

His hand clamped around my wrist, and I gasped loudly. I hadn't even heard him move. I didn't know he'd gotten so close.

"Cut the crap, Sabrina," Rush said, yanking me around. I stumbled and pitched to the side. He yanked me up, shoving me back to my feet. "You know, don't you?"

"Kn-know?" I stuttered.

He laughed, his face twisted into a vile expression. "I know you aren't stupid. Daniel made sure of that. He thought he was teaching you to protect yourself. Instead, he just made you more of a target."

"What are you talking about?" I asked, my voice weak.

"He just couldn't mind his own goddamn business. I warned him, but he kept poking around. Hell, I even offered him a generous cut."

My brows furrowed, and Rush pulled my wrist, making me tumble closer to him. "He could have retired off what I would have paid him. He could have spent the rest of his life fawning over his baby sister. Instead, what's left of him is rotting away in some hole-in-the-wall country where no one gives a damn."

His words shocked me and conjured up an image I would be haunted by forever. Anger burned through my veins, fighting some of the weakness I felt. I wrenched free of his grip, ignoring the pain burning through my wrist.

"How dare you?" I yelled. "What have you done to my brother?"

"I only gave him everything he deserved." Rush fumed, his nostrils flaring. "That stupid son of a bitch dug around until he had enough evidence to not only shut down my operation, but bury me in a jail cell for the rest of my life. He was such a fucking Boy Scout, refusing to look the other way."

My head was spinning. Disbelief clung to me like a second skin, making it hard to wade through what I was hearing. "You mean you killed my brother?"

Rush clicked his tongue. "Not me, but I was the one who ordered it."

The confession robbed me of thought for a few moments. Then blinding anger took over. With a yell, I lunged at him, my open palm connecting with his face. "You son of a bitch!" I screamed, lunging for him again.

He caught my arm and twisted it around behind me, but I continued to struggle. Rush wrapped around me from behind, locking his arms in place. "That wasn't very smart," he intoned against my cheek.

I turned and spit on him.

He shoved me away, and I fell into the couch. Before I could stand up, he grabbed the back of my shirt and pulled me around. He backhanded me across the face, making my head snap back on my shoulders.

The stitches I had before were gone, but the wound was still healing. Feeling the warm trickle of blood run down my face, I knew it reopened.

I lunged at him again, and he shoved me back. "I will hit you again."

"How could you betray my brother that way?" I yelled. "Your country!"

"They betrayed me!" he screamed, the first real sign he was unhinged revealed. "I gave them everything when I was enlisted, and all I get is a measly twelve hundred dollars a month for keeping this country from falling apart!"

"This is about money?" I asked. "Have you no loyalty?"

"Loyalty is for cowards. Look where it got your brother."

I gasped, picked up the mug of coffee nearby, and threw it at him. The ceramic hit him in the cheek, hot liquid splashing all over his face and chest. The mug hit the coffee table when he batted it away, and it cracked almost perfectly in half.

"You bitch!" He snarled and came at me. I skirted back just out of reach.

"You're going to pay for what you did to my brother. I'll kill you myself!"

Calm washed over Rush. It was more frightening than anything else he'd displayed since stepping into this house. He pulled back, straightened to his full height, and adjusted his clothing as if his appearance meant something. "I came here today to see what you knew. I thought maybe I could let you live. Maybe you would be so broken about Merc's death that you wouldn't put the pieces together."

"I hope you rot in hell."

He smiled. "Silly girl. I've been to hell. More times than most could ever imagine. I thrive there… It makes me feel *alive*."

I ran toward my phone, but he beat me to it, picking up the device and throwing it against the wall, shattering it.

"I was hoping I wouldn't be the one to do this. I thought maybe sending men after you would get Mercer to back off."

"Daniel would never back down from you!" I hurled the words at him, chest heaving.

"Yes, well. Too bad for him it killed you both."

I took a step back when he took one forward. A light came into his eyes, one of enjoyment, one of animation. It showed me something.

I wasn't broken. Not really.

This is broken.

Something Rush had seen or done, or maybe a combination of heinous missions, shattered him. It turned him into a monster whose only way of feeling was through killing.

"This way is better for you, though. Those other men, I told them to make you suffer. I planned to let them do whatever they wanted because the more tortured you were, the greater the pain for Mercer. It's all mostly over now. Our secrets are protected, and my cover is intact. You're the last loose end, Sabrina. An annoying little fly buzzing overhead. Come over here to me. Come over and don't fight. I'll make it fast."

"Like hell I will," I said, picking up a lamp and swinging it like a bat.

It hit him in the center of the chest. He slumped forward in pain, and I dropped the light. The bulb shattered when it hit the floor, and I rushed toward the door.

Rush laughed, vaulted over the back of the couch, and grabbed me by the back of the neck.

I screamed and kicked, but my feet left the ground when he lifted me as though I weighed nothing at all.

"You're starting to piss me off," he disclosed.

I wrenched forward and bit his nose.

He screamed in pain and slapped me so hard with his free hand I flew out of his hold and dropped to the floor. Wrestling against the ringing in my ears, I moved to my feet. Large, dark boots appeared as I was scrambling. One toe drew back, and I braced myself.

His boot buried into my ribs, and I felt some of my bones snap.

I slumped to the floor on my side, balling into a fetal position as pain clouded my thoughts.

Rough hands reached down and grabbed the front of my sweatshirt, wrenching me up off the ground. I struggled to breath. The pain in my side was tremendous as I stared up into the eyes of a madman.

He smiled, eyes wild, and wrapped a hand around my neck. I began to choke and wheeze, sounds that seemed to make him happy.

Laughter rang out overhead, and his other hand closed around my neck. The pressure he applied was unmatched. It felt like a vise was crushing my windpipe. My vision began to dim, and thoughts of Alex filled what was left of my consciousness.

The faraway popping sound cut through some of the pain, and then I was gasping and writhing on the floor, sucking in air I thought I would never breathe again.

"Sabrina!" Alex fell to his knees beside me, his hands gentle when he pushed me onto my back. His eyes were dilated and wide, but everything else about his face was calm. "You're okay now." He promised. "I'm here now. Everything's okay."

I wheezed and coughed, tears streaming down my face.

A shadow moved behind Alex, and I screamed.

Swiftly, he stood and reached behind him, grabbing Rush and slamming him against the wall. I struggled to sit up, knowing I still had to fight.

Alex rammed his fist into Rush's stomach, and the man doubled over in pain. When he lifted his head to look at me, there was blood dripping from his lips, dribbling over his chin.

His face was ghostly, sweat dotting his forehead.

"I have to know," Alex said, his voice calm but cold. "Were you the one who gave us up that night? Were you the one who got Wells killed?"

I gasped. It couldn't be! Rush was dirty even then? He was the one who tipped off that village… the one who got Wells killed?

My God! They all could have died that night!

Rush coughed, more blood leaking from his mouth. "You all should have died that night. Then all this would've been over. You all should have died!" Rush hollered. "But no, you went subzero and ruined it all!"

Disbelief left me shocked and numb. All these years we'd been living with a traitor. My brother had been trying to bring this scum down on his own.

If only he'd told someone… If only…

"Death is too good for you," Alex spat, yanking him off the wall. Rush fell onto his knees, gasping, and that's when I saw the bullet wound in his back. Alex must have shot him when he was strangling me.

Rush laughed, the sound more like a cough. "Merc could've killed me once. He should have. If he had, he'd still be alive." He lifted his head and looked at me. A twisted smile contorted his expression, and he reached out, slapping his hand over my ankle.

I screamed and tried to kick him away.

Alex appeared over him, straddling his back and reaching around his body with both arms. Lifting Rush partway off the ground, he leaned around him, his subzero temperature permeating the room, leeching all the heat from the space.

"I'm not as good as Mercer was." He spoke matter-of-fact. "And though death might be too good for you, it's all you're going to get out of me."

The sound of Rush's neck breaking made me wince. The crazy glint in his eyes went out like a light, and his body dropped onto the floor in a heap.

Alex didn't even give him a second thought, stepping over his body and reaching down to lift me off the floor. "If you had told me where you were going, I wouldn't have been so late."

I crumbled into him, weeping in shock and despair.

His arms supported all my weight, and his lips moved in my hair. "It's okay now, kitten. It's over. This time, it's really finished."

I cried against him until my throat was raw, and he peeled me away from his tear-soaked chest.

"Why would you leave and not tell me?" he demanded, cross.

"I wanted to say good-bye to my brother." I hiccupped, trying not to look at the dead body staring at us from the floor.

"You couldn't have told me that?" He fumed.

Finally, some anger beat back the numbness, and I found my voice. "There was no body to grieve over. No funeral, no place to bring flowers. This is his funeral. This is my way of saying good-bye. My brother died for me. All I wanted was to come here and say good-bye."

The crystal blue of Alex's stare penetrated me, a bit of relief passing beneath the cold. "You were coming back?" he whispered.

I blinked. It never once occurred to me Alex would think I wouldn't come back. "I was always coming back," I confided. "I wouldn't leave you. I couldn't." My eyes found his. "You're home."

A sound of distress ripped out of him, and I was yanked into his body. He hugged me so tight it hurt, but I didn't utter any complaint.

"I forgive you for leaving," Alex said. "I forgive you for almost getting yourself killed."

When I didn't reply, he pulled me back, and I sucked in a painful breath and winced.

His face darkened with concern. "Sabrina?"

"I'm okay," I wheezed. "Just some broken ribs."

He glanced down at the man he'd just killed and then back at me. "I have to make some calls. If I want to keep this quiet, I have to make them now."

"How will you do that?" I asked, new fear creeping into my awareness. I pressed my lips together, then asked, "You could go to jail for this?"

He shook his head definitively. "No. That won't happen. I'll call my contacts. They'll come clean this up. Rush was a traitor and a killer. They won't want it to get out that one of their own did something like this."

"Are you sure?" I worried, my eyes involuntarily straying to the man on the ground.

Alex moved to block me, his face wary. "I'm sorry you had to watch me do that. If it changes the way you feel…"

I rushed him. My body screamed in pain when we collided, but it was worth it. "I love you," I dashed out. "You could kill a thousand men, and I would love you still."

He hugged me, his chin sinking onto my shoulder. "I wish I'd figured this out sooner. Maybe I could have saved your brother."

I thought a moment, and then I smiled. Pulling back, I gazed into Alex's eyes. "The loss of my brother will always be my greatest pain, from now until the end of my life. But thanks to Daniel, I have my greatest love. He brought me back to you, and as long as we have each other, I can survive anything."

All the ice in Alex's eyes melted, leaving behind the warmth of a blazing fire.

"You might look like a kitten, my love, but inside you beats the heart of the fiercest tiger I will ever know."

I smiled under his admiration. "Tell me you love me, Alex."

"I love you."

His words infused me with strength.

Pulling back, I gazed around the apartment. "Good. Now let's get this cleaned up so we can go home."

Alex

One Year Later…

The sun had barely risen, the sky just beginning to show signs of day, when I woke. I kept still, listening to the silence, noting nothing out of the ordinary.

But something was.

I might not have heard it. But I felt it. I trusted that feeling over any other senses my body had.

Slowly, I drew away from Sabrina, careful not to wake her but tucking the blankets up over her body a little farther. Soundlessly, I lifted the gun on the table beside me and pulled the knife out from between the mattress and box springs.

I crept out into the living room, heading for the door.

"Alex?" Sabrina's sleepy voice stopped me.

Rotating, I let her see the weapons in my hand and watched her eyes grow wide as both palms went toward her belly.

She made such a beautiful sight that a rush of frigid ice rose in me, and I welcomed it. That deep cold inside me was the first thing I'd let out if I needed to protect my girl.

"Stay inside," I ordered, then continued moving.

May God help the poor bastard who stumbled onto this property this morning.

The triangular window was lit with string lights, and beyond it, I noted a shadow of movement in the tree line. I went to the back door, glancing out the window from behind the curtain. Moving lithely, I slipped out onto the back deck, which was littered with leaves and lined with pumpkins.

The cold air slapped my bare chest, and I breathed in deep. Staying against the house, I looked out across the yard where I'd seen the movement before.

A dark shadow moved again, and I raised the gun, ready to fire.

A familiar sound cut through the morning silence. A sound from my past that I wouldn't ever forget. It was the call of allegiance, the signal we always gave when there was no threat.

I didn't lower the gun, but I held back on firing as a man stepped out from the cover of trees and into the yard.

I lowered the pistol immediately and shook my head.

I was a lot less quiet when I went back into the house and dumped the knife on the table as I passed. In the bedroom, Sabrina was standing in the center, her bare feet curled against the rug. My flannel was buttoned around her, and her hair fell down her back.

"What's happening?" She fretted the second I stepped into the doorway. Her cheeks were pale, and her eyes were giant orbs.

I smiled, letting her know it was okay. "Someone is here to see you."

A confused look crossed her face. "Me?"

I nodded.

She started forward, but I caught her shoulders and waited for her to lift her golden-green gaze. "You better be careful. You fall out there while you're running, things will get ugly."

Her face screwed up, and she rolled her eyes. "You're being ridiculous."

I let her go, trailing closely behind.

Sabrina pulled open the back door as though she expected someone to be standing there, waiting to be invited in. When she saw the space was empty, she glanced back at me, unsure.

"Outside, kitten."

She went out, and I had to bite back the command for her to put on some shoes.

I was just at the threshold when I heard her sharp intake of breath. Sabrina rushed toward the railing, knocking over a pumpkin, and gripped the wooden rail so forcefully her hands turned white.

"Daniel?" she whispered.

The man in the yard took a step closer and lifted his hand.

A sob ripped out of Sabrina, and she tore across the deck, down the steps, and went running across the yard. I followed at a much slower pace, but my heart beat to the tune of her running feet.

She was crying, her sobs blowing behind her like the dark strands of her hair.

Daniel came across the yard, meaning to meet her until his feet stalled out and he stopped. Realization slammed into him, and his eyes widened.

"Daniel!" Sabrina cried out and launched herself at her brother. She hugged him tight, then began patting his back and shoulders, wrenching back to stare at him. "Oh my God! Is it really you?"

"It's really me."

Another sob cut through the morning, and she smacked him in the chest. "I thought you were dead! We all thought you were dead!"

Before he could say anything, she fell into him, sobbing. He put his arms around her and held her tight. Our eyes met over her head, and I stepped up nearby.

"You knocked up my sister."

"I married her first," I said, showing him the silver band around my ring finger.

"I guess I'll let you live, then," Daniel announced with a smirk.

Sabrina made a rude sound and shoved at him. "You stupid jerk! You let us think you were dead! Do you have any idea what I've been through?"

"I'm sorry, Brin-Brin. It was the only way I could make everyone safe again," he told her, eyes eating up her face and body.

Daniel looked rough, and I knew what he'd done wasn't anything he wanted. It had probably been a year of hell for him, a year of moving constantly, barely sleeping, and eating only when he had the chance.

I respected him for it because he was right. If he hadn't done this, Brina might never be safe.

"It's been a year!"

"I'm well aware," Daniel remarked dryly.

"Oh my God!" Brina declared and hugged him again. As she cried, she wiped her nose on his shirt.

"It's the hormones," I informed him.

Daniel patted her on the back, then hugged her tighter. Over her head, his eyes deepened. "Thank you," he mouthed.

I nodded, swallowing past the sudden lump in my throat. "It's good to see you, bro," I said, holding out a fist so we could bump it out.

Brina sniffled and wiped her face on his shirt again before stepping back. "You smell."

"It's been a while since I had a shower."

"You're too skinny." She went on.

"Was hoping my little sis might make me a meal."

She made a sound. "I'll make you ten!"

He smiled, his eyes warming as he took in her face. "Shit, I missed you."

"You have no idea." Her voice was watery and deep. "I don't even care you lied for an entire year."

"It was necessary, kitten," I added.

She glanced over her shoulder, her eyes narrowing. "Did you know he was alive?"

I shook my head. "No. But I understand why he did it."

"I can't believe you're pregnant," Daniel said, gazing at Sabrina. He lifted his hands to hover around her round belly.

She smiled, gently took his hand, and brought it to rest on her stomach. "I was going to name him after you."

Daniel's eyes flew to her face. "It's a boy?"

"Two of them, actually."

Daniel jolted. "Twins?"

Sabrina laughed and nodded. She still radiated the same amount of joy she erupted with the moment we found out.

Pride swelled my chest, as well as a little arrogance. "Hell yeah, two. I don't do nothing half-assed."

"They're identical," Sabrina told him happily, then made a sound and glanced down at her stomach.

"What was that?" Daniel asked, jumping back. "Something's wrong!" he demanded at me, pointing to her.

"Nothing's wrong." Sabrina assured him, grabbing his hand again. "He just moved."

Daniel seemed skeptical and a little out of his element. "He moved?"

Sabrina held his hand on her stomach, and I knew when someone in there moved because Daniel's eyes went wide.

"Does that hurt?" he inquired, then looked at me, his eyes narrowing. "I know I gave you my blessing, Ice, but you better not be—"

"It doesn't hurt." Sabrina quickly spoke over him. "Your nephews are excited to meet you is all."

His eyes widened. "They are?"

"I've told them all about you." Her eyes welled up again, and tears slipped over her cheeks. A cold wind blew, and I stepped in.

"C'mon, kitten. It's cold out here. You're going to freeze your toes off."

"I'm fine," she insisted, still blubbering.

"The boys want some breakfast." I scooped her up and cradled her against my chest. "Mercer does, too."

"It's just Daniel now," he said quietly as we went toward the house.

I slid a glance in his direction.

"I'm out," he added. "It's better if everyone believes I'm dead."

In the house, I sat Sabrina on a chair and moved to put on some coffee. "Is it safe for you to be here?" I asked—because I had to.

Sabrina gasped. "It doesn't even matter!" She scolded me. "He's not leaving."

"I'm not suggesting he's got to go, sweetheart." I cajoled. "But a man needs to know what he's working with. I have a wife and kids to think of."

She made a harrumphing sound. But given the way she caressed her stomach, I knew she understood.

"You know nothing is one hundred percent," Daniel allowed. "But I'm pretty sure it's clear. It's why I hid out for a year. I wanted to make sure no one else came out of the woodwork. I wanted to make sure everyone believed I was dead."

I nodded.

"Rush was in on it," Sabrina confided. "He tried to kill me."

Daniel's face was grim, and anger sparked in his eyes. "Yeah. I figured as much." He met my stare. "You got the message I sent?"

I nodded once. "I took him out."

"Good."

"Daniel, where have you been?" Sabrina asked.

"Here and there," he answered, vague.

"You aren't leaving again, are you?"

"Was thinking I might stick around here. Apparently, I got nephews to spoil and a brother-in-law to harass."

Sabrina jumped out of her chair and tumbled forward. I vaulted over the island, but Daniel caught her, keeping her upright.

I pulled her away from him and into my arms. "You tryin' to kill me?"

"You can stay here with us," Sabrina said, not even fazed by almost ass-planting on the floor. She gasped. "I know! Daniel can live here after we move out!"

Daniel blinked. "You're moving out?"

"It's a one-bedroom, and we have twins on the way." I reminded him. "We aren't going far."

"Right," he said, gazing around. "I could maybe rent this place from you. Once I get a job."

Sabrina bounced around in my arms, and I made sure to keep a tight hold on her. "I have all your money!

I haven't spent anything out of it at all. I'll sign it all back over to you," she informed him proudly.

Daniel's eyes widened. "You saved it all?"

She seemed offended. "Of course. I wasn't about to spend your money." She blanched. "Well, I did use it for one thing."

"What's that?" he asked, curious.

"I bought something for the boys." Her lower lip wobbled. "I was going to tell them it was from you."

Daniel pulled her out of my arms and hugged her. "Aww, Brin-Brin. I love you."

She sniffled. "I love you, too, bear."

It was good to see her like this. The suspected death of her brother had altered something inside Sabrina, and I was hoping now that deep wound might begin to heal. "I'm sure we could find some work at the resort for you, too." I offered.

"I'd appreciate that." Daniel agreed.

"Welcome home, Daniel," Sabrina said happily and nearly danced toward the fridge. "I'm going to make you a huge breakfast."

He watched her a few moments with love and relief mixed in his eyes. Finally, he pulled them away to where I was standing nearby. He came forward, offered his hand. "I won't ever be able to repay you for keeping her alive."

"There's no debt here," I said, shaking his hand. "You bringing her back to me was the best thing that ever could have happened."

"So we're even?" Daniel asked.

I shook my head. "No. There's no keeping score with family."

Daniel smiled. "I was wrong to keep you apart before. I'm sorry."

I smiled. "Forgiven."

"You know," Sabrina asserted from beside the stove. As she spoke, she punctuated each word with the spatula in her grip. "*I'm* the one who decided to stay."

She turned back to the eggs, muttering about men taking all the credit when she was the one who was carrying around twins. "Probably going to act just like the both of you, too."

I threw back my head and laughed, going up behind her to slide my arms around her and my boys. "Now, kitten, you know I'm happy as hell you married me, filled my deck with pumpkins, and turned this house into a home."

"This house was empty before I got here."

I made a sound of agreement. "And now it's overflowing." I pressed a kiss below her ear, and she sighed, turning in the circle of my arms.

"I suppose you were worth all the trouble," she mused, then leaned up to whisper against my lips, "I love you."

Between us, the babies moved, and I smiled down at my beautiful wife. The ability to go subzero was always going to live within.

I accepted it.

Now I knew without a doubt it would never control me because the rest of me was filled with so much warmth.

THE END

If you enjoyed Subzero, *please consider leaving a review online.*

Reviews help authors!

Thank you for reading the BearPaw Resort *series!*

AUTHOR'S NOTE

Writing a book is hard. Very profound, right? LOL. Though it's not profound, it is the truth. Especially when you are writing a book about a character people have been asking for since the first book in a series. I'm not really sure why, but Alex was one of those characters that everyone wanted to know about almost from his first appearance on page. I might even say some of you probably like him better than Liam. Me? I couldn't choose between them. But I do love them both, and I do understand why Alex was so intriguing. He had that mysterious, dangerous past and that sometimes cold interior that, when you got a glimpse, made you shiver with anticipation.

I have no idea if I did Alex justice. I know I tried. I hope you all think that I did and are satisfied with his story. I did enjoy writing this book. I enjoy writing flawed characters that we all like anyway.

I really enjoyed Sabrina as well. I like her tough, take-no-shit attitude and the way she didn't back down from Alex.

Though I enjoyed writing this book, it was at times stressful. It took a while to nail down the plot and certain aspects of this book. I would say the hardest thing about writing *Subzero* was the timing. Halfway through writing this, I hit my stride and was ready to pound out the entire book. Then we were evacuated for the large hurricane that hit the East Coast. It was the first time we'd ever been mandatory evacuated for a hurricane, and it was sudden and stressful. We were gone for a little over a week, staying with friends. It pulled me out of my routine and the headspace I was in for writing. When we arrived home, there was a lot of cleanup and things to deal with. We were lucky our home only had minor damage. Unfortunately, so many people here lost everything. It is very heartbreaking to witness such things firsthand.

Even as I type this, my kids are still not back in school. Kids in this county have missed a full month of school so far due to damages.

Suffice it to say, the most challenging thing about this book was timing and getting back into the right frame of mind to write this story. I will say it was a good escape at times, but other times it was a challenge.

Now that the *BearPaw Resort* series is ending, I look forward to new projects on the horizon, and I hope you all will stick around to see what comes next!

As always, thank you for reading and for all the amazing support you have always shown my work.

See you next book!

XOXO,

Cambria

ABOUT CAMBRIA HEBERT

Cambria Hebert is an award-winning, bestselling novelist of more than forty books. She went to college for a bachelor's degree, couldn't pick a major, and ended up with a degree in cosmetology. So rest assured her characters will always have good hair.

Besides writing, Cambria loves a caramel latte, staying up late, sleeping in, and watching movies. She considers math human torture and has an irrational fear of birds (including chickens). You can often find her painting her toenails (because she bites her fingernails) or walking her Chihuahuas (the real rulers of the house).

Cambria has written within the young adult and new adult genres, penning many paranormal and contemporary titles. She has also written romantic suspense, science fiction, and male/male romance. Her favorite genre to read and write is contemporary romance. A few of her most recognized titles are: *The*

Hashtag Series, GearShark Series, Text, Amnesia, and *Butterfly.*

Recent awards include: Author of the Year, Best Contemporary Series (*The Hashtag Series*), Best Contemporary Book of the Year, Best Book Trailer of the Year, Best Contemporary Lead, Best Contemporary Book Cover of the Year. In addition, her most recognized title, *#Nerd,* was listed at Buzzfeed.com as a top fifty summer romance read.

Cambria Hebert owns and operates Cambria Hebert Books, LLC.

You can find out more about Cambria and her titles by visiting her website:
http://www.cambriahebert.com.

Please sign up for her newsletter to stay in the know about all her cover reveals, releases, and more:
http://eepurl.com/bUL5_5.